DEDICATIONS

My heartfelt thanks go to all my family and friends who have been generous enough to believe in me, especially Kath, Pauline and Karen who have encouraged and pushed this odd ball pensioner to realise her dream.

To the people of Norway and the Shetland Islands many of whom paid the ultimate price in defence of their freedom during the Second World War.

And my unshakable belief in my mantra, 'If it's to be, it's up to me'

An epic novel of mystery, danger, hope and love. "From first proof, I couldn't put it down".

Kath Graham. G.F.

ABOUT THE AUTHOR

Living happily retired in Northumberland I fill my days with hobbies and friends, fresh air and writing.

'The Shetland Eagle' came to me in a dream many years ago. It was complete with characters, location, twists and turns and the all important ending. Where it sprang from I have no idea, but I'm glad it did.

I visited Shetland to do lots of research and fell in love with the place, the big skies and stunning beaches. The Shetlanders I spoke with were happy to talk about island life and share stories. I have taken some artistic licence with the geography which I hope they will forgive.

It has all been a wonderful and fulfilling journey.

Anne Taylor

CHAPTER ONE

She stood a few feet from the edge staring out at the North Atlantic. The pale evening sun had just dipped below the horizon leaving the sky a slate grey. It was a cold October night and the wind was building into a storm. Dark rain squalls were sweeping in from the west like shadowy attackers. Huge waves crashed onto the rocks five hundred feet below sounding like a thousand war drums. She had stood here many times, on these massive cliffs at Eshaness. Shetlanders were battening down for the night and the clownish puffins tumbling back to the safety of their clifftop burrows. She wrapped her shawl tightly around her as she stood thinking about this little island. The place she'd lived since being brought here from Russia as a baby by her father. Although it was a beautiful place, deep down inside she felt like a stranger. Not because she was Russian but something else that she was never able to explain. She pushed these feelings away and turned to make her way back to her father waiting in their little cottage nestling in the lee of a hill. She hurried long the path past the ghostly white lighthouse as it began to sweep out its warning.

She was freezing cold by the time she reached the cottage door but once inside, she felt the welcoming heat in the cosy room. Loosening her shawl she went to sit beside her father, her hands held out to the warmth of the big peat fire.

"Well, is the Atlantic still there?" he asked with a smile looking across at his daughter.

She shivered briefly, "Stop pulling my leg Pa, of course it's still there and as stormy tonight as I've ever seen it." Tally returned the smile then she stared into the fire. He looked at her, this tall, dark haired gentle girl knowing she needed to walk the cliffs and spend time on her own. He wasn't sure why and found no need to ask, although the thought of standing on that cliff edge filled him with dread. He had learned to live with his acute fear of heights but had never quite overcome it. Even during his career as a submarine commander during the First World War, standing on the top of the conning tower was something he had tried hard to avoid.

Their cottage was a simple place with a thatched roof and thick stone walls keeping out the harshest of weather. Inside was warm and cheery with one main room where the fire burned and a basket of peat sat on the flat stones of the hearth. The walls were rough and whitewashed and oil lamps gave a comforting glow from the table and the sideboard. Shining pots and pans hung from the ceiling over the stove. Two doors lead from the main living space, one was her father's room the other was Tally's with a traditional box bed and its heavy woollen tapestry curtain. A deep-set window looked out over the beach to the sea. Yellow checked curtains brightened the view even on the dullest of days. Against one wall were shelves full of books with stories from far away places, travel, adventure and Russian history; her special treat was to spend time at the library in Lerwick.

On her dressing table stood a flowered china washbowl and jug along with an assortment of combs and brushes and a few shells. A beautifully carved driftwood box, a gift from her father, sat on her bedside cupboard. On the floor was a 'hooky' mat of different colours, brightening the room and warm under her feet.

Next morning, a steady cold wind blew in from the west but the sun was shining and patches of blue sky showed between the clouds. Although it was early, Tally already had a pan of porridge bubbling away. Her father appeared from his room and put his sea boots by the hearth.

"Good morning girl, it looks to be a fine day, yes? The storm blew itself out during the night." Without waiting for a reply, he sat down to eat.

"Don't forget I'm helping Lowry Nicholson with the fishing today so I'll not be back 'til dusk," he said.

"Yes I know Pa," Tally dished up the steaming oats, "so you must eat plenty and I've put some bread and cheese in your bag enough for you both. I'm going to have a walk over to Katy's place and Jenny's going to meet me there, we're going to catch up on all the gossip, and I want to make the most of the lovely sunshine."

Katy Graham and Jenny Amundsen were two of Tally's closest friends. Katy had been a young teacher at the school Tally and Jenny attended. Their friendship had grown over the years. Tally was a keen student and fast learner, enjoying all aspects of school life. Jenny was not very academic but a budding artist and such a dear friend with a wicked sense of humour, everyone liked her.

After they'd eaten, Tally helped her father on with his waterproofs, gave him his canvas bag and walked him to the gate.

"Have a good day girl," he smiled, "give Katy and Jenny my regards."

"I will," said Tally giving him a quick kiss on the cheek before he set off to the harbour. She watched him as he walked away, this big powerful man with his thick black curly hair not quite tamed by the woollen hat he wore.

"I'll have to knit him a bigger hat," Tally mused to herself.

She set about feeding and tending the few animals they kept. The chickens, always hungry and knowing the sound of the feed bucket came scurrying around her feet. She took fresh hay to the two sheep, which were her favourites.

"Good morning to you," she said and gave them both a hug, their coats were thick and warm and smelled of oil, salt and seaweed. Their big brown eyes were looking for anything that might be edible. These lovely beasts supplied the wool she spun then knitted into shawls, hats and socks.

After feeding them she went back indoors humming a tune that she'd heard her father whistle many times. She didn't know what it was called and made a mental note to ask him.

She dressed in her warmest clothes and tugged a brush impatiently through her long unruly hair, but with a sigh and a little shrug, gave up and put on her shawl, picked up her work-bag and left the cottage.

Once outside she hurried over the grass to the path that would take her to Hillswick. She took out her knitting and worked as she went.

Katy Graham's cottage was immaculate inside and out. The garden that surrounded it was full of vegetables grown safely behind the wire mesh fence. None of them yet victim to the rabbits.

It sat at the end of a lane, its rough walls were painted white and the window frames a pretty pale blue. Even the metal stove-pipe sticking through the roof was shining, though that had more to do with the bleaching winds carrying salt and sand. The thatched roof was neatly trimmed and strapped.

Tally could see through the window that Katy was busy in the kitchen.

"Hello Katy, it's just me," she shouted walking in through the back door. The two women hugged as Katy was trying to wipe her hands on her pinny.

"It's lovely to see you Tally, sit yourself down and I'll boil the kettle."

The cosy kitchen was full of the smell of baking and Tally started to feel quite hungry. The tea was just being put onto the table when Jenny Amunsen's smiling face popped around the kitchen door.

"Hello, I've arrived," She laughed and came quickly into the room and gave both Katy and Tally a big hug.

"Oh it's great to see you both, I feel as if we haven't met for weeks."

"We haven't," laughed Katy and they sat down for tea.

There was always something going on in a tiny place like Shetland and the girls managed to work their way through just about everyone they knew.

Katy blushed when they got onto the subject of Lowry Nicholson the fisherman. Over the years this shy and kindly man had shown a great fondness for her. In the winter he would call to make sure she had enough peat in the shed and fresh fish in the pantry. Katy never did mind his visits; in fact she quite enjoyed his company, in her own quiet way.

"Yes, I like him but no more than that," Katy said rather too quickly, "anyway he's got his life and I've got mine."

"Yes we know," laughed Tally, "and you are definitely in his." The two girls giggled.

"I'll get some more tea," said Katy, blushing as she went to fill the kettle.

"If he asked you out Katy would you go?" asked Jenny.

Katy turned to look at them noticing the cheeky smiles and sensing an air of conspiracy.

After what seemed only ten minutes but had actually been nearer two hours, Tally and Jenny said their goodbyes to Katy and left to go their separate ways but not before they had planned a day trip to Lerwick town in a week's time.

CHAPTER TWO

It was dusk as Lowry Nicholson's fishing boat appeared at the harbour entrance, easily riding the incoming swell with the little lantern on the stern giving a soft yellow glow. Tally could see her father and Lowry packing away the heavy nets and getting the fish boxes ready to land onto the jetty wall. A couple of the local lads had wandered along the harbour and saw Tally standing there.

"Hello there Tally," said the taller of the two, "how are you keeping, I haven't seen you for a while?" Tally turned to him and smiled,

"I'm keeping very well Jac Smith and hello to you too Jimmy." she said looking at the other lad. Jimmy mumbled a hello, blushed and turned to watch the boat come in. Tally had liked Jac from their school days, and he was very fond of her but living away up at the top of the island she didn't see him very often. The last time was at a school reunion months ago, organised by the rather unpleasant headmaster Mr Johansson.

Jac smiled, "It's been a while now since the school get together, I should have been in touch before but I've been helping my father." Tally had also remembered the reunion, when they'd sat and talked for hours about life on this island and what their futures might hold. He made Tally feel safe and had a quiet strength, which made her want to be close to him. He was also very handsome, tall and muscular, with big blue eyes that seemed to soften whenever he looked at her. Tally often thought of him as her Viking warrior with his shock of shoulder length blond hair and tanned skin.

Jac had chosen not follow his father to the fishing grounds. His mother was already worrying herself into an early grave about her husband being at sea. He saw no reason to cause her any more upset, and fancied being a sheep farmer. There were good breeds on the island and good money to be made.

Lowry Nicholson's boat was now bumping gently against the harbour wall and her father was smiling up at her noticing that Jac was with her.

"What are you doing here girl?" he asked glancing at Jac. "Good to see you Jac, how are your father and mother?"

"They are both well thank you Mr Gregor, have you had a successful trip?"

"Of course," shouted Lowry from the boat as he heaved the heavy boxes of fish up onto the harbour wall. He smiled and slapped Peter Gregor on the back, "but I couldn't have done it without the help of this man. He can sense where the fish are like no other man I know." They moored the boat safely and carried the fish to Lowry's waiting van. Tally turned to walk with her father as Lowry shouted,

"I'll see you on Friday then Peter and thanks for a good day."

"Yes, of course my friend, I'll see you then," Peter waved back.

Tally linked her arm into her fathers and looked at Jac.

"How long are you in Hillswick?"

He said, "I have to return home tomorrow, I'm staying at my aunt's house tonight but would you mind if I called on you next week, it will be Wednesday when I'm back here.

"That would be nice Jac; I'll look forward to it." She smiled and looked at her father who pretended to be busy with the box of fish given to him by Lowry. Tally and her father said their goodbyes and walked away up the harbour bank toward home.

"He's a good man that Jac Smith," he said, "and I'm pleased he is calling on you." They walked on taking the beach road; two dark figures bent against the wind.

They arrived at the cottage with just enough light to see. Tally went straight in and piled the fire up with peat, then hung the kettle on a hook above it.

"I'll make us some supper Pa, and then I'll clean those fish."

"How was your day?" her father asked. She told him about going to Katy's and teasing her about Lowry and how they'd love to see them get together one day.

Her father smiled, "If that is what they want, then that's what will happen."

"Lowry says his boat is getting too old and he can't afford another one just yet so it may be better if he could work for someone else." Peter took off his heavy boots and stood them on an old mat beside the fire. "We'll be going to Lerwick to see what's about"

Tally looked surprised at this news, "Does that mean you are going to look for other work too Pa?"

"No girl, I'm only going to keep him company, but obviously if he sells his boat I'll have to get work somewhere, in the meantime I'll get some supplies for us.

We'll be there a couple of days so why don't you Katy and Jenny get the bus down and join us.

Jac called the following Wednesday looking handsome in his tweed winter coat with a huge blue woollen scarf. He took Tally walking to the nearby beach their feet sinking into the soft yellow sand as they headed for a small outcrop of sheltered rocks and sat down, thankfully out of the wind.

The weather was cold but sunny with the ever-present wind blowing in from the west, Jac talked about his plans and his hopes of one day having his own house with a good number of sheep and a decent amount of land. He looked quickly at Tally to see if she had caught the implications of such a plan, she had but did not show it. Her father depended upon her working the smallholding while he was away fishing.

They sat for a while, easy in each other's company. Just talking about anything and everything.

Soon Jac said, "Let's go back; it's getting too cold out here."

He took her arm and helped her back up the beach. When they stopped at the cottage he looked at her with such gentleness Tally's heart nearly melted, he rested his hands on her waist.

"Can I call again, and you can tell me all your plans?" he asked quietly.

"Of course you can Jac."

He kissed her lightly on the cheek and turned to go.

"I'll look forward to it," she called after him and went inside.

CHAPTER THREE

The day of the trip to Lerwick arrived. The old bus rattled along the road into Hillswick and picked up the three women, all wrapped up warmly as was everyone else.

Greetings of the day were exchanged as folk settled into the journey wiping condensation off the cold windows with gloved hands.

Mr Johansson the headmaster appeared none too happy and was sitting at the back of the bus watching everyone. Looking to see who was sitting with who and trying to overhear conversations. Mrs Johansson looked her usual timid self, her red ringed eyes staring out of the window as she clutched her shopping bag on her knees. Oh dear, thought Tally, looks like there's been another falling out in the Johansson house.

The driver picked up another four passengers. Two older men sat a few seats in front of Tally and began talking quietly and shaking their heads, both looked very serious. Tally overheard the word 'war' but couldn't catch what else they were saying. War, she thought, and shivered.

The women left the bus with their bags and headed to the town. Katy set off towards the High Street.

"Where are you going first?" Tally asked hurrying to keep up and Jenny trailing behind.

"I'm off to Larsson's, come on."

Mrs Larsson was a fearsome woman of wide girth, middle-age and wild grey hair tied up in a bun and ran 'Larsson's Stores' with military precision. Her two shop girls just had to take one look at her face in the morning to know how their day was going to go. Her voice could be heard far and wide when she berated her poor suffering husband Archie, her standards were very high and he didn't always reach them. All the same, she was a woman with a kind heart. The shop was beautifully clean and tidy with polished wooden shelves, which held everything from buttons to boots, pans to pinafores, wool to wire but mostly it was known for the quality hand knitted garments. Tally and Katy had knitwear in her shop and both had brought more.

As soon as they opened the shop door they could hear Mrs Larsson with a customer telling him there was nowhere on Earth he could buy better socks than the ones she sold. Katy was pleased to see the socks were ones she'd knitted. The customer, a big Russian fisherman smiled good-humouredly at this larger than life animated woman. Holding his hands up in mock defeat he agreed to buy six pairs.

Mrs Larsson looked up as the doorbell jangled, "Won't be long girls, just let me finish here."

The Russian touched his cap in greeting as he left, Mrs Larsson clapped her hands and a young girl came scurrying round the counter.

"Yes Mrs Larsson?" she squeaked.

"We'll be in the back Lizzy, look after the shop." It was an order.

"Yes Mrs Larsson." Lizzy was very fortunate to work at the store, her mother kept telling her so, but Lizzy wasn't so sure.

The women sat in Mrs Larsson parlour with its red velvet chairs and large round table with a chenille tasselled cover. China dogs on the mantle, oil lamps on the sideboard and a stuffed falcon in a glass-covered case, gave the room a feeling of Victorian clutter.

Tea was served in the best china and all the gossip gone over and over.

"What of this Adolf Hitler fellow in Germany? I have a feeling he's a trouble-maker and has his eyes on Britain," said Mrs Larsson. "He'd better not try coming over here." She sounded as if she'd take him on herself.

"It's all very worrying, but I'm sure it will not come to that," Katy said, though not too convincingly.

The girls left their goods and finally said their goodbyes to Mrs Larsson then went on their way.

"Look," said Jenny, "there's your father and Lowry, best say hello."

They waited until the two men caught up with them, Lowry smiling at Katy.

"Well ladies, how about looking for somewhere to have a cup of tea?"

"I must get on," said Katy, a little undecided as to what the girls wanted to do.

"In fact we've just had a cup of tea and a rather longer chat than we anticipated with Mrs Larsson. She kept going on about the bad news from Germany, and we should all be aware and prepared. I must say she sounded quite put out by it all. I just hope there's not going to be another war. Well, we'll see you later gentlemen?" Katy hurried away.

"Of course, and I hope I'll see you soon in Hillswick," Lowry nodded at Katy.

Katy had caught the look between Peter and Lowry when she mentioned Germany and noticed how grim their faces became.

She'd heard similar news last week from Meg and Maisie Donaldson who ran the post office. They listened to their radio every night and said Adolf Hitler was 'up to no good' and threatening war.

They were tired and it was getting colder as they climbed aboard the bus for home. The sun was beginning to set and they watched as two boats left the safety of the harbour for a nights fishing.

On the way home Tally thought of her father and Lowry still in Lerwick for another night and wondered whether he too would be tempted by the work on the large Russian trawlers, she was also worried about the threat of war. Shetland had already lost many a brave man to the 1914-18 war, their headstones stood proudly on a hillside near Eshaness. Tally was lost in her own thoughts while Katy and Jenny chatted happily about their day. Jenny glanced at Tally sitting by the window and wondered at her friend who often closed up and lived for a while in her own little world. They eventually arrived at the road ends where Tally and Jenny got off the bus waving their farewells to Katy who smiled at them through the steamy windows.

There was something about her father's solemn face when he arrived home next day; Tally knew all was not well.

"So, it appears we are at war again with Germany." He paced the floor and looked at Tally and took her hands,

"Lowry and I have decided that we must do all we can to help protect the islands."

"What can you do?" she asked quietly and felt a flutter of panic in the pit of her stomach, some old stirrings of long ago, of remembered noise and commotion, which unnerved her. Not knowing where these feelings came from, again tried to ignore them.

"We're going back to Lerwick very soon to call at the Admiralty offices which are being set up in the old fish market building. We'll get more information there; don't look so worried girl I'll let you know how we get on."

Peter sat in front of the blazing fire and mulled over this awful news he'd heard earlier. The war seemed even nearer as word of Nazi atrocities came out of Europe. The USA recalled their ambassador, which to Britain was an ominous sign.

Some thought Hitler was a madman and planned to invade Britain, and at this moment in time it looked as if nothing was going to stop him.

Peter had also heard that the Admiralty in Shetland had requisitioned three local ships the 'St Magnus', 'St Ninian' and the 'Viking' and was keen to know what was going to happen to them. His night was a restless one; his thoughts were of the years he'd spent on Russian submarines during the First World War.

He remembered the first time he'd seen the huge submarine that he would command. It was a 'Narval' class called 'Galina' and was part of the Baltic fleet. Back then, Germany was once again the aggressor much better organised and well armed catching Russia very much unprepared. He prayed it wouldn't happen to Britain.

A few days later Peter and Lowry arrived in Lerwick to the noise of trucks streaming off the ships that were tied up at the harbour. Men in army uniform waved vehicles out of the town to destinations north and south.

"They must have come in last night," Peter shouted above the noise, "they certainly know how to keep a secret. I didn't hear a whisper that any of this was going to happen today, did you?" He looked at Lowry.

"No, I didn't and it looks like some of them are on their way down to Sumburgh where they're building a new runway."

Dark green and camouflaged trucks shook the ground as they rolled past filled with soldiers, supplies and machinery.

"Things are moving pretty fast Lowry we must go and find out what else is happening, come on." Both men hurried away along the harbour to the temporary Admiralty Headquarters.

A few minutes later they arrived at the old fish market and found that the offices had been set up in the grey stone building that stood on the western end of the harbour. The big wooden front door was almost devoid of paint but neatly fixed in the middle of it was a smart square sign, which read 'Admiralty Offices first floor'.

Peter pushed open the door and they climbed the wide stone staircase to the next floor, their footsteps echoing in the vast hall. There was another sign pinned on the wall in front of them, which said 'Admiralty Office, Room 1' with an arrow pointing to the right. Another smaller hand written sign informed them 'Please wait as all visitors must be checked in'.

"Where do we check in then?" whispered Lowry, just as a door opened and out walked a man in naval uniform. Peter saw by his insignia that he held the rank of captain; the man smiled and asked if he could help them.

"Yes, I hope so sir," said Peter, "we're looking to check in so that we can speak to someone about the situation we find ourselves in and whether we could be of any assistance."

"'The situation we find ourselves in'," the captain repeated slowly looking carefully at the two men.

"Interesting terminology sir, if you don't mind me saying so. Here, we call it war." He let the words hang in the air.

"I'm Captain Howard and in charge of this set up here in Lerwick." He shook hands with both men. Turning back into the room, he walked over to the far window and indicated for the two men to follow; Peter closed the door behind them.

"It's a terrible business, terrible," he said wearily as he stared out of the window with his hands behind his back.

There came a knock on the door and at his shout of "Come in," a young, smartly dressed junior officer popped his head into the room, his eyes registering Peter and Lowry.

"Ah, sorry to disturb you sir, I just wanted to know where these two gentlemen had gone. I had 'em in my sights then they disappeared, they need to check in."

"Its ok, Jackson, I'll see to that. I brought them straight in here with me, thank you."

"Ok sir, thank you sir," and he backed out of the room and closed the door.

"In his sights, what did he mean by that?" asked Peter.

"Oh that, we just have to be careful and I suppose he watched you come in to the building and then heard you on the stairs. He has a set of mirrors that allow him to keep 'toot' on anyone entering, quite the Sherlock Holmes that one."

Peter didn't know whether to believe him or not so stayed quiet.

The captain finally turned to face them, "Sit down gentlemen please."

They sat on wooden chairs in front of an old desk that looked as if it had been rescued from a rubbish tip. It was covered with papers, which the captain scooped up and tapped into some form of order then placed them to one side.

The meeting went on for a long time. Peter and Lowry explained who they were and why they'd come down to Lerwick and hoped they could be of help. The captain was very thorough but asked more questions of Peter than of Lowry and seemed very interested in the fact that he had been a submarine Commander. Plus he knew the waters off northern Russia, Norway, Finland and Sweden and had a working knowledge of the coast around Murmansk, this may prove useful.

Finally the meeting was over. Captain Howard stood up and gave a shrug as if he was feeling the cold; he looked tired his face lined with worry.

"Many thanks for calling, please tell others that we are enlisting men to help with the building of the new runway at Sumburgh."

"Of course." They both said together.

They shook hands and walked back down the stairs to the chilling wind outside.

"What now?" asked Lowry, "I'm not too keen to go out back out to sea, there may be German subs already in these waters."

"There probably are," said Peter matter of factly, "I think things are going to get a hell of a lot worse my friend, so let's go to Sullom Voe like the man said and see what we can do there."

They made their way back to the van Peter had borrowed and drove along the harbour to the road that would take them back to Hillswick, and the Voe.

On the way they saw the masses of machinery and equipment being unloaded onto the harbour side. The ships that had crept in under cover of darkness were rolling in the swell making the iron gangways squeal and screech on the stone surface of the quay. They saw armoured vehicles of all sizes. Diggers and trucks carrying small cranes and lorries loaded with cement; tons of cement.

"I'll have to tell Tally what we're doing and where we're going, she'll worry if I don't, then again she'll worry once I've told her, I can't win." He smiled wryly at Lowry.

"Yes ok, but we'll have to get a move on its getting dark."

Back in Hillswick, Peter went into the cottage and found Tally sitting knitting by the fire.

"You're back, good, do you want to eat now or wait 'til later?"

"Later girl I've got Lowry waiting in the van outside, we're off to Sullom Voe to take a look at what's happening there."

"Pa, I spoke with Maisie Donaldson from the Post Office today and she told me a ship has been sunk off Muckle Flugga.

Peter was shocked, "Dear God, what ship was it, do you know?"

"No, but they think it was a Swedish steam freighter and that it could have been a German sub that attacked it. Could it be true Pa, are they going to kill these innocent men going about their work, they can't do that." Tears of anger were welling up in her eyes.

He put an arm around her shoulder and just held on to her; she looked up at him,

"It's ok Pa, I'm alright, I'm just angry that's all."

Next day Tally's father told her about his trip to Sullom Voe and the plans that were in place for the hundreds of British and Norwegian soldiers plus many more personnel to be stationed there.

"There are going to be flying boats, Catalinas and Sunderlands probably, plus a lot of other hardware. I'm going back with Lowry today to help them make detailed maps of the area. A bit of local information about the waters around the bay may prove helpful."

Over the next few weeks Peter and Lowry spent more and more time at the Voe. They went on exercise with different crews showing them how to get in and out of the areas that could be used in emergencies.

Tally's life had become one of concern for her father. She knew and understood his great love for the sea and felt that if he were to be given the chance, he would go back on board a ship so long as it was against the Germans.

CHAPTER FOUR

Jac Smith called on Tally late one afternoon and she thought he'd become a little older looking, perhaps it was the war.

He smiled that familiar smile and presented her with a little bunch of wild flowers.

"These are for you, I picked them on my way here, I know you like your flowers."

Tally smiled and kissed him on the cheek

"They're beautiful Jac, thank you, please come in and sit down its freezing out there, want some tea?"

She found a little old china vase for the flowers and stood them on the window-sill.

"Yes thanks," he said as he eased himself in to a chair, "how's your Pa, did he hear about the sinking the other night, what a terrible business. My father's gone to Sullom Voe to see if he can help up there."

"So has mine Jac, he's helping the crews with a bit of local knowledge."

"Have you seen anything of Giles Johansson recently?" Jac asked casually.

Tally turned slowly to face him,

"You mean the headmasters son, no, why what has he done now?"

Giles Johansson was a strange one. About the same age as Tally and Jac, they'd all gone to school together. He was a thin slip of a lad with dark lank hair and pale pock marked skin. He had few friends and spent most of his time hanging around anyone who would listen to him. Unfortunately, his shifty behaviour endeared him to no one, and it was common knowledge that he cheated a lot at school, thanks to his father.

Not many liked Mr Johansson either. He was a very strict headmaster who made no secrets about who he liked and didn't like in school. Tally was well aware that she was not one of his favourites.

As they got older Giles would still leer at her whether it was when passing her in the village or at church, even though he knew she had no time for him. Once he asked her for a dance at the village summer party. She had given him a very firm 'no thank you' but he followed her around the dance floor until the ever-protective Jac had a quiet but forceful word in his ear. Giles had never forgotten the humiliation and had certainly never forgiven Jac.

"It's just that he's been hanging around Sullom Voe. My father saw him and asked what he was doing there. Giles said he was looking for work. Well we all know Giles Johansson doesn't even like the sound of the word let alone do any and my father got a bit suspicious that's all."

"Hm, Pa didn't mention anything but he's been out on the boats all day and may not have seen him, what do you think he's up too?"

"I don't know, I just don't trust him and we're all trying to look out for each other, he's a bad'un Tally that's all I know, a real bad'un." Jac's hand was shaking as he put his cup onto the table.

"Are you ok Jac, you look a little pale, I bet you've been working too hard again?"

"I'm fine Tally; I just keep getting these headaches and haven't got time to go to the docs."

"But you must Jac, please, I can't have you getting ill." She smiled at him, his heart melted, as usual.

"Ok, ma'am, will do, just for you, when I get the chance." He chuckled at her and finished his tea.

After a short while he said, "I've got to go," and stood up, straight away grabbing hold of the chair to stop himself from falling.

"Jac!" Tally jumped up and held onto him, "what's wrong with you, that's not just a headache. You sit right there and I'll run for Katy."

"I'll be fine Tally honest, just give me a minute then I'll be ok to get home."

"You will sit down and wait for Katy." Tally's firm but kindly voice was ringing in his ears. He admitted to himself that he felt quite sick and was glad to sit still and try to manage the pains that were exploding in his head.

"Tally, I won't let you go for Katy. I'll be fine; another cup of that lovely tea might help though." He smiled but his face was deathly pale.

CHAPTER FIVE

Night was drawing in as Peter, Lowry and their old friend Duncan Cameron stood on one of the old timber jetties at Sullom Voe.

"Damn this war, damn it to hell." Duncan's anger spilling over as he turned and pushed passed Peter and Lowry and walked down the jetty to the wooden hut that served as a shelter. They followed him in and Lowry shut the door behind them. There was an old iron stove burning in the corner that gave out welcome heat and pungent smoke as the three stood warming their hands. Duncan Cameron was one of the biggest men Peter and Lowry had ever met. At six foot eight and built like a bear not many men chose to cross him. Particularly now as they knew his only son Rob, a fisherman, had been killed at sea just two weeks ago, his small boat hit by a German torpedo. It broke Duncan's heart and now he was man possessed, swearing that he would kill any enemy he found regardless of who or where they were.

"Peter, we have to do more, we just have too." It was as if he didn't know what to do with his anger. He moved to the little window, which was dirty and hanging with old cobwebs and looked out onto the darkening skies, "God help us all Peter," he said quietly as if in prayer.

"Duncan, why don't we take a look over at Lunna Voe I hear that there's something going on at the big house and that the military are setting up some kind of safe anchorage? It's got to be worth a look, what do you say?"

"Aye, I've heard the same story but I'm not sure the military will like us snooping around. But, I suppose it's worth a shot. Do you know anyone down there?"

"No, but there's only one way for us to get to know someone."

"Aye ok, pick me up at seven sharp in the morning."

"Sorry lads I can't make it tomorrow," said Lowry, "I've got a last trip to do, just the one to collect my pots then I'll join you."

"Ok Lowry, for Gods sake take care of yourself and we'll see you soon."

The three men left the shelter of the hut and stepped out into a wild black night. It was starting to rain and the wind whipped at their coats as they made their way back to the truck and set off for Hillswick.

The morning weather was much the same as Peter and Duncan drove to Lunna House.

They travelled south then turned left in the little hamlet of Voe. After a few miles of potholed and bumpy road they could see the house by the shore and on through the mist, out to the wild Yell Sound.

It was cold and lonely and there was a bleak isolation to the place. A few sheep were grazing on the rough grass of what had once been a garden and even they looked cold and miserable. They drove slowly down to the gate where Peter stopped the truck as the old worn wipers continued to screech their way across the windscreen. He quickly switched off the engine; no one emerged.

"Well," he said, "there appears to be nobody at home, better go in and have a look around see what we can find." He started up the engine again and went through the gate pulling up beside the yard wall.

Both men got out of the truck and walked toward the main door. The stone house was huge and solidly built. There were many outbuildings and storage sheds to the south side. A quay ran into the bay, which looked suitably sheltered and would indeed take good-sized boats. This was invaluable for covert comings and goings and no doubt why this isolated spot had been chosen.

"Hello," boomed a very English voice from behind them, "what can I do for you gentlemen?"

Both men turned and found a tall rather elegant looking man standing in front of them. He wore an Air Force greatcoat. His smile was warm but his eyes were steely. He walked toward them his right hand holding a pipe in his mouth and his left hand stayed deep in his pocket, perhaps a gun, thought Peter. Strangers hanging around, caution at all times that was the way of things now.

Peter noticed there were no insignia or badges with which to recognise his rank.

"I'm Peter Gregor from Hillswick and this is my good friend Duncan Cameron, we've come to find out if you were in need of any men or boats."

The airman looked at them for a few seconds taking in all he had to.

"Follow me please gentlemen and let us get in out of this dreadful weather." De'ja vu thought Peter another office another interview.

They went into a large stone hallway with five doors leading from it. There was a great wide staircase with panelled walls and a decorated ceiling. The airman led them upstairs where it was obvious by the beautifully carved doors and ornate plaster work that this had once been a very grand house, but now it was suffering from a deal of neglect and had the musty smell of damp. They turned along a wooden floored corridor Peter and Duncan glanced right and left into some of the huge rooms. They saw an odd assortment of boxes, rolls of wire, stuffed canvas bags and what appeared to be oil drums stacked into every corner. The rooms had long floor to ceiling dusty windows. Most looked out to the east where the threat of war loomed largest.

The men were led into what could have once been a sitting room; the deep rich red carpet had seen better days and was now frayed and faded. There was a roaring peat fire burning in the overly large fireplace. Dark velvet curtains were hanging in front of the new blackout blinds and a big round table with six chairs sat at the far end of the room. The airman took them to a corner near the fire where an old desk and a few chairs had been set up. The two men noticed that all the papers on the desk had been turned over so that there contents could not be read. Must have done that as soon as he saw us coming thought Peter, so he could have been watching us for a while.

"Please sit gentlemen, make yourselves comfortable and let me introduce myself, I'm Captain Vickers, that's all you need to know at this point and that I am in charge of all operations at Lunna House, now please, tell me more of yourselves." The Captain sat at the desk and emptied his pipe by knocking it against a battered old metal wastepaper bin. He proceeded to refill the bowl from a packet of St Bruno, which he produced from his left hand pocket. So, it was tobacco thought Peter.

It looked like a scene from a Sherlock Holmes film, the three men sitting near to the fire talking in hushed voices with Vickers casually smoking his pipe but listening intently to what the two fishermen had to say. Peter and Duncan told him that they had sailed regularly into Norwegian waters and knew the coastline well and they also knew of the operations, which were in progress between Shetland and Norway.

"Gentlemen, we are on a war footing here and we need all the local knowledge and help we can get on the understanding that for the time being you tell no one why you are visiting Lunna House or what goes on here, although on such a small island nothing is secret for long eh?" He smiled wryly.

"We have moved operations here from Flemington, the house along the coast. Work is still going on there and is of great importance and secrecy, but here we can make better use of the outbuildings to store the supplies we need to keep the boats sailing and the channels open. First we need to repair and make good the jetty and fix up one of the larger sheds to make it a suitable workshop. So as you can see gentlemen, there are lots of things to do if you are willing to help and we would be glad to have you on board as it were. Now I must press on so let me show you out." The time spent with Captain Vickers went quickly but now both men knew they were going to be part of a very important time in the life of Shetland in the coming months and even years. The men emerged into a lighter sky with no rain and a lessening wind, Captain Vickers touched Peters arm and asked.

"Tell me, what part of Russia do you hail from Peter?"

"Sverdlovsk, it is east of the Urals. I left there with my baby daughter after the death of my wife in 1919, and strangely it was friends I had in the Russian Navy who helped me choose to come to Shetland."

"Is that so," he raised his eyebrows, "it is not so strange, things happen for a reason Peter, you have good friends." Vickers looked at Peter with interest.

"I want you to come and see me again we need to talk more. My colleague in Lerwick told me that he'd already spoken to you and another friend of yours, I look forward to our next meeting, please make arrangements with the young officer at the desk."

The men shook hands and Peter and Duncan walked toward their truck knowing they were probably being watched from some dusty window.

"We must go back there as soon as we can Peter," said Duncan settling back into the truck with a feeling of satisfaction, knowing he will at last be doing something to help ease the pain of losing his son, "there's certainly plenty to do."

"I'm going back in a couple of days; I suspect he wants to pick my brains about my time in the Russian navy. I have no problem with that and he'd already heard of Lowry and me from our trip to Lerwick. I think they know quite a lot Duncan, perhaps more that we think they do."

"We'll go and check with the rest of the lads tomorrow at first light, they've all agreed to let their boats be used. I have a feeling he might want them at the quay pretty soon."

They drove north to Hillswick.

CHAPTER SIX

Back at the cottage Tally had prepared a simple meal of mutton broth and bread cakes. Hearing the truck pull up she went to the window and watched her father coming in the gate. He smiled a weary smile as he entered the room hanging his overcoat on the back of the door.

"Well girl how went your day?" he moved to the fire to get warm.

"Oh fine Pa," as she began to set the table, "I had Jac here today and I'm worried about him, he looked so pale and as he was about to go home he nearly took a tumble. He says he's been getting lots of headaches recently, but of course he hasn't been to the doctors, say's it's too far and he's too busy."

"Hm, what's he been up to lately then?"

"Just the usual I think. Working the smallholding and helping his father, if you see him Pa will you have a word with him, please?"

"Yes of course but I doubt I'll see much of him now because Duncan and I visited the house at Lunna Voe, had a long chat with the chap in charge, and I might be spending time there for a while"

"Oh, I see."

"Yes, and they'll be needing men and boats as soon as possible. Lowry will be joining us soon but not a word to anyone about this, you understand, caution my girl"

"Of course Pa," they sat in silence and ate.

"Talking of caution Pa, Jac mentioned that Giles Johansson had been to Sullom Voe and is asking for work."

"Hah," he laughed, "since when has that useless lad ever thought about work, when was he there?"

"Jac said his father saw him a couple of times last week and again the night before last but he seems to be more interested in just hanging around. I don't trust him Pa and neither does Jac or his father."

"I've never had much time for that lad but I don't suppose it's entirely his fault. His father is a cruel man and his poor mother has struggled with the boy. No matter, I'll ask around when I'm next there, it may be that he just wants to get out of the house."

"No Pa, I don't think so, if he just wanted to be away he wouldn't go all the way to Sullom Voe."

"Aye you could be right girl, something's not quite right."

Tally cleared away the dishes and put more peat on the fire then they sat in amiable silence, Tally knitting and her father reading.

The fire was burning low when they both heard the drone of an aircraft approaching from the east. Tally turned down the lamp as her father went to the window and pulled back the blackout curtain just a chink to look out into the darkness. All they saw was blackness. No stars, no lights, as the noise of the big engines got nearer and louder. It was a German aircraft; certainly not the noise of a Catalina or a Sunderland.

"Get into the storehouse, now!" He shouted to Tally, he quickly turned out the lamp, grabbed his torch and joined her. Little did he know when he'd built this stone room for storing wood and supplies that it would become a place of safety. They waited huddled down in a dusty corner glad of the thick walls around them. Soon the aircraft was almost overhead though Peter reckoned the pilot wouldn't be able to see very much and hopefully be unsure of the terrain.

The first bomb fell and the ground shook.

"Dear God Pa, where do think that went?"

"It sounded about half a mile or so to the south of us, hopefully no damage but there will be another one or two yet, then he'll want to get away back over the sea and home."

Another bomb fell, but further to the south west and hopefully onto the moors or into the sea. They sat for a few more minutes but there were no more, then they heard the aircraft turn to the northeast as it made its way back to its base.

Tally and her father emerged from the storehouse and returned to the cottage.

"I'm going down the road to check folks are ok, you stay here, keep the lamp down low and listen out for any more visitors, and I'll not be long."

"Take care Pa."

Peter couldn't quite make out the shape at first, but he was aware that someone was standing by the gates that led to Lowry Nicholson's place. He hoped that whoever it was hadn't heard him coming. The night was still and black and he was curious. His instincts told him something was wrong so he waited knowing whoever it was would have to move sooner or later, and as he was in no great hurry he settled down beside an old stone wall. Nothing happened for a while then he heard footsteps walking quietly and carefully along the gravelled road towards him. He stayed very still, managing to keep below the height of the wall until the figure was level with him. He stood quickly and quietly and saw that it was Giles Johansson.

"Good evening Giles, or should I say good morning. What may I ask are you doing here hiding at the entrance to Lowry's place?"

Giles Johansson nearly jumped out of his skin as he spun round to face the dark large shape of Peter Gregor, he gave a choking gasp.

"It's nowt to do with you why I'm here." His voice was shaking uncontrollably with the shock of being caught and the fear of what might happen next. He tried to stand up to Peter but he was a puny little man whose legs were about to give way under him so he put an arm out and leaned on the wall.

"I want to know what you are doing here and why you are out after dark. You are aware of the curfew are you not? I don't think your father will be too pleased, in fact we will go and see him now and you can explain yourself to him."

"No, please, my father will kill me; he thinks I'm in bed." Giles squirmed as Peter held on to his collar, determined to get to the bottom of Giles's nocturnal wanderings.

"Well, either your father will or the Germans, didn't you hear that bomber come over and you walking around as if you don't care, come on we're going to your place."

Giles looked the picture of misery as he walked beside the big man; he knew he was in a lot of trouble. It didn't matter what he did, his father saw no good in him and took every opportunity to let him know. And yes he had seen the German bomber; he wasn't stupid but was absolutely terrified when the bombs dropped.

They soon arrived at the Johansson's house which was in darkness so Peter switched on his torch shielding the light with his coat. They made their way carefully up the steps to the front door. Giles took out his key and after fumbling at the lock they stepped into the hallway. Minute's later Mr Johansson red faced and almost growling rushed down the stairs to be confronted by his son and Peter Gregor.

"What the hell is going on here, and what are you doing in my house?" yelled Johansson toward Peter, almost apoplectic. Then he turned on his son, "and what, may I ask, are you doing out at this time of night?" The blood vessels standing out on his thick neck.

"Actually its morning," said Peter calmly, "and I found your son wandering around Lowry Nicholson's place, why do think that is Mr Johansson?"

"How on earth do you expect me to know that," he screamed, "he does as he likes and anyhow what has it got to do with you there's no law against walking." Johansson was obviously torn between wanting to punish his stupid son but also curious to know what he was up to and being well aware of the curfew.

The noise of the bombs had already woken Mrs Johansson who now appeared at the top of the stairs, wondering what the further commotion was about. Her salt and pepper hair sticking out from under a hairnet and her worn pink woollen dressing gown tied with an old black pyjama cord, in her bare feet and her eyes red and blinking in the light.

"Giles my dear, what's going on?" She asked nervously as she walked down the stairs towards her son.

"Nothing Ma, I was just out for a walk and he," Giles waved a limp finger to where Peter Gregor stood, "thought I was up to something so brought me home, honest Ma I've nothing to hide." he whined and looked as if he were about to faint. Mrs Johansson went to put her arm around him and take him to the kitchen.

"Just a minute," yelled his father, "get back here, I want some answers lad."

"That would certainly be a start," said Peter who by now was leaning casually against the front door frame with his arms folded.

"So, can you ask your son what he was doing at Nicholson's place?"

"Well?" boomed Mr Johansson in to the face of his son, "I want some answers and I want them now."

Mrs Johansson knew better than to intervene so shuffled off to the kitchen safe in the knowledge that she was not going to get anymore sleep this night.

Mr Johansson took hold of his terrified son and shook him violently before Peter could get to them, the poor lad wobbled like a rag doll with its head about to fall off. The result was that from the folds of his coat a huge flashlight fell with a clatter onto the stone floor, the three of them looked at each other in stunned silence. His father let go of the lad and picked up the light.

"Where did you get this, who gave it to you?" His voice rising again as the flashlight was waved in front of his face, which made Giles hold his skinny arms over his head just in case there were more blows to follow.

"Hold it," said Peter taking the light from Mr Johansson and looking at it closely, turning it in his hands. His steady gaze met Giles's and he could tell that the lad's brain was trying desperately to think of a suitable reply.

"I found it," he whined up at the big man.

"Where, and I would appreciate the truth?"

"TRUTH, he doesn't know the meaning of the word," shouted his father.

"I did, I found it when I was out walking, honest."

"Where do you go walking Giles?" the question from Peter Gregor was quiet but firm. Giles felt it was almost threatening, he knew Tally's father didn't like him much but in his simple mind he still wanted to win her affections, so didn't feel the need to upset the big man.

"Oh, you know out and about nowhere special," he wanted to walk casually away to the fireplace but he couldn't trust his legs to work properly so he just stood there.

"I'm waiting Giles," the tone of Peter Gregors voice suddenly didn't seem quite so friendly.

"Sullom Voe," he blurted out.

"And why have you been going there for a walk, it's a hell of way from here," Peter asked quietly.

"To look for work, honest."

"You," gasped his father, "honest and work, don't make me laugh. You've never worked a day in your life so don't kid me lad." His father's anger was still boiling away. He was just as angry at his stupid son, as to have this Gregor man in his house. This big Russian fellow that everyone liked...Except him.

"Tell me Giles, who have you seen there to ask for work," again the voice quiet, controlled.

"Eh, some bloke called Tam, I think."

"Some bloke called Tam, you think?"

"Aye, that's right but he said there was no work so I left and never went back, that's when I found the flashlight."

"So, you have only been to Sullom Voe once is that what you're telling me Giles?"

"Aye that's right, just the once," he lied.

"When was that Giles?"

"Last week, aye, last week." By now Giles felt as if he was going to collapse in a heap on the floor but knew if he caved in now his father would keep on and on at him. He would ask more stupid questions which he had no intentions of answering.

"I'll be on my way then and I'm taking the flashlight back to Sullom Voe. It will belong to one of the workers who I dare say is looking for it. Good morning to you both and please give my regards to Mrs Johansson, and Giles?"

Giles stood arrogantly but shakily beside his father as Peter turned slowly and looked straight at him, his eyes as cold as ice.

"Yes, what?" Giles croaked nervously.

"I really hope you know what you are doing." It was a slow and measured statement, Peter's voice sounding hard and menacing. Giles had the distinct impression that Peter Gregor knew more than he was letting on. It frightened him. With that, Peter left the house and made his way to see Lowry.

Peter thought long and hard about what had been said at the Johansson's place. He knew the lad was lying, but was that to stop his father asking too many questions. He suddenly felt very uneasy. Was there a connection between the German bomber and Giles with a flashlight as bright as a lighthouse? Could the boy really be that stupid? He pressed on to Lowry's place. It was very late but Peter knew it was important he share this information with his friend.

He tried walking quietly to the back door but the geese that Lowry kept were already screeching out their warning of an intruder. So, he stood with his hands above his head, waiting for the door to be opened by his friend probably holding a gun. Lowry appeared rather bleary eyed, holding the predicted weapon, and was shocked to find Peter standing there very calmly telling him of the nights dramas. After going in to the parlour the two men had a large whisky each and Lowry listened to what Peter had to say. In the end he said he was not surprised, saying it was just the sort of thing the lad would do. Giles had never thought about the consequences of his actions. So to wander around with a big torch when an aircraft was overhead would to him seem pretty exciting. Peter still felt very uncomfortable and both men agreed to keep a careful watch on Giles whenever they could.

CHAPTER SEVEN

The day of Peter's second meeting with Captain Vickers had arrived. He made his way up the great staircase of Lunna House to Vickers' office. Papers covered the desk as they had before only this time they were not turned over and it would have been easy to read any one of them. In fact Peter was surprised to find that one or two were written in Russian.

"Ah Peter, good to see you again, please sit down." Captain Vickers shook hands firmly and sat at his desk.

"Thank you sir, good to be here."

"Tea Peter? Now that's something I will not travel without" Vickers smiled.

"Yes, thank you that would be good." He said as he looked for somewhere to sit that wasn't covered in papers.

"Oh just put that lot on the floor," Vickers indicated to a chair rather overwhelmed by boxes. Peter picked them up carefully and placed them on the floor.

"Don't worry too much about them they're only fuses. "Well, to business, I haven't much time and I have a proposition to put to you. I'm afraid I can't give you too many details or too much time for you to think about it; in fact I want you to say yes today. We need you to go to Russia."

Peter's face must have registered the shock he suddenly felt.

"Yes it's true, Russia. You will have guides, mostly resistance workers, all the way through Norway and Sweden and across Finland. Your final destination is a town you know well, Sverdlovsk. It might sound insane to you but we need to get vital information to one of our groups there and the only way to do that is to send it with someone overland. That someone has to be Russian speaking with some knowledge of the area in question, that's why we want to send you."

"I see," said Peter, "and I take it that's why you asked me about the town during our last meeting. You weren't too subtle"

"Yes, that's right and I knew you were aware of the direction of my questioning but I could tell you little at the time until certain checks could be done you understand. Plus I needed to know that our groups would be in the correct position to meet you, I only hope you choose to help us."

Peter's mind was racing, memories of his last visit to Russia were beginning to surface and he wondered how he would feel to be back in the very place he last saw his beautiful wife and heard her final words.

"Of course I'll go," he said, quickly pulling his thoughts together.

The two men talked for a while but Captain Vickers gave Peter only the bare facts and details of the trip. Peter was going to have to trust this man and all the others he was going to meet along the way

He said, "There are one or two things I need to do before I travel, I have a daughter and will need to explain my absence."

"We are aware of your daughter Tally, and you will tell her nothing. Your mission is of the utmost secrecy. I suggest you tell her you will be away to look at a new boat for yourself, you'll think of something and will see her on your return. Is that clear?"

Captain Vickers stood up and walked around the table and looked closely at Peter.

"Remember, you tell your daughter nothing of the mission and little of how long you will be away. You need to be packed and ready to leave this Saturday at seven o'clock in the evening to catch the tide. You will meet me here at Lunna House and I will give you any last minute details and your papers. You will also meet the captain and crew of the boat that will take you to Norway. I wish you all the luck in the world and may God go with you and bring you home safely."

Thank you Sir, I'll do my best."

"I know you will, I know you will," he said quietly.

The two men said goodbye and Peter went back downstairs and out into the sunshine. Taking in deep breaths of cold salty air he thought over what he'd just agreed too. Vickers looked grimly out of the upstairs window wondering if he'd ever see this man again once he had left for Norway.

CHAPTER EIGHT

Tally sensed there was something wrong as soon as her father walked in to the room.

"Pa?" she said taking his coat and laying it over the back of the chair.

"Sit down Tally, there's something I have to tell you and the sooner the better." He sat on one of the benches by the table. Tally waited.

"I'm going away for a while. The problem is, I can't tell you where, but I can tell you I'm leaving on Saturday nights high tide," he held up his hand toward her in a gesture of silence, "you are not to ask me any questions, and if anyone asks where I am you tell them I'm off looking for a new fishing boat. And you have no idea when I'll be back, do you understand?"

"This is why you've been to Lunna House today isn't it?" she asked.

"Yes, it is."

"Can't you tell me anything Pa?"

"Afraid not girl, you'll just have to trust me. I have to be at Lunna house on Saturday seven o'clock ready to go. I have agreed to do something and that's that," he looked at his daughter with a mixture of pride and sadness. This trip was going to be a dangerous one and the less said the better.

"Who else knows you are going away Pa?

"Apart from my contact at Lunna House, no one and that's the way of it. And I repeat, if anyone asks, you tell them I'm away looking at new boats, ok?"

"Not even Lowry?"

"No, not even Lowry and I feel bad about that but there's nothing I can do. I only hope when he does find out that he understands."

"Ok Pa, I'll manage. Is there anything I can do to help?"

"Yes, see if you can find my old black waterproofs, and I'll sort out some warm clothes."

Tally went to the shed for his jacket. She lifted it off the big hook and hugged it. It smelled of him. His soap, his hair oil and sweat. She knew he'd probably agreed to undertake something dangerous. Many stories were being bandied about of Lunna House, no one quite knew what to believe, but she did know that dangerous missions were being planned there.

What scared her most was there was only one other man who knew where her father was going. She didn't have a name for him but by God she'd find him if anything went wrong.

Everything was as ready as it could be for her father to go to Lunna House; he left without fuss early Saturday evening. Just a hug for his daughter, who he left standing at the gate in the gathering darkness. His voice whispering a prayer as he climbed into the truck and headed south.

CHAPTER NINE

There didn't appear to be anyone at Lunna House as he pulled into the yard. All windows were blacked out and no machines or generators could be heard. To all intents and purposes the place was deserted, but he knew better. Walking slowly round to the seaward side he could see in the dusk the shapes of two boats that were moored at the jetty. He had seen neither of them before and so suspected they were Norwegian and ready to make the return journey before too many people could ask any questions. As he reached the house it was then he heard the soft hum of an engine coming from the nearest shed. He made his way over to the old building and shone a little glimmer of light from his torch into the dusty interior. He saw nothing, but the sound of the engine was a little louder now, and he wondered where it was coming from.

"We have the generator in the cellar," said the voice from behind him.

Peter turned and saw Captain Vickers standing in the doorway, "We have a lot of room down there and it is certainly good for muffling the old sound don't you think, helps to keep any snooping strangers away too?"

"Yes of course, and with a little bad weather thrown in, you probably wouldn't hear a thing."

"Quite so, let us get on then." He went into the house and opened a door into what looked like a pantry. There were a few empty shelves and a single light bulb hanging from the ceiling and a fine metal grill covered the window. Vickers pulled a package from inside his jacket. "This is the envelope I wish you to deliver. Carry it about your person at all times. Follow the instructions I gave you earlier and remember you must trust your guides." Vickers watched as Peter tucked it into a wide canvas belt he had fastened around his waist. The two men looked at each other; there was little more to say. "Ok, I'll now introduce you to your travelling companions, grab your things."

"Right, lead on."

The two men went into the darkened hall of the house and made their way to a downstairs room at the end of a stone floored passage. Captain Vickers knocked quickly and went in. Peter followed and found himself in a big well-lit room where six men were sitting around a table playing cards. They were all dressed in dark warm clothes with their oilskins hanging over the back of their seats. All had the look of hardened fishermen and they glanced up as the two men walked in. Some smiled, some didn't. Peter nodded to them as he stood beside Vickers.

"Attention men," called Vickers, "as I informed you earlier, this is your 'cargo' for tonight," putting his hand on Peter's shoulder, "to be delivered safely to Norway as planned. He's going to meet with our friends in Bremanger. We have been there before have we not gentlemen? The tide will be right for you to sail at eight o'clock, so eat your fill and get prepared. If any of you need anything else for your journey, please don't hesitate to ask. Ammo, clothing, anything, you all know the drill.

I will return in thirty minutes with final instructions, thank you men." With that, Captain Vickers quietly left the room.

The men got up from the table and shook hands with Peter and wished him well but asked little of him. They were all used to keeping their mouths shut, what they didn't know they couldn't disclose if captured. And if Captain Vickers wanted him delivered to Norway then that is what they would do. Vickers had earned their trust many times over.

"You must eat with us Peter," one man said with grin, "it could be your last meal on Shetland."

There was a scraping of chairs as they all sat down again.

"Take no notice of him," laughed another, "he's the joker of the pack and never stops eating, always claiming it may be his last meal."

Peter smiled his thanks and sat amongst them and ate all the same. He knew that his next meal might be a long time coming. The food was good, roast lamb and some locally caught fish with an abundance of potatoes, it was excellent fare.

They ate in quiet companionship each with their thoughts on the night ahead, outside the wind was rising.

It's going to be a rough old crossing thought Peter but he wasn't worried. He was thinking of Tally who had no idea where he was going or of the danger he was putting himself in. He hoped that one day he would be able to explain it all to her.

After the meal and the final packing of kit, the men left for the jetty. Peter checked the precious envelope, wondering what the hell he was carrying. He grabbed his kitbag and went up the shaky wooden gangway onto the deck. The increasing swell made the vessel bump against the jetty and strain at its moorings

The boat was a wooden Norwegian 'More' fishing boat without a name and a blacked out number. She was seventy foot long with a single cylinder semi-diesel engine whose top speed was only about eight knots. Not very fast in wartime, thought Peter, they would not have the speed to outrun any other craft. The card playing crew knew exactly what they were doing, dark shadowy figures moving around the deck in eerie silence. The boat was ready to go at the appointed time.

Peter was shown to the cabin by the 'dealer' of the card game, Jan, "This is it my friend, eight bunks one table one window, home sweet home, that's yours there," as he pointed to one of the bunks, "we will need you on deck as soon as you like, the more lookouts the better, oh, and you had better change that jumper you've got on. Here take this one and throw yours back onto the quay."

The man gave Peter a big black woollen polo necked sweater with no labels or pattern. Peter changed quickly.

"That Shetland jumper's a dead give away to the Germans, if you're caught that is," he laughed good humouredly as he left the cabin, but to Peter, it was a sobering thought nonetheless.

"I'll be right there," Peter shouted as he stowed his bag in a locker and had a quick look round.

This was to be his home for the next couple of days. Like many fishing boat cabins, the wooden walls had been varnished many times and were covered in tobacco tar and drawing pin holes that looked like an infestation of woodworms. This is where pictures of wives, children and film stars could be looked at every day. They were all gone now. The captain couldn't risk any form of identification being found by the Germans. Peter went quickly up on deck where the salt spray hit him and the ever-increasing wind tugged at his clothes. He'd been too late to throw his sweater onto the quay so it went overboard into the waves. He watched it sink like a slowly drowning man hoping it wasn't an omen.

The boat had cast off and was making slow headway to the entrance of the small harbour; the wind blowing spumes of water over the bow. Once out into the open sea and away from the shelter of land, Peter felt the full force of the wind as the heavy craft rolled and dipped, chased by a westerly. The tilting boat would rush forward and rise up on a wave only to surf perilously down the other side, the massive hull juddering into the troughs. A heavy sea was running and huge white topped waves towered behind them breaking on the stern flooding the deck. All the men took shelter in the wheelhouse and Peter joined them, hanging onto the wooden rail, which went around the stuffy smoke filled cabin. Shouting was the only way to be heard above the 'toink toink' of the big engine and the howling wind.

"I'll take first watch on the bow, ok?" Peter yelled as he picked up a pair of binoculars

"Aye, ok," the captain called back, and watched him struggle to get out of the door that was being forced shut by the wind.

"I'll take stern watch," shouted Jan as he too battled outside.

"Aye and for God's sake watch yersels."

Jan staggered his way to the stern where huge oil drums were tied against the rails. He huddled down jamming himself between them, got his binoculars out and looked skyward. It took nearly two hours of constant buffeting to reach the Outer Skerries and then set course for Norway. Winds were nearing gale force and the boat was struggling to cope with the huge swells. Still, they made canny headway and the steady rhythm of the big diesel engine gave much confidence to the crew.

In the darkness, all Peter and the crew could hear was the screaming of the wind and the crashing of the sea over the decks. Throughout the night the watches changed and the men who'd been on deck were grateful to return to the relative warmth of the cabin. They would stagger below and eat some hot food and shiver their way into an uneasy rest.

Dawn broke with a sliver of light showing on the starboard bow. The wind was no longer gale force and the boat rode easier in the water, although the pitching was constant.

Peter was back on watch in the shelter of the high bows of the boat. It wasn't long before he heard an aircraft coming at them from the east. He shouted to the captain in the wheelhouse and pointed over the bows indicating the direction of the noise. The captain poked his head out of the tiny window and cupped a hand to his ear and peered into the distance.

"All men on deck, man the guns. We appear to have a visitor, let's give him a good old Norwegian welcome," he shouted with an almost cavalier attitude to the danger. He rubbed his big hands together and a huge smile crossed his weather beaten face.

Men came running from below and went to their stations. They began pulling tarpaulins off the big oil drums and lifting off the lids to reveal Twin Lewis machine guns. The rest of the crew had sub-machine guns, and all were now swinging round to meet the enemy.

"It's a German sea plane lads, fire at will," the captain shouted at the top of his voice.

The plane flew low and loud over the rolling boat firing cannons and machine guns. The crew replied with a barrage of firepower, and judging by the tracer bullets many looked as if they'd hit their target, although trying to hit the plane from a heaving deck was not easy. Splinters of wood from the cabin went spinning past Peters head but he just gripped the machine gun even tighter and kept on firing. His heart was thumping and the noise was overwhelming as the others fired continuously. All guns were now pointing at the single aircraft that was tormenting them. It was a short but fierce fight. The German finally made a turn for home with a small trail of smoke from one of his engines. The men congratulated each other with pats on the back and big smiles; even though they knew the pilot would have given their position to any nearby German submarines.

"Is everyone ok?" shouted the captain.

"Aye sir, all present and correct," replied the crew.

"Good, four men on deck at all times from now on, we're nearing land and that bastard will have told all his friends where the party is."

The wind had gradually swung round, dropping slightly and was now coming from the north, much to the relief of the captain. He knew from passed journeys it was almost impossible to enter the little bay on Bremanger Island with a westerly blowing. And that's where he was headed.

Everyone was now watching the approaching shoreline for any sign of Germans or movement of any kind. This was a very quiet part of the island and the little harbour at Vetvik was in a calm and sheltered bay. Although there was still quite a swell, the captain brought the boat expertly alongside the jetty. One of the crewmen jumped off and secured their mooring ropes. When the engine was switched off the silence was eerie, just the slap, slap, of water could be heard under the wooden pier.

Peter looked around at the stunning scenery; mountains rose up high on three sides of the deep bay leaving only the westward side open to the sea. How lovely this place would be without the war breathing over it, he thought. Then wondered who was going to meet him. All he'd been told was that his guide was called Kit and he was to wait hidden in a cave, which the captain would show him when all the supplies had been brought ashore.

The men shifted nearly two tons of supplies and by the end of it, were exhausted. The boat was soon ready and the winds were favourable but Peter was becoming a little anxious as to when or if he would meet his guide.

"I suspect your contact will have been watching us since we arrived and won't make himself known until we are gone. Don't worry my friend go to the cave, they know where to find you." The captain chuckled, although Peter did not share his optimism at this moment.

"I'm sure you're right as you've done this many times before."

"Yes friend I have, I know nothing of your mission nor do I want to, but I wish you success and may God go with you." The two men shook hands and the skipper walked back to the boat and as he untied the moorings the big engine burst into life and it turned slowly and made its way back out to sea.

Peter had never felt as lonely in his life as he stood and watched it leave. The noise of the engine could be clearly heard and sounded far too loud.

Making his way to the cave hoping his contact would soon turn up; he settled himself beside some of the newly delivered boxes and looked out to sea thinking about the next few days and what they might bring.

CHAPTER TEN

At first he thought the screech was a seagull, the familiar sound of a hungry bird but it wasn't quite right. He froze and took out his gun aiming slowly and steadily at the entrance to the cave. The sound was nearer now, not a seagull but maybe another type of seabird. He hid himself behind a pile of supplies then he heard the footfall of someone in a hurry on the shingle path outside the cave. A shape appeared at the entrance. Someone was standing there, looking in, getting their eyes used to the darkness. Peter held his breath. Then again the most eerie screech echoed around the cave.

"I'm Kit the seagull, is anybody there who can feed me?" The voice was squeaky like a child, but here stood an adult.

Peter was totally bemused, no one had told him to meet someone who pretended to be a seagull. He didn't move and still had his gun aimed toward the man.

"I'm Kit." The man repeated as he came further into the cave.

"I know you're there Peter Gregor and you have been sent by Captain Vickers," he whispered loudly moving slowly forward.

"Come out, we don't have much time." His voice was now urgent.

Slowly Peter stood up and watched as the man walked towards him with a big smile on his face.

"I wouldn't fire that thing in here if I were you." He laughed looking at Peter's gun.

"There must be a couple of tons of explosives in these boxes and I think old Fritz may just hear the bang if it all went up, don't you?"

Peter put away the gun, climbed over the boxes and shook hands with his guide. The man was tall and looked extremely strong. He wore old worn camouflage trousers, black sweater, leather boots, which looked as if they'd walked a thousand miles and a brown woollen hat. Over his shoulder he carried a rifle and a bandoleer full of ammunition. He slid a small rucksack off his back, placed it on the boxes and pulled out a map.

"Come; let me show you where we are headed tonight," he smiled.

"Tell me. Why do you make so much noise does no one ever hear you?"

"Oh you mean me screaming like a seagull?" he laughed.

"Yes."

"A German patrol came here once. No one knew they were in the area; they must have come in under cover of darkness. It was at the same time that I was to meet an agent in the cave so I had to think of something fast. They saw me running around flapping my arms and screeching like a bird. They tried to talk to me but I convinced them I was totally mad, you know, the village idiot," he said tapping the side of his head and laughing some more.

"I do it most days I'm here so when they see me they just leave me alone, but come, we must go now, it will soon be dark enough to travel but first we must get our supplies together." He quickly showed Peter an area on the map that was to be their target for that night. It wasn't too far away but they both would have to have their wits about them and as Peter was told by Captain Vickers, 'trust your guides'. They picked up their gear and Kit led the way out of the cave and away from the harbour.

They followed the path to the other side of the island, and in the gathering dusk Peter could see the shape of a small wooden building near a sheltered beach.

"What's this place?" he asked quietly.

"This is where we are going to pick up extra supplies for our journey and check out our transport."

The building was an old boathouse, which looked in a state of collapse, weeds three foot high grew from the roof and there were holes in the end wall big enough for a man to walk through. Peter wondered what could be kept in here of any worth.

Once inside Kit switched on a very low light torch and shone it forward. The shed had the smell of decaying fish. Peter could see a small sturdy looking boat with bits of old sacking draped over it. It was tied to a rickety looking pier by a piece of frayed rope. Kit went to the corner of the shed and started to pull some ragged tarpaulin off a pile of wooden fish boxes.

"Here Peter help me with this and get yourself some ammunition and anything else you need then we must be away."

"Thanks, but how come the Germans haven't found any of this stuff?"

"Ah, we keep moving it about. There are quite few boathouses on the island and as you can see everything is kept in fish boxes. We just put them on the boats and motor to another place. All this will be gone by tomorrow, now hurry."

"Is this the boat we're going to be using?"

"Yes, she's a good seagoing craft, so if God is with us we'll make the mainland in good time. We will have to hope that the Germans are all tucked up in their beds tonight and not on fishing control duty." He had his rucksack open and was packing it with a waterproof cape, a warm jumper, some water and batteries.

As Peter looked through the boxes he found a gun. It was a Browning P 35 qnd better than the gun he'd brought with him. He turned it over in his hands feeling the weight and solidity of the black deadly weapon.

"Any chance I could have this?" He asked Kit holding it up in the torchlight. "I will return it if at all possible."

"Of course my friend you must take what you need. The ammunition for that is over there in that box marked 'cod'. And don't worry about returning it. If you ever come back, you will have earned it as a souvenir." Peter stuffed the pocket on his backpack full of ammo, thinking about what Kit had just said.

Looking from the entrance of the boathouse the two men could see how near the island was to the mouth of the Nordfjord on the mainland of Norway. That was the stretch of water they would soon have to cross to reach their destination.

They quickly gathered what they needed and all was soon stowed away and ready. Kit began reading a note he'd picked up from the wheelhouse.

"What's that?"

"It say's there are no cod in the straights but a shark was spotted earlier today in the fjord." He smiled as he lit a match and burned the paper, letting it fall harmlessly in to the water.

"What does it mean?"

"It means my friend, there are no German ships in the straights between Bremanger and the mainland but a small patrol boat was spotted somewhere in the fjord so we must take care."

Peter untied the mooring rope and jumped aboard as Kit started the engine. The little boat slid out into the main channel with hardly a sound. The engine was remarkably quiet and Peter was thankful for it; a German patrol was not what they wanted to see or hear at this moment in time. Kit handled the boat with ease and the journey to the coast went without incident. They entered the mouth of the fjord hugging the left hand shoreline. Kit knew this was the least likely area for the German boats to be hiding because of the treacherous rocky skerries that needed great skill to navigate. They motored slowly and carefully toward the area where Peter would be put ashore and met by his next contact.

He could just make out the dark shapes of the towering mountains; they looked sinister and plunged for thousands of feet into the black depths below. He scoured every rock with his night vision glasses for signs of enemy activity or any thing that looked out of place or threatening.

"Keep a look out for a small green light on the left shoreline about a half a kilometre ahead that is to be your drop off point Peter."

"Ok," he said as he moved to the bow. After a few nerve-jangling minutes and straining his eyes, he saw what he was looking for. "There look, I can just see it, a flashing green light on top of that rocky outcrop. Pull in, in about a hundred metres." said Peter as he indicated off the port bow.

"There is a very small jetty be ready to jump when I say so. The man who is to meet you and take you on the next leg of journey is called Lars. I'll not be stopping for any longer than it takes you to get ashore, ok, so be ready?"

Kit put the engine into neutral and coasted in. The little craft bumped gently against the tiny landing stage and out of the darkness a pair of hands reached down and held onto the bow. Kit shook Peter's hand, Peter saw a weary concern in his eyes but neither man said anything

A whispered voice out of the darkness said, "Quickly, its Lars, give me your bag."

Peter passed it to him as he heaved himself out of the boat.

"Goodbye and good luck my friend," said Kit quietly as he reversed the boat back out into deep water.

With that he set off to his own village on the other side of the fjord.

The sound of the little boats engine became lost in the darkness, and Kit was gone.

"Come we must hurry, do you speak any Norwegian?" said Lars picking up his own bag and slinging it on his back.

"A little but I'm a bit rusty," said Peter, falling into step beside his new guide. Lars was smaller than Peter, very wiry with long sandy coloured hair hanging in great strands down his back. His face from what Peter could see was weathered and creased; his smile welcoming and his voice confident.

"Ok we will stick with the English, follow me and don't make a sound," as he set off on a path along the waters edge. Soon he took a turn to the left toward the mountains. Peters mind was thinking only of getting to his final destination and had little intention of talking. He had learned quickly that all of his contacts so far had said very little, either of themselves or of anything else. It was obvious they had been told to get him to Russia via the routes that were being kept open. And that's what they were doing. It was for everyone's safety that mouths were kept shut. Now he had to concentrate hard on where he was going. He could see very little of what was ahead of him so had to follow Lars quite closely. The path was narrow and steep and he tripped a few times over tussocks of grass, cursing quietly to himself.

They kept a steady pace for about two hours as the path went ever upwards eventually coming to rocky ledge.

"We will stop here and eat because the next part of our journey will be a four hour hard climb, if all goes well, and it will be cold."

Peter felt the old, horribly familiar fear of heights return. His head felt a little light and his legs didn't want to move. He didn't go near to where he suspected the ledge was although it was sometimes worse to imagine what was there, than to go and look.

Lars was watching him, an amused smile on his face, "Don't like heights eh?" he said as he sat on the ground.

"No, but don't worry, I'm fine," Peter lied as he sat next to him.

"Just don't sleepwalk that way," Lars smiled again and pointed over the edge, "there's quite a drop and you won't be found."

They unpacked a few of their rations and ate a simple but welcome meal.

A faint glow from the moon made eerie shadows on the ground sending Peter's weary mind and imagination into free fall. Small rocks looked like animals and larger ones became the enemy and he stared for some moments trying to get his thoughts in order. He knew he was tired but didn't realise how much it was affecting him. He concentrated on eating. The distant snowline was barely visible in the ghostly glow and he knew there was a hard climb ahead. Wind was rushing up from the valley and the temperature was dropping. He pulled his coat tightly around his shoulders.

"So, you are hoping to get to Russia," it was a statement rather than a question from the Norwegian. Peter nodded but stayed quiet.

"Oh don't worry all I know is your destination, I don't know why you are going nor do I need to. My time with you will end tomorrow when we reach the safe house when I will hand you to another guide and they will take you on the next part of your journey."

"Yes I'm headed for Russia; I only hope the damned Germans have the good grace to stay away."

"Ha, I wouldn't worry too much about them," the Norwegian said casually, "we have many groups in these mountains watching any movements of troops or patrols."

They sat for another few minutes staring toward the fjord though they could see very little. A black vastness stretched out before them and there was a smell in the air that told you there was water below, a long way below.

Peter was keeping a tight rein on his fear.

He felt a sudden surge of sadness; this was not how he had imagined his return trip to Russia would be. He wanted one day to have enough money to take Tally to her place of birth. Tell her all about her beautiful mother and the life he had planned, but it was not to be. Now he wondered what would be left of the town and of the people who might have survived in war-torn Russia.

"Finish your food Peter; we will not stop again now until we camp for the night." Lars pulled his water bottle from his bag and sat with his back against a tree. "See this?" he patted the trunk of the bowed old tree, "it is the last one we will pass until morning. We will soon be above the tree line, easier for us to spot any Germans but of course they can see us too." He smiled.

"Ok, we must keep moving and now we should now wear these," he pulled a couple of white capes from his backpack and handed one to Peter, "we'll soon be in the snow and we'll need all the camouflage we can." With his cape on and rope tied at the waist he hooked his arm into the strap of his rifle and slung it over his shoulder then started up the path again. Peter quickly put the big cape over his head picked up his rucksack and followed.

The path was difficult to see. It was a case of putting one foot in front of the other and hoping you didn't go down a rabbit hole and break your ankle. They just kept walking, in silence, in the dark.

The wind was still blowing hard up the valley and Peter was starting to feel cold and tired. The muscles in his legs were burning and his lack of sleep was beginning to tell. Their climb up into the mountains was strenuous, though Lars appeared to make light work of it. The snow was deceiving, some would be covering firm ground, the next it would be disguising a bog and they would sink in over their boots.

It was an energy sapping effort to keep on the move. After what seemed a lifetime of bursting lungs and aching muscles, Lars beckoned for them to stop. They had reached a flat area, which was in the shelter of a massive rock. The huge monolith looked so finely balanced on the edge of the bluff; it seemed that just touching it would send it crashing down the mountainside.

"We'll make camp here, it will be safe enough and no one can reach us without us seeing them first." Lars said. The pair took only a few minutes to set up their flimsy bivouac, pulling one corner of it over a rock and anchoring it down with stones. The other end was the door, which would be held with more rocks. It was very simple but it worked and before long they were inside sheltering from a blizzard that had blown in from the west. The night was one of freezing cold and very little sleep. Lars took the first two-hour watch while Peter settled into an uneasy rest with his head on his pack and his body curled up saving as much precious heat as he could. Lars, outside, looked east toward the valley they would travel through tomorrow. While Peter slept, he checked the rocks round about; these were the hiding places for messages and warnings to and from contacts and guides. There were none. Good, he thought, so far so good.

After a couple of hours he woke Peter. The big man crawled to the entrance of their makeshift shelter and looked toward the valley as Lars had directed. He felt a little better after his rest but his feet and hands were as cold as ice.

He held the canvas sheet of their tent around him like a shawl hanging on to try and stop it blowing away.

The night watches followed the same pattern, two hours on two hours off until they could make out a thin strip of weak morning light. Peter was now able to see the vast area of pine forests and pastures with a river running through the valley bottom. This is the route they were to follow today. It was startlingly beautiful.

"Our breakfast is simple fare." Lars handed him a bread roll filled with smoked meat. "Thanks, that's good. So you will be leaving me today?"

"Yes, we need to travel another few miles yet but with the weather getting better we should make good time. How are you feeling?"

"A lot better than yesterday, thanks. I was definitely feeling tired by the time we got here, but now I'm fine now." The men grinned at each other.

"You have done well, not many have managed the journey to this point in the time you have, you are a strong man Peter, but come we must move on."

They packed away their gear and set off. The trek to the 'safe house' was easier than Peter thought it would be. The weather had definitely improved with sun flashing on the snow and the sky a clear blue. They soon left the snowline behind them and took off their white capes. The walking became easier on the heathery grassland down to the valley floor. After a few miles Lars pointed to a cluster of little wooden houses that sat in the shelter of a hill. They all looked very old and deserted.

They made their way cautiously into a little muddy street. There was not a sound, and the air had the faint smell of wood smoke.

Together they walked up to one of the houses. It was a weather beaten place with grubby windows and ragged curtains. It's wooden porch leaning slightly. The front door looked as if it would fall down if you knocked on it. But Lars didn't go to front door. He walked around to the back of the house where there was a large overgrown garden covered with a jumble of old farming implements. A broken plough, which seemed to have become rooted into the ground. Bits of machinery that were rusted solid, and an old van that had seen better days with its green paint worn dulled by wind and weather and doors tied up with wire. Lars glanced at it as he walked toward the man standing at the back door with his arms out in welcome.

"Lars, Lars it is so good to see you and you have our traveller with you, hello Peter." The man held out his hand and gripped Peter's like a vice and hugged Lars like a bear.

"Hello," said Peter wincing at the strength and noticing how the two men looked remarkably alike. They were both the same height and build with the same long blond hair and their clothes almost identical

"Good to be here," said Lars laughing, "Peter this is Joachim, just call him Jo. He will take you on the next part of your journey. He is a good man and will look after you well, just you do everything he says and you will be ok."

"Please come in and have some warm food. I've been watching you come down off the mountain for the last hour you must be hungry," Jo said turning toward the house.

He led the way into a small dark kitchen. A large square table with four odd chairs stood in the middle of the stone floor. There was an open fire where a pan was simmering away, the smell was wonderful.

"Please sit," he said as he pulled out chairs for Peter and Lars, then got three dishes and started spooning out the hot soup. There was some rough bread already on the table.

"Eat now, I made this broth two days ago and so it's now at its best." Jo laughed as he sat down and started to pull the bread apart.

"Tell me of your journey Lars, did you see any German Patrols?"

"It was better than expected," he glanced at Peter who had a wry smile on his face, "Peter is a good companion and strong, so we made good time and no, we saw nothing of any patrols but heard a light aircraft during the night. It was difficult to tell whose it was but I suspect it would be a German. No harm done though."

"Hm, that's good, when we've eaten we will get packed and on our way again Peter. It will not take me long to get prepared but you can put your head down for a short while if you like," Jo said as he got up from the table.

"Ok, but I'd rather be on the move, what can I help you with?"

"Well, if you're sure," they ate heartily and soon finished the meal.

"Come with me Peter," Jo said as he got up from the table and went outside walking over to the old van, Peter's heart sank; he'd hoped this wasn't the transport.

"Right," said Jo, pointing, "go over to that old water tank and bring me the wheels from inside it."

Peter went to the other side of the muddy yard and took the wooden lid off the big drum and instead of water there were four good wheels, a wheel brace and a large jack. He quickly got everything over to Jo who by now had removed the sheets of wood that had hidden the bottom half of the van. He saw that it was up on big blocks of wood therefore it was easy to fit the wheels back on. Then Jo took all the wire off the door handles, and opened the van. He climbed in and looking at Peter, he grinned and started the engine. It sounded as sweet as any engine Peter had heard and he felt he had a lot to learn from these men.

"Right my friend are you ready?" Jo said, wiping his hands on an oily rag.

The three men said their goodbyes and Peter and his new guide climbed into the van while Lars stood at the door. Peter looked at him; this is exactly how Jo looked when he arrived.

A little way down the rough road, Peter commented on how alike the two men were.

"He's my twin brother," grinned Jo, "we have done this many times before. The stupid Germans know there is an old man living in that house but don't really bother him because he never seems to go anywhere, little do they know. So we stand in for each other. Lars works with the resistance groups in the west and I work on the east, see?"

"And the Germans don't suspect anything?"

"We are very careful not be seen much at the house together. We always wear the same clothes, and being twins, we tend to act in the same way just going about our business on the little land we have. So unless the Germans have reason to come and see us, they leave us alone. Mind you, we do make sure that any passing patrols that do stop get the best of the food they think we have. There was one night when a patrol of two men came in and ate with me, they were starving and hated the war just wishing to get through it without killing anyone. They swore me to secrecy because they would have been in big trouble fraternising with the enemy. I suspect they are deserters. Trouble was Lars was hiding in the barn freezing his bits off waiting for them to go. That was a close thing I can tell you but we can smile about it now."

"My God." Said Peter hanging on for dear life as the van rattled and shook its way down the slippery mountain track. It felt as if it was going to fall apart at any minute as Jo wrestled with the huge steering wheel. Old tyres, wooden planks and assorted junk jumped about in the rear of the van making a hell of a racket.

"It's all good for the image," he shouted to Peter.

It wasn't long before they reached what could be called a half decent road and Jo floored the van even harder. They hurtled through little villages, which showed no signs of life, and passed thick, dense black forests.

"Don't be deceived by the seemingly empty houses," Jo said, "we have many friends in the countryside and they know how to keep us informed if there are any German patrols about. I was going to stop for fuel at a little house back in the first village but there was a yellow paper flower in the window. That means the Germans have called on them in the last two days so now we must go to another place and hope they haven't had a visit."

They eventually came to a deserted looking hamlet and the van rolled into a yard behind a large house. Jo switched off the engine and sat for a while. Peter's ears were ringing and he was glad of the silence.

"Ok, it's too dark to go any further without putting on the lights so we'll bed down here for the night. You stay here in the van for a while and keep your head down, I'll go and check for fuel and come back for you," said Jo as he jumped out and made his way quietly to the house.

Peter looked around but couldn't make out very much apart from the house, a barn and some old tumbled down outbuildings. He risked winding down his side window and breathed in the night air, all was very still and quiet. He looked again at the barn. Was that a faint light he could see or was his mind playing tricks? No it was a light from a cigarette. He could now smell the smoke from it. Whoever it was, they were standing very still by the end of the wall. Peter just sat there quietly wishing now he hadn't opened the squeaky window. His hand went to his gun, which had become his close companion. He felt the cold metal of the P 35 under his fingers and hoped that whoever was having the sly smoke was friendly.

They must have heard the noisy van and seen Jo going into the house, so, were they now waiting for him to come out? Peter's mind was working overtime. His heart was thumping fast. Why did Jo say wait in the van. Where was he, and if Peter did have to shoot, the noise would wake the dead in this tiny quiet place. A few minutes past and the smoker threw the cigarette end onto the ground making a little shower sparks. His boot ground out the evidence and all was dark again. Now Peter didn't know where the smoker had gone. He stared toward the barn straining his ears and eyes for anything that moved but he saw only the black shape of the building. Then he heard a sound from the house, it was Jo with some cans of petrol. He tried to see where the smoker had gone and what Jo was doing. If the smoker decided to attack now all hell would break loose. He figured they wouldn't have moved very far from the end wall because that's where they would have a good view of the van and the house. So he kept his gun pointed in that direction, his other hand on the door handle ready to jump out.

"Alright there Jo; do you need a hand?" came a man's voice from the barn. The smoker thought Peter.

"No thanks Ulf, we are here for the night, I'll fill her up in the morning."

"Goodnight then."

"Goodnight."

As Jo looked into the van he could see by Peter's face that he was a little puzzled.

"It's ok Peter; Ulf is a friend of ours. He knew we were coming and just kept and eye open for anything unexpected. I must tell him not to smoke though I can still smell it and that could get a person shot."

You don't know how near he came, thought Peter as he put his gun back into his belt.

The night passed peacefully and they slept well in the big old beds in the attic of the farmhouse. In the morning they ate a quick breakfast of bread and cheese served to them by a young girl who smiled but said nothing. Peter thought she may be the daughter of whoever it was who lived there but knew better than to ask any questions.

After they had fuelled up the van and tied another few cans in the back they were soon on their way east.

They made good time through lush green valleys trying to stick to the back roads and those used by farmers. Jo chatted about himself and his brother and how they would fight to the end to stop Germany from winning the war. Peter told him about his life on Shetland and his beautiful daughter who he missed dearly and prayed she would be ok.

"She sounds a very special lady; I may even come and visit you after this mess is done with" he smiled at Peter.

"You will be made very welcome Jo; I hope you can make it, you and your brother, and yes she is special, you don't know how much."

The two men travelled in easy silence but both keeping an eye on the sky as well as the road.

After a day of bone shaking and noise the little green van stopped at another village and pulled into the courtyard of a stone house. They were greeted by a sombre looking man and shown into the kitchen. Jo hugged the man and spoke in whispers for a few minutes before coming to the table, which was set for a simple supper. Very little was said by Jo or anyone else in the house other than a few courtesies. Peter was uneasy. He had the feeling that something was very wrong and perhaps it wasn't safe to stay the night but Jan assured him they would be ok. The owner had asked that they leave at first light and of course they agreed. Peter was glad to have another warm bed for the night but he was just as glad to get back on the road. It was a freezing cold grey morning as they drove quickly and quietly away from the house settling in for another long day's journey.

"What a strange place Jo," he said wrapping and old blanket around him. "All seemed very quiet, have they had trouble from the Germans?"

"Yes," Jo said, "sadly they have. They are good people and friends of mine and have been helping agents from Norway and Russia since the occupation. A couple of days ago they had a visit from a German patrol. Their son was taken away and they have no idea where he is or even if he's alive. The lad knew something of the work his parents did so that of course puts him in great danger. He's only twelve years old, God help him, and I don't think the Germans will show much mercy."

"How come the patrol didn't take the parents?"

"They were both out of the house at the time and the boy was just doing some work around the place."

"So how did they know the Germans had taken him?"

"There were two British airmen being hidden upstairs. They'll have heard it all I'm afraid, and had to sit tight of course. I don't imagine they would have told the parents exactly what the Germans did to the boy but there were bloodstains on the floor when the parents got back and their son was gone. The airmen had to be moved that day, and that poor lad had the guts to keep his mouth shut." Jo shook his head slowly.

"My God will this ever end?"

"Oh it will end, but not until we lose many more friends and even family. We must be more vigilant now than ever," they continued in silence.

Jo drove steadily, "We will be going onto more back roads soon, just until we get over the border into Sweden, then we will make better time"

It was now only two hundred miles to the coast, the roads were good and for once they could relax a little.

"This is more like it," said a grinning Jo, driving with a bread roll in one hand and a lump of cheese in the other. "We will be there in no time." They pressed on stopping only to fill the van with petrol from the cans they carried.

Their route took them through the mountains and down toward the coast. About halfway, Jo turned off onto a quieter road through Kalarne that followed the railway line on toward Umea on the coast.

"You know that Sweden is playing the neutral card, don't you?" Jan asked

"Of course, yes, why?"

"Well the Germans are being allowed to use Swedish railways to transport their heavy tanks and guns, and I wonder just how many Swedish people actually know that?"

"Then the Swedes must be getting something out of it, mustn't they?"

"I suppose so, they're at least able to track where all this stuff is going and pass on the information to the Allies, though it does just seem a bit rich to me."

"Hm," said Peter, glancing out at the railway line that ran next to the road.

"I don't suppose you know what time the next Nazi train is," he smiled.

"No, I don't, though it would be interesting to see it blow up. We have the goods," laughed Jo.

"We will soon be in Birch City and from there we go to Finland."

"Birch City, where is that?"

"Its correct name is Umea but it's known by the trees that were planted after the great fire in 1888. It's a very nice place but we're going only to get on the boat I have waiting for us."

He swung the little van onto another bumpy road and put his foot down, Peter hung on. He was beginning to wonder at the great network of men, women and children who were all part of a massive force trying to outwit the German war machine. He felt humbled that so many were willing to help him.

Ahead he could see a huge wide river with Finland on the far bank. The weather was being kind; it was clear but very cold so it was certainly going to be bitter on the water.

"We will of course be posing as fishermen for the journey so you will feel quite at home Peter; you might even catch us some supper," Jo chuckled.

"I'll see what I can do."

They slithered to a halt on the icy mud in front of an old wharf. The boat sat in the water in front of them. As fishing boats go, this one was good. Peter could see that it had been well looked after and appeared to be fully equipped to go to sea, he noticed too that it had a large covered oil drum on the stern.

He jumped aboard while Jo parked the van behind an old shed, lifted the bonnet and took the rotor arm out of the engine and put it in his pocket then walked back to the boat.

"That will only stay hidden until someone comes snooping around but that's the chance I'll have to take. Without the rotor arm they'll not get anywhere and I might still have a lift home." He smiled at Peter.

The two men stuffed their bags and supplies into the seat lockers. Jo retrieved the key which had been carefully stuck behind a tide table pinned to the cabin wall and put it in the ignition. He prayed it would start first time; they couldn't afford to make too much noise attracting unwanted attention.

The engine didn't start; both men looked at each other. He tried again, and with a cough and a puff of smoke from the stern the engine fired up. Jo signalled to Peter to cast off.

They were soon heading east and the coast was fast approaching. Peter's heart was thumping, he suddenly felt as if the whole mission was indeed possible whereas before he doubted he would make it to Norway. It was bitterly cold and the ancient paraffin stove gave out less heat then a candle. They motored without lights into the gathering gloom, toward where they could just make out the faint glimmer of a lamp. Peter stood on deck with the paraffin fumes drifting around him.

"See that?" asked Jo pointing ahead to where the lamp was.

"Yes I see, is that where we're headed?"

"It is. I've arranged to meet someone who will transport you further on your way east; I just hope it's him."

The light on the shore pointed straight at them, and then began to move up and down, Jo steered towards it and switched off the engine when just a few metres out and let the boat drift quietly into a tiny horseshoe shaped beach. There was a soft scraping sound as it bottomed and glided to a halt. Jo jumped into the shallow water with a mooring rope in his hand and started up the beach. Peter quickly grabbed his bag of supplies and followed. Jo tied the boat to an old wooden post and started talking quietly to the man with the lamp. This was a perfect place to come ashore. The beach was steep and had large sand dunes around it, sheltering it from prying eyes.

The man's face was hardly visible, hidden by a dark hat pulled down low and he wore the same black clothing as many of Peter guides. Jo introduced the two men then they walked to a waiting car which unseen from the beach was parked on a narrow track behind the dunes. Jo grasped Peters hand and shook it hard, there was nothing to say that hadn't already been said so they just parted there on the track and Peter got into the waiting car as Jo hurried away back to the boat.

The big Mercedes was warm and smelled of old leather and oil. The seats though very worn were comfortable and it didn't take long before Peter could feel himself starting to drift off to sleep. The man in the driving seat was silent and big so Peter stayed quiet.

"You can grab some sleep if you want," the man said after a while, Peter jumped; he must have already started to doze.

"Thanks, I will." He relaxed again and could feel the heat washing over him. He was asleep within minutes while the car went quietly from the track to a road. He soon awoke to the sound of voices and found that they'd stopped at the edge of a wood. The driver was talking to someone inside a makeshift cabin. Peter found his gun and held it gently, pointing in the direction of the men, just in case it was a trap.

He didn't know who the driver was or where he was being taken. He only had Jo's word to trust these people and they will help him reach his final objective. The driver came back and got into the car and presented Peter with a bag, which contained bread, cheese, sausages and milk.

"Thanks, I'm sorry I didn't catch your name back on the beach."

"Sig. You eat now," and Peter did just that as he was very hungry and the food was welcome. The big car started moving over the muddy track through the wood, crackling small branches under its wheels. Peter wondered whether Sig was really this mans name but was not about to ask, Sig was fine by him.

It was now pitch black and he began to wonder where they might stop for the night. He soon found out when the car pulled off the road into a field. They bumped along its rutted edge for about a hundred metres towards a barn and the car didn't stop. Sig drove it straight into the huge wooden structure, did a quick u-turn and parked facing back out of the big doors. The barn was dark and dusty and there were old bales of hay stacked on one side, neglected now and of no use to anyone, the farmers long gone.

"This is us for the night, sleep on the hay, not in the car, make yourself comfortable, but you mustn't go outside." He got out of the Mercedes and walked over to the big doors pulling them partly closed then came back and opened the boot. There, wrapped in oily rags was a machine gun, which he set on top of some boxes, pointing it toward the doors.

"We can't take chances." He said. He was a man of few words and Peter wondered how long he would have this quiet travelling companion.

The smell of sun dried hay in this dusty barn brought back fond memories for Peter. Growing up as he did on a farm with his parents and his older brother. Many a day was spent running around playing 'hidden comrade' in their barns. Thoughts of this long ago life of sunshine, laughter and love helped him drift off to sleep.

His guide was not so relaxed. The man sat on a bale of hay with his back against the wall and arms resting easily on the box, which held the gun. He did not sleep. He was listening and looking, eyes wide open, concentrating, not making a sound.

It came from the left side of the barn; a sound of movement. Someone was trying to walk quietly over gravel and frozen earth. Sig crept over to where Peter lay and clamped his huge hand over the sleeping mans mouth. Peter jumped, and tried to sit up. He soon realised he couldn't move because of the weight of the man who held a finger over his lips to tell him to be quiet and then pointed at the door. Peter got up slowly and took out his gun. Holding it in both hands arms outstretched pointed toward the doors. Sig went silently to the machine gun on the boxes. They waited. The sound of a release bolt on the big gun was like a twig snapping in a silent wood but they could still hear the movement outside getting nearer and nearer.

With their eyes used to the darkness it wasn't hard to see the shape of a man appearing in the thin shaft of dull light between the doors. Neither man moved. The intruder crept slowly into the barn towards the car. He put his hand on the engine cover to see if it was still warm. Then he edged silently to the driver's door and tried the handle. It suddenly opened with a muffled bang sending the intruder flying over backwards dropping his gun on the way and leaving him in shock on the floor. Sig rushed to where he lay and grabbed him by the scruff of his neck dragging him to his feet.

"Who are you?" He hissed.

"Please don't hurt me." He looked dazed and confused holding his arms over his head, his face bleeding from the blast. His accent was broken Norwegian.

"Hurt you? I'll fucking kill you if you don't tell me right now who you are and what you're doing here." Sig shook the man violently and swiped the back of his hand across his face bringing more blood from his mouth.

"Please, please, I just wanted to know who you were. I saw the car come in earlier and was curious that's all." He licked some of the blood from his lips and grimaced at the taste.

"What time did you see us arrive?" asked Sig as he tightened his grip on the man's collar. Peter picked up the intruders gun and moved to the door to keep a look out wondering what Sig had done to the car door.

"I think it was about five hours ago. I was walking home and saw you." His voice and body were trembling uncontrollably.

"You stinking liar, we were not here five hours ago and I suspect you weren't walking home. Who are you, who sent you and do try to get it right this time. This may help your memory?" He punched him hard in the stomach, the man fell forward but Sig kept hold of his jacket collar and brought his knee up sharply into the mans face bursting his nose and spurting more blood out onto the dust. As the man headed for the floor he received a massive rabbit punch to the back of his neck. He lay there groaning and looked up in terror. Sig took out a knife from the back of his trouser belt and held it to the man's bloodied face.

"You have less than a minute to save yourself, so, if you do not tell me what I want to know, you are a dead man."

The man just looked at Sig and gave a twisted bloody smile, he tried to move but couldn't. His eyes strained to see what Peter was doing by the door. He tried to turn his head but he was having great difficulty doing so. In fact he was having difficulty moving at all.

"Having trouble are you?" asked Sig menacingly, watching the man struggle, "you are now paralysed, and I think you've just found that out, eh?" he said in a hoarse whisper. The look of utter disbelief on the man's face as the full horror of what had happened dawned on him. Sig bent down and said something to him but Peter couldn't hear what it was. The man was pleading for something, and then through bloodied teeth with his face twisted in fear he cried, "Ach nein mutti, hilf mir, Gott! Ich kann mich nicht bewegen." Sig took his knife and with one swift movement cut the man's throat. There was a rush of blood onto the floor and a sickening gurgle from the man's mouth, then silence.

"My God did you have to kill him?" Peter whispered.

"Yes, I think I did," Sig said calmly wiping the blood from his knife, "you didn't hear what I said to him did you?"

"No, but…"

"Simple, he could have told me who he was, and who sent him, but he chose not too. So I told him to pray and ask his mother and his God for forgiveness."

"And?"

"Oh he prayed alright, in German; remember Peter, fear is a great leveller. Come we will have to leave now."

After the two men packed the weapons into the car Sig walked to the barn door and scratched a simple heart with two crosses on it

"What's that for?" asked Peter.

"It's 'our' language, it will tell the group we are safe and on our way and we pray we'll meet again."

"How will they know we are both safe?"

"One heart, that means we have gone, two kisses one for each of us, romantic eh? Come." Sig gave a wry smile.

The two men drove for hours, every mile taking them further from the barn. They had left the body hidden under bales of hay. It wouldn't be too long before it was found, Sig didn't care. He reckoned that whoever discovered him wouldn't spend too much time wanting to know what had happened, unless of course it was the Germans.

The weather was freezing and the landscape was white and bleak. Crops were dying in the fields and the few cattle looked starved and unattended. Sig didn't seem to notice anything; he just drove and sometimes struggled to keep the big car on the road.

"Tell me, what did you do to the car door back there?"

"Just a small charge, but enough to catch anyone unawares."

"What if I had gone to the car to get something?"

"You didn't," he just kept looking forward and left Peter silent.

"Soon we will come to the border where there may be a patrol so I'm going to get off this road, so be prepared." Peter just nodded and put his hand on his gun.

Suddenly, the car lurched to the left skidding into a farmyard and on through an open gate into a field. The border ran along the small river at the bottom of a snow-covered bank at the edge of a field. It came and went in a shower of mud and snow as the big car hurtled across the rough ground crashing onto a ford over the icy stream. Its roof snatching at some low hanging branches on the way. Any guards who may have been standing on the main road would no doubt have heard the noise but would not have been quick enough to do much about it.

There were clouds of steam and inside the car was the smell of an overheating engine and an even hotter exhaust as it hit the freezing water. Peter hung on for grim death, his feet pressed hard against the floor and a hand jammed on the roof to stop him being thrown around. Sig gripped the steering wheel as if his life depended on it. He put his foot to the floor as the roaring mud spattered vehicle growled and slipped its way up the bank on the other side of the river and on to another track. He didn't stop or slow down; he drove even faster as if the Devil himself was on his tail.

They had reached Russia.

"You ok?" he shouted as he looked at Peter with a wicked grin on his face.

"Yes thanks, woke me up though," Peter smiled.

"I like to give them a run for their money if they're there, but I didn't see anyone. Now, get some food out, we can eat as we go."

Peter retrieved the bags of supplies from the back of the car with some difficulty as everything had been flung around onto the floor. He squeezed himself between the thick leather seats, not easy for a big man and at seventy kilometres an hour on a bumpy road.

"Where are we headed now?" He asked giving Sig a sandwich or what was left of one.

"I have friends in Medvezhegorsk, our next stop. It's a long drive but we should be ok, so long as this rattletrap keeps going." It started to snow.

Peter had never known such weariness. This whole journey was like a dream, which could fast become a nightmare. He touched the broad belt around his waist that held the documents he was carrying, and began to wonder just how important they would turn out to be. With no knowledge of what they contained he couldn't make any judgement but felt that he had somehow, back in Shetland, walked into a rather nicely set trap.

CHAPTER ELEVEN

Peter Gregor had grown up with his brother Stefan on their parent's farm, which sat on the outskirts of the little town of Revda. It was a little grey town in an anonymous landscape. The whole of this vast open countryside was dotted with small farms. Most of them grew wheat but in recent years some had ventured into cotton crops and then seen the vicious winters wipe them out. The Gregor's farm was a substantial two storey wooden house, which sat half a kilometre from the road. Surrounded by beautiful birch and pine trees it was sheltered from the worst of the north winds. Wooden outbuildings formed a quadrangle around a large yard. Two were used for storing the grain harvest throughout the year. One was for keeping all the farm equipment. The other had pens for the cows that would be brought in at wintertime to survive the freezing weather. Peter and Stefan would have to help with all the cattle before they went to school. Life back then was hard but happy and safe.

Both boys attended the local village school, which was a small two roomed building on the main street backing on to the river Chusovaya. In winter the place was so cold there was ice on the inside of the windows all day. Many of the children huddled in their coats while at lessons and sat with chattering teeth. At break time they were able to get out into the sunshine to play and laugh as they watched their breath dancing in the frosty air. Even in summer the rooms smelled of damp and still had the coldness of winter in the walls. There were only two male teachers both of whom had limited views of achievement. If a boy or girl could describe and draw different parts of a tractor and explain the function of them, then as far as they were concerned that child had a future. Stefan loved school; he was a star pupil and could talk about crops, tractors, harvesters, motorbikes and anything mechanical all day. Peter on the other hand was desperate to learn about the world and physics, geography and languages. He became frustrated with the teachers and was given little encouragement to learn anything other than 'traditional' lessons. He was often told that subjects, 'not in the interest of Mother Russia' were no good to anyone'. His parents applied for him to attend college in the nearby town when he'd finished at the village school. And finally the day came when he said goodbye and set off for a new life in Tagil to the north of Redva. It was here that he met a tutor who encouraged him to pursue his ultimate dream to become a submariner. Peter wrote often to his parents and his brother telling them how he enjoyed college life in this beautiful city and had met many new friends, though he missed his childhood sweetheart Zhanna and his mothers cooking. He hoped to join the Navy very soon but that of course meant that he would have to go even further away to Archangel.

It was a September morning, the sun was shining and the leaves on the trees were fiery red and gold. The ground was covered with a cold sparkling frost and Peter was looking forward to his last days in college before graduating. He was about to leave his small apartment when a single envelope dropped through the letterbox onto the hallway floor. He picked it up. His heart began to race at the sight of his fathers writing. His father never wrote to him, it was always his mother. Putting down his bag of college work he walked slowly back into the kitchen and sat down tearing open the old envelope with its pencilled address. His fathers' writing was scrawled and shaky and it took a while to grasp what he had written. His mother had taken very ill and was not expected to live many more days. Peter felt sick. He immediately contacted the college and asked the principle for leave to go home. He left Tagil within an hour, taking a bus to the local train station hoping and praying that his mother would be well when he arrived home. The journey seemed endless, nothing but forests and fields. A bleak landscape that was a study in white. Finally he arrived near to his home but had to run the last mile from where a neighbour's wagon had dropped him off. He banged on the door gasping for breath. His brother opened it and just stood there, his eyes red raw from crying. He turned back into the house and went to the room where their mother lay. Peter followed snatching off his hat and walked straight to the bed falling on his knees. His mother's body lay silent and unmoving on a bed of brightly coloured blankets. He took her hand; it was barely warm, and looked at his father and brother, tears streaming down their faces neither of them knowing quite what to do.

"Is she's dead?" Peter asked choking back tears.

"Yes," said his brother, putting his hand on Peters shoulder, "just minutes before you arrived"

"Oh God, what happened. I came as soon as I got your letter?"

"Poisoned," Peter's father cried his face creased with anguish

"What, what do you mean poisoned?"

"She ate some mushrooms that she'd gathered from the field," his father broke down again, wiping the tears away with the grubby sleeve of this shirt.

"Mushrooms! No, Mother knew which were safe and which were not, we've eaten them before," Peter said incredulously

"Well this time the poor thing got it wrong," Stefan said through his tears.

"The doctor was here yesterday. He said her kidneys and liver had given out. There was nothing he could do."

Peter just looked at this mother laying there, her wispy grey-brown hair framing her strong pale face. He remembered all the good times, and the hard times too. How he had wanted her to see him make something of himself. His world had just come crashing down around him and he wept like a baby. A day later she was buried at the village church. A simple service was given by the priest, the three men standing by the grave in stunned silence. A few good neighbours were huddled in a group saying quiet prayers. The following week Peter returned to Tagil and made preparations for his move to Archangel. He began to question why he'd left home to carve out his own life and career and not stay at home to help with the farm. Was he being selfish or was he following the dreams his mother had always encouraged him to follow? He could not decide and only hoped she would have been proud of him.

CHAPTER TWELVE

Arriving in Archangel on a freezing cold day he met with his commanding officer and fellow crewmen. They were shown their land quarters, which were in a rather fine block of apartments near the base. This would be their home until they were ready to sail. Then they were taken to the dock to see the submarine for the first time.

This was to be a sight Peter would never forget.

The massive sub was riding low in the water, moored there with great ropes and fenders. It looked grey and menacing against the huge concrete harbour walls. A weak winter sun shone pale on its surface.

The boat was called 'Galiana.' She was a Holland type built in nineteen fourteen and the best the Imperial Navy had. Driving her were six huge powerful diesel engines, giving her a surface speed of over nine knot

He was to be part of a crew of forty-seven and his intense training moved him quickly through the ranks taking promotion whenever it was offered. Now he took in the sight of this amazing fighting machine.

War was raging in Europe, Germany the aggressor was powerful well armed and organised, but when Russia entered the theatre of war it was in a ramshackle inefficient way. All powers were decentralised; bureaucracy incompetent and no one knew who was running the Government. A growing body of unrest against the Tsar was beginning. In the countryside there was a lot of talk of revolution, there was a widening gap between workers and officials. Peasants began rioting as their land was unfairly divided by faceless bureaucrats who were power mad and greedy. There had been various Prime Ministers and Foreign Ministers over a period of just a couple of years leading up to the war. Russia's transport systems were old, worn out and inadequate and the closing of both the Black Sea ports and the Baltic left the country almost cut off from its allies. The only port open, when not icebound, was Archangel. And it was here Peter stood, about to enter a whole new chapter of his life.

He remembered his father telling him that Russia was being torn apart by the people of the land, the Government and the Tsar but mostly by war, and that he must make his own choices in the world, "There will be revolution son and it will be bloody."

Peter spent two years on the *'Galiana'* then returned home to the farm for some well-earned leave.

It was here back in the village that he married his sweetheart, Zhanna.

They had grown up and gone to school together. Their families had neighbouring farms and helped each other through harvest and the bad times. Peter had fallen in love at an early age and knew that one day he would marry this beautiful girl. As they grew older they knew that they were meant for each other. Peter was the tall, strong, gentle man and Zhanna was the dark haired fiery beauty who stole his heart. In summer they would walk through the wheat fields for hours just treasuring each other's company. Sometimes Zhanna would sit quietly and sketch a picture, which she would then give to Peter as a memento of their day.

The wedding was a simple affair with only their families and a few close friends. The weather was sunny and warm as they walked from the church to the little old school, which had been decked out with ribbons and flowers for the wedding breakfast. Music played and everyone danced and sang long into the night. Peter and Zhanna laughed and hugged each other with a passion that comes from knowing they were soon to be parted. Six days later Peter had to return to his post so left his wife with the promise to return at the first possible chance.

It was to be nine months later at his base in Archangel that a telegram arrived. It informed him that his wife was soon to give birth but her health was giving rise for concern and he should try to return home as soon as possible.

That journey was to be the worst of his life and memories of his mother's death were clouding his mind. War was crawling across Russia. The Bolsheviks had come to power the previous year and Lenin, ruthless and single minded was stirring up trouble against the Government. Peter had no idea what he was to find in his own town but was desperate to get there. There were no trains to speak of, those that were running were ferrying supplies to the army and so was not an option. The only way he could get home with any speed was to buy some sort of transport and drive the hundreds of miles. He knew of a garage not far from the docks so went that day and bartered with the old man who was only too happy to part with an ancient black van. Wiping his hands on an greasy rag he said it may not look much but he had just overhauled the engine and it would serve Peter well. Peter said he'd be back to see him if he found out the man was lying, the man recognised a threat when he saw one. He also knew better than to argue the price offered by the officer standing in front of him.

Stopping only for fuel and snatched meals on his journey home, Peter pressed on thinking every minute of his wife. He arrived at the outskirts of his hometown of Sverdlovsk and realised that something was very wrong. Winding down the window as he drove he heard the sounds of gunshot and could see fires burning in the streets. His heart was racing as he headed into the town.

Times were not safe; the great revolution that Lenin had spoken of to peasants and workers and anti-Tsarists had arrived. People had taken to the streets and were finally venting their feelings against the rule of the autocrats, and privileged classes.

Driving through the darkened streets he decided to park away from the house and so not draw attention to himself. He pulled up in a lane where few people would choose to walk. The area was dark and hidden from the main road. He locked the doors and put the key into his pocket not knowing whether it would be there or not when he came back. From there he ran down the back alleys and narrow lanes to his home passing a gang of men who glared at him and noted his uniform. They were not to know whether he was friend or foe so he kept on running. By now the sweat was trickling down his face. His breath was coming in short gasps as he slipped and slid on the cobbles. He kept saying his wife's name over and over hoping that she could hear him. Noise was everywhere. Crowds were gathering on street corners, some smashing windows and he noticed there were flames coming from the local government offices. The mood of the people was ugly and unpredictable.

At the block of apartments where Peter and Zhanna lived, another crowd had gathered. Their home was in an elegant suburb of Sverdlovsk. Many business people chose to live in this leafy part of town with its broad tree lined streets and beautifully manicured parks. Now it felt a very different place. As Peter approached he could see a crowd milling around on the muddy wet grass, which had once been well kept lawns. They were agitated, sounded loud and ready for a fight. Some had sticks, some had knives but all looked angry as they shouted abuse at a government worker who happened to live below the Gregors. Peter pulled his coat around him and hurried to the rear of the building and ran up the concrete staircase so as not to be seen. He stopped outside his own apartment and banged on the door as he searched for his key. He was breathing heavily and wiped a shaking hand over his face. All he wanted was to see his wife. There was no answer and fear grew in his gut. He looked through the little window by the door but could see nothing; the place was in darkness. There was no sign of his key as he cursed and looked around for help.

He banged again but knew anyone inside would have heard him the first time. He walked up and down the long dimly lit corridor either side of his apartment but found no one or any signs of his wife. He looked over the balcony to another group of people below and wondered if he should ask them if they'd seen anyone about, it was his only chance. The man who seemed to be the ringleader looked up and spotted him, so Peter asked if anyone had left this block recently. The man shouted up to him that two women had left about three hours ago. One of them appeared to be quite ill; she was carried away on the back of a horse-drawn cart. He didn't know where too but he pointed in the direction of the woods at the back of the apartments. Peter thanked him and started running back down the stairs. He knew that Zhanna's maid Eva had a little place nearby so headed in that direction. His lungs were fit to burst by the time he spotted the cottage. He could see that the lights were on and that the horse and cart were tethered up outside. He was cautious as he approached the door and stood for a couple of minutes listening. There was the sound of a baby crying and a woman weeping. He knocked gently on the door and the weeping stopped suddenly. There was a movement and the door opened just enough for Eva to peer out, her face wet with tears.

"Oh thank God it's you Peter, come in come in," she cried, wringing her hands and pacing the floor.

"We waited so long for you to come, it is Gods will," she continued to cry and hugged Peter with such force that he had to ease her hands gently from his arms.

"Zhanna, Peter has come," she called out, "you must be strong my child."

Peter looked puzzled,

"Where is Zhanna, where is she?" he turned on Eva.

"Where is she?" he shouted at the maid who couldn't stop crying or walking round and round the tiny room.

"She's so ill Peter, it has killed her. You must take your beautiful baby daughter and go, go and go now," she pleaded through her tears.

"What do you mean Eva where is she?"

He rushed through the door at the back of the room.

"Oh God," wept Eva as she followed him to where Zhanna was lying in bed. Her face was pale and sweating as she looked at Peter holding up her arms to him.

"My darling Zhanna," he said cradling her gently and kissing her face. "You'll be ok; I'll take you away now and get you to a hospital." He was starting to panic, what had gone wrong.

"Darling Peter," she looked at him with tears in her eyes, "I am dying. I know that. The doctor has told me I will not recover, please listen to me." Her breathing came like quiet whispers; her body looked emaciated.

"You must take the child and look after him. Give him all the love that you have given me. Show him how to be strong like you and let him live his life in the sunlight." her voice was fading.

Eva was weeping uncontrollably beside the tiny cot,

"You had a girl my darling Zhanna, a little girl remember?" Eva said through her tears.

Peter turned to look at Eva wondering what she was talking about, and then he looked into the cot and saw the face of a beautiful tiny girl. "We have a daughter my darling, a beautiful daughter," he said holding onto his wife.

"No, we have...a...son, call him...Sergei...I love you." They were the last whispered words Peter was to hear from his wife.

He sat with her nestled in his arms, not wanting to let go. He closed her eyes very gently and it broke his heart. He could no longer see the love when she looked at him. It was the look in those eyes that melted his heart all those years ago.

Eva quietly took his hand and told him to go into the other room while she attended to Zhanna. He didn't think he had the strength to stand up so just sat staring down at the body of his wife. He felt as if he'd been frozen in time. His mind went dark and his body felt calm and peaceful.

How could this happen to him, the death of his beautiful wife giving birth to their child. It brought back all the painful memories of when his mother died before he could get to her. He just sat there listening to Eva weeping. He didn't care anymore; he was not worried, not frightened, and hardly capable of any thought. He kissed his wife's cool lips and just held her. He talked gently to her about all the things they were going to do. Where they were going to live and all they'd planned together for a future full of children and laughter, a couple of dogs, some chickens and goats. And how they'd laughed when Zhanna said she wanted a white horse to ride out into the hills. Well, she would now have her white horse, if there was God in Heaven.

Peter's last image of his wife was of her lying on the little bed covered in a blue blanket. Her face still beautiful in death and her eyes closed forever to the world.

All through the night Peter and Eva talked and wept for Zhanna, their hopes and dreams.

Zhanna's funeral took place in the local church the following day. It was a simple service with only Peter, Eva and the baby there to say goodbye. The priest seemed to find it difficult to look at them but Peter wasn't going to worry about this strangely reticent man of the cloth. As they left the church and walked out into the drizzling rain, Peter left a small bunch of flowers at the graveside. He felt numb and useless.

He looked at the child in his arms and felt so lonely; she was beautiful just like her mother. Her hair was dark and thick; her eyes staring up at him were of the darkest blue. She just lay quietly as if waiting for him to speak, eventually he did.

"I will look after you. You are now my world," he sobbed quietly and kissed her head.

Eva was insisting he take the baby and leave as soon as possible. Her persistence was beginning to irritate him. Something didn't feel right. All he wanted to do was go back to their apartment and surround himself with Zhanna's things. Her clothes, that still held the faint smell of her perfume. The little toys, which she'd kept since childhood and the pictures she'd painted hoping one day to decorate their home.

Eventually he packed up a few of his and Zhanna's belongings. Then he sorted out some food and provisions for the journey. Eva had given simple instructions as to how to look after the baby hoping and praying they would be safe. Peter walked back to where he had parked the van, and was surprised to find it safe and still locked. He had a quick look around it to make sure it hadn't been tampered with then drove to the little street near Eva's place and put their meagre supplies in the back. He took the tiny cot and tied it with an old rope to the front seat. On leaving, he faced Eva hugging her gently. She looked wretched and hadn't stopped crying and fussing around the baby since Peter had arrived, so it was almost with something of a relief that he said his goodbyes,

"I know that you and the doctor did everything you could to save Zhanna, please do not blame yourself," he was finding it difficult to speak to Eva.

Eva flinched and broke away from his arms, fresh tears coursing down her cheeks and great sobs shaking her body.

"I will get word to you as soon as I can Eva," he said gently.

"You must go, and take good care of that precious, precious girl," Eva said, sobbing as she kissed the baby.

"Goodbye."

Eva pulled a small cotton bag out of her pinafore pocket and handed it to Peter.

"You must take this, protect it with your life, it is now the child's, she is the only one now." She pushed the bag into Peter's hand and wrapped his fingers tightly around it squeezing hard. Her hands were shaking uncontrollably.

Peter looked puzzled but put the unopened bag into his pocket.

"Goodbye darling child," he heard her whisper, as he turned to walk away.

Then Peter stopped suddenly and looked at Eva, "Why did Zhanna think she'd had a baby boy, she even wanted me to call him Sergei?"

"I don't know Peter, she was very ill, her blood was poisoned. You must understand the pain she suffered made her quite delirious. She was confused, and the birth of the baby came as a great relief from some of that pain." Eva sounded scared which Peter thought strange but this was a time when a lot of Russians were scared.

"What happened to my son Eva?" he said it so quietly, his eyes never leaving hers.

"I don't know what you're talking about," her voice a whisper but she looked terrified.

"I think you know exactly what I'm talking about," his voice icy now.

"No, please God, it's your child, you must believe me, it's your child."

"My wife told me we had a son," his voice rising with anger, "you tell me we have a daughter. I want to believe my wife Eva, do you understand?" His voice louder now, "If we had a boy, where is he, where is he? As God as my witness if you know anything and you're not telling me, I will come back and personally see you punished." His face was only inches away from hers.

Eva fell to her knees and held onto his coat, "Take the child please. You must believe me. Your wife was so ill and confused and I know God is watching. I know He is my witness. Please let Him forgive me."

"I don't know what to believe anymore. Are you lying? You call her my child Eva but not my daughter. Why is that, tell me?" Still holding the child in his arms he couldn't get hold of Eva to pull her away from him. He moved backwards but she just dragged along the pavement in the icy wet dirt.

"You have to take care of the girl; you have to take care of the girl." She finally let go and fell to the ground weeping.

"I will get the truth Eva, believe me when I say it, I will get the truth one way or another." He turned and walked away holding on tightly to the baby.

Eva lay in the gutter watching him leave, praying the girl would be safe but dreaded Peter Gregor ever coming back. Getting slowly to her feet she hurried back inside her cottage slamming the door with some force, then leaned with her back to it shutting out the world. Then she made the sign of the cross to a crucifix hanging on the wall. Wiping her tear stained eyes with her pinafore she prayed out loud for what she had done and asked most humbly for forgiveness. She could hardly stop herself from shaking but the appointment she'd made earlier with the priest was near. She put on her coat and headscarf and left by the back door to walk the few hundred yards to the church. She saw him standing, waiting for her as arranged. A gaunt old man, who looked as if he never saw any reason to smile. He was dressed in his long black robe with a silver chain and crucifix hanging almost to his waist. His thin white hands folded in front of him as if in prayer. What they had done would haunt them for the rest of their lives. He made the sign of the cross as she approached.

"Batushka, Batushka." She sobbed as she fell to her knees on the wet stone before him, kissing the ragged hem of his cassock.

"Woman, come inside." He said quietly helping her to her feet.

CHAPTER THIRTEEN

Peter's journey back to Archangel was a difficult one. The country was in turmoil. Ordinary people had seen what revolution could do and hoped it would lead them to a better life. There were mutinies among Russian troops and strikes within the police. Many army barracks were captured and soldiers inside were refusing to fire on the demonstrators. It was on this journey that Peter Gregor decided that he could no longer stay in Russia. His decision was made, not for himself but for this baby girl. What life would she have here? How could she grow up in a system that was tearing itself apart with a government that had lost its way and he could not be around to take care of her. It became an easy choice once he had thought it through. He would find help to bring up his daughter for a short time until he could leave the navy, and Russia.

That day came about one year after his arrival back in Archangel. He was told that his submarine was to be taken out of service for repairs and he could take some well-earned leave. His resignation came as a shock to his commanding officer but he understood the circumstances as he and Peter had been friends for many years. Bringing up a child without a mother was difficult enough and to have her looked after day after day by well meaning friends while he was at sea was not what he wanted. Now he could see a much better future. His retirement from the navy was going to be for him and his daughter.

At first he didn't know where he wanted to go. Getting out of Russia was going to be difficult enough. Then he began thinking of Britain. 'Our Allies in the west' To the north, there was Scotland where moorlands stretched for miles and a man could be free. The sea was near, so near. He just wanted to live somewhere that was safe and quiet, somewhere that he could build a life for himself and his beautiful child.

It was in the dining hall in the company of his fellow officers that the conversation came around to hopes for the future and dreams if life were perfect. The men were voicing their 'wishes'. Who would you like to marry? The names of many film stars were bandied about amid raucous laughter. Who would you like to meet? Where would you like to live? Where would you like to travel? It was all done with much merriment but it was at this point that one man said he'd like to go to Scotland and visit the Shetland Islands. He'd heard of them from his old uncle who had worked on the whaling ships out of Fetlar and had fallen in love with the place, and also with a local girl. The islands sat off the north coast of the Scottish mainland. There was work on the whaling ships and at the whaling station. The island was sustaining many a fishermen and sheep farmer. It could be reached easily across the North Sea from Norway. Peter thought about what this man had said and it began to form a plan. Why could he not take his daughter and begin a new life there? By the end of the evening Peter's heart was a little lighter.

Over the next few weeks he spoke with friends who would know of boats that travelled to Britain. It wasn't long before he'd been given the name of a Russian fishing boat that was headed for the waters around Shetland and a promise to be put ashore at Lerwick. He was finally introduced to the captain who had agreed to take him and his daughter on this one-way journey. The man may have been called a captain but he certainly didn't have the appearance of one. He was a man of indeterminate age; his clothes were dirty and ill fitting. A black cotton vest was stretched tightly over his huge stomach. Peter couldn't decide whether the man was slightly drunk or thought he was out at sea, but he was not too steady on his feet. When he shook Peters hand he nearly crushed it. His face had the look of a fighter who had won nothing. His mouth with its crooked smile contained very few teeth and those that did show were brown and broken. His black greasy hair hung down to his shoulders. Peter could see that the man was weighing him up as to the amount of money he could charge. As far as the captain was concerned, here was a commander who was leaving the Great Russian navy when the country was in a state of turmoil. To his way of thinking that was worth a lot of money.

"So, you're running off to Shetland are you?" the taunting thick in his voice. Peter stared straight back at him his eyes not leaving the greasy pock marked face.

"If I thought it was anything to do with you, I would inform you, but it hasn't. So I suggest you just get on with the journey for which I have paid you very handsomely. And for your further information, I have served for years in the Russian Navy and fought for Russia and all Russians, that includes you." Peter spat the last few words out and paid no mind to what the captain had to add but heard him mumble some obscenities as he went to the wheelhouse.

Peter and the baby girl Tally finally boarded the fishing boat *'Saidy'* out of Archangel and began their journey to Shetland with the hope of a new life. Peter had called his daughter Tally from a name his grandmother used to call him and his brother when they were children. She had explained that it meant 'special one' and they were her little 'tally children'.

CHAPTER FOURTEEN

The deep pothole the car smashed into jolted Peter out of his seat. Sig fought with the steering wheel to bring the big vehicle back into a straight line.

"Have I woken you up again?" he asked, smiling at Peter,

"Sorry I must have been more tired than I thought," he said hanging on and rubbing his tired eyes.

"We will soon be on the outskirts of the town so I want you to keep a look out for anything, anything at all, you understand what I mean?"

"Yes of course," Peter was suddenly alert and watchful.

The car slowed down to about twenty kilometres an hour on what looked to be a back road into Medvezhegorsk. The engine was sounding very rough but Sig was not about to stop. Peter glanced down a street leading to the city centre and saw the beautiful Karitonov Palace, standing large and white against the darkening sky. It brought back wonderful memories of the time he'd walked there with his wife in the evening sunlight, beneath its tall, carved walls. He could almost hear her laughter. Night was falling and there were not many people about although Sig felt sure that they were probably being watched. The noise from the big car would see to that. They passed rows of old cottages spattered with mud from the road, faint lights showing through the slats of their shuttered windows. They arrived at the industrial part of the town, where the buildings either side of the road were old factories and warehouses. Signs hung on fences, warning intruders of severe punishment if found on the property. Peter could see that a great deal of heavy industry had moved from the west to the city since the beginning of the war. Now there were armament factories where once there had been grain stores and huge sheds where heavy artillery was being produced to be ultimately sent to the western front.

"Three kilometres up this road there's a signpost to Archangel. There will be another car waiting for us, so I want you to get your things together and be ready to move. In case you're wondering why we need to change cars, I want something that is not going to fail me on my journey back. This beast is about finished," he said patting the steering wheel affectionately.

Peter asked no questions, and was the first to see the sign and the car beside it. Sig pulled to halt, "Quick, get into the other car." Peter opened the door and threw their gear onto the back seat. Sig followed with a hoard of weapons and ammunition, which he transferred from one boot to the other. He started the motor and raced off down the road headed for Kirov then on to Perm.

This was becoming familiar territory for Peter, the bleak plains and the snow covered mountains and winds that cut like a knife. They travelled the back roads and forest tracks hidden by pine trees for the last few miles. Passing between the lakes of Baltym and Isetskoe, all the beautiful places Peter remembered from a lifetime ago. The warm summer days he would come here with his brother to go hunting for rabbits, then take home their day's kill to a very proud mother and father.

The car finally pulled off the road and under a big stone archway into what looked like a castle courtyard. He quickly switched off the engine and just sat quietly breathing deeply as if glad this part of his journey had ended. He peered out of the window. After a few minutes there was a movement from a doorway over to the left. A figure wrapped in a dark hooded coat appeared and walked slowly towards them. The sound of frozen snow and ice crackled under their boots. In the darkness it was difficult to tell whether it was man or woman but all the same Peter was asked to get out of the car and follow them. He only had a second to say his goodbyes and thanks to Sig who was already settling himself in the car ready to travel back the way they had just come. Peter quickly followed the figure into a small stone room dimly lid by a single candle. There he saw a wooden table with four chairs, a cupboard and not much else. An old tapestry curtain hung limply at a dark window overlooking the yard he'd just walked across. He heard the car moving quietly away into the night.

The figure turned to Peter and offered a hand in greeting. Peter took it and not only was it pleasantly warm but tiny.

"My name is Zoya," she pushed back the hood of her coat, "I will escort you to your final destination after you have eaten and had some rest." There was a slight smile and it came with a confident but wary look in her eyes.

"Please, sit down. Are you hungry?" She took off her coat and slung it casually over the back of one of the chairs.

Peter had not yet given anyone his final destination but it was obvious this woman had prior knowledge and he had no need to ask how. He smiled his thanks. She appeared to be no more than a girl as he watched her go to the cupboard at the end of the room. Zoya was slim and tanned with dark hair tied back with what looked like a strip of white, blue and red fabric from a Russian flag. She wore dark coloured army trousers and a black woollen high-necked sweater, a leather belt was tied at her very small waist. Her fur lined boots looked old and comfortable. A scar ran from the corner of her left eye to the hairline above. It looked angry as if it was still in the process of healing. She put a flask of tea and a box containing bread, cold meat and cheese onto the table.

"I'm afraid it's not much but it's all we have and you are welcome to it," she wiped hers hands on her trousers.

"It's fine, really, and very kind of you."

Zoya left the room as Peter was eating and returned with a map which she spread on the table. The candle gave a flickering glow to the image of Sverdlovsk once known as the city of Yekaterinburg.

"You know this area I believe?" she said spreading her small hands over the paper.

"Yes I do," he said, feeling the nearness of this woman.

"Good, you have the address of the house we must go to?"

"Yes," he was now so near to his old home and wanted to visit his father and brother. First he had to fulfil his promise and deliver the package to the person whose name he had kept safely in his head, and he would find this person in Sverdlova Street.

"Do you have a name for when we get to this address?" she asked.

"Yes, I do," he looked straight at her.

"Let us not play games Mr Gregor we do not have the luxury of time, please tell me the name that Vickers gave to you," she was leaning on the table her face just a few inches from his, her voice soft and calm but with a steel edge. He found her nearness disturbing but not unpleasant.

"Believe me, I am the last one to think of playing games, but we both find ourselves in a situation where we know nothing of each other and I am expected to trust you without question."

"Mr Gregor."

"Please, call me Peter."

"Mr Gregor, I know that you have been given papers from Captain Vickers on Shetland to hand to a contact here in Sverdlovsk. I will tell you anything you wish to know about myself, if that is what you want but I will not and cannot tell you anything else. I think you should think about that before you start doubting me."

"Forgive me, I'm sorry, I feel so tired and that is no excuse and I didn't mean to ignore your question. The name of the person I am to give the papers to is Vasily K. That is all I know."

"I accept your apology, and we already knew where you were to go and who you were to meet. We too must try and trust you without knowing much about you. I know Vasily well; he is good man and a good friend. You must get some rest now, come I will show you to your bed." She picked up the candle and lit another from it and gave one to Peter.

Peter suspected that when she said, 'without knowing much about you' it was an indication that she probably knew more about him than he cared to think.

"Follow me." she said and left the room. They walked along a dark passage and up a flight of stone steps leading into a room, which had a wooden framed bed an old chair and a small table. "You will be safe in here tonight and I will call you in the morning, Goodnight".

Zoya closed the door and left.

"Goodnight," he kicked off his boots and climbed gratefully into the bed, which was a lot shorter than his six foot five but it was not long before he curled up, pulled the blankets over him and was asleep. It seemed as if he'd just shut his eyes when Zoya was tapping on the door to wake him up. His still felt very tired and his whole body ached from sitting rather uncomfortably in the car for hours. For a minute he sat on the edge of the bed then rubbed his hands quickly through his hair and tried to blink the gritty feeling out of his eyes. He pulled on his boots and went to meet Zoya who was waiting for him, with the map in her hand.

"You ok, you look a bit rough?" she smiled at the sight of him.

"So would you if you'd slept in that bed last night," his smile gentle, then he realised what he'd said and hoped that she wasn't offended.

Her smile told him she wasn't as she let her gaze last a fraction longer than was necessary. His presence stirred some old feelings of longing in her that she had fought since the death of her husband a year ago.

"I'm fine, though I could have just done with a couple of days longer," he smiled back.

"Come on then, let's get you to Mr K.," she said leading the way.

It was freezing outside. The temperature must have dropped to minus fifteen during the night and the wind was not helping. Light snow was whipping around them as he followed her to an outbuilding, which housed a large truck.

"Get in and don't slam the door," she said.

Peter did as he was told and climbed up into the cab, the seats were old and worn, and their leather covers dirty and split with stuffing hanging out. There were old pieces of carpet on the floor to try and keep in the warmth. The whole cab stank of diesel. Zoya got into the driving seat and pulled the starter, Peter wondered why she had told him to close the door quietly because the noise of the old engine was like a tank. They pulled out onto the road and made their way to the city. There was little traffic and the roads were slick and dangerous with icy mud, but Zoya handled the truck well.

They drove for a short time beside the beautiful Iset River, which ran through the town. It was another place that Peter knew well; he had spent some happy times here in the summer messing about in an old rowing boat with his brother; him pretending to be a sea captain. The river was frozen and low tree branches were stuck fast in the ice and they would stay there until the thaw. The body of a swan was splayed out on the ice as if it had frozen the instant it landed. The early sun was shimmering on its motionless pure white feathers.

They drove to a quiet wide street and got out of the truck. Zoya walked around to the pavement side and pushed the lorry door shut after Peter got out. She cursed at the same time having pushed it too hard and the window dropped inside the door and disappeared.

"That's why?" Peter smiled at her.

"Shit," she said looking into the gap where the glass had gone, "I'll have to fix that now or we'll freeze to death on our way back."

Peter opened the door and ripped off the old lining to expose the mechanics of the window. It only took him a couple of minutes to lift the glass back in to place and jam it closed with an old piece of carpet.

"That will have to do for now, I'll have another look at it later if you want," he smiled.

"Thanks, I'm grateful. Ok, let us go and meet Vasily," Zoya stepped carefully on to the icy pavement.

Number one hundred and sixty, Sverdlova Street was a large stone four-storey town house in a row of similar buildings. All had an air of old faded elegance about them. Carved stone porticos sat either side of the grand wide steps leading to the front door. Long windows showed white wooden shutters opening into the rooms inside. There were footprints in the snow on the steps, evidence of the comings and goings of recent days. On the wall to the side of the door was fixed a brass plate, which showed sets of numbers. Beside them were three large white porcelain bell pushes. Zoya quickly pushed bell number two. After a couple of minutes the door was opened by a middle aged man who looked as if he had been a wrestler in a previous life, his huge body bursting out of his ill fitting suit. He greeted Zoya with a typical Russian hug and then looked at Peter with something like distrust, immediately wary of the big stranger standing there, with wild hair and unkempt beard.

"We have been waiting for you," he said, finally holding out his hand to Peter.

"It's been quite a journey one way or another but I'm glad to be here," the two men shook hands. Zoya led the way in to a large hallway with its curved stone staircase leading to the upper floors. Large paintings hung on the cream walls. Many were of Cossacks charging into battle with their red uniforms, silk flags and eager horses.

"Is Vasily here?" Zoya asked the wrestler as she walked past him.

"Yes, he is in his office, he knew you had arrived last night so is expecting you," his voice rising in volume as he watched Zoya and Peter disappear up the stairs. Then he walked away, his boots sounding alien in the grand hallway.

Arriving on the first floor, Zoya turned left along the blue and gold carpeted corridor. She stopped outside a door, which had a brass figure seven on it, then knocked and walked straight in.

"Vasily, my dear," she said walking up to him and kissing him on both cheeks.

Peter stood for a while looking at this man who had been the very focus of his long journey. He looked of medium build although it was difficult to tell because of all the clothes he appeared to have on. He had a ruddy smiling face and a grand display of black hair, both on his head and on his chin.

"This is Peter Gregor who has finally made it here safely," she extended her hand to Peter, smiling and touching his arm and again feeling that she liked being near to this man.

"You don't know how glad I am to meet you," Peter said reaching out to shake Vasilys hand.

"How was your journey; please sit down and tell me all about it."

"First let me give you the papers I have carried from Captain Vickers," he reached inside his jacket and handed them over, "I must admit I'm very glad to see the back of them if the truth were known."

"Thank you, yes, I'm sure you are. Now, Zoya can you get some drinks and we will first celebrate then we will talk for a while."

Peter wondered about the papers and there importance. The mere fact that there did not seem to be any great hurry to read them made him curious but, he was rid of them and that was a great relief.

Zoya came back with a bottle of vodka and three glasses, placing them on the desk in front of Vasily, who quickly poured generous measures.

"Let us toast this brave man and his safe journey here."

The three of them touched glasses and downed the vodka in one.

CHAPTER FIFTEEN

Tally worked hard on the smallholding while her father was away but sometimes when she was alone in the cottage at night, she had too much time to think. With no idea where he was or even if he was still alive though felt sure she would have heard if it were bad news. She couldn't ask anyone, apart from the contact at Lunna House. Last week when she was in the Post office, a couple of women asked when her father would be home. Tally had calmly told them that it wouldn't be long; and knowing that these women were chatter-boxes, she just thanked them for their concern and walked away, knowing she was fuelling further curiosity.

Katy Graham noticed how anxious Tally had become during her fathers absence and knew that there was more to the 'fishing boat search' than Tally was letting on. But knowing her friend as well as she did, asking questions would get her nowhere; she knew she would be told in time. Katy was well aware of the comings and goings of boats to Norway and Lowry had hinted at what was going on at Lunna House and Scalloway. She didn't have to think too hard as to what Peter Gregor might be up too. All the same she feared for his safety. The girls still met up for a chat and tea but the sunny edge to Tally's smile had all but disappeared. Katy and Jenny hoped that her father would come home soon.

Sometimes it looked as if Shetland had become the busiest place on earth. The roads from Lerwick to Scalloway on the other side of the island were full of the sound of rumbling trucks. The whole rhythm of the island had changed. Boats were leaving Scalloway harbour on a regular basis heading for Norway and their business was not always fishing but lips were sealed and casual talk discouraged. Many families had to bear the loss of a son, father, brother or friend when the Germans decided to target a working boat.

Tally was sitting in Kate's cottage late one afternoon when the subject of Jac arose,

"Have you seen him lately Tally?"

"No, he said he would call by last Thursday but he didn't turn up, have you seen anything of him?"

"I haven't, but Maisie Donaldson from the Post Office told me she saw him coming out of Doctor Helmsuns in Lerwick on Monday morning. She was just getting off the bus."

"Oh, I hope he's been to see about those horrible headaches".

"Maisie said he didn't have time to speak but that he looked quite pale and she was a little worried by it all," Kate said looking anxiously at Tally.

"I will try to get up to see him as soon as I can. You remember I told you he felt a little dizzy when he visited me. Well I'm sure there was something wrong then. I mean, a headache doesn't make you dizzy to the point of falling over, does it?"

"Well, not necessarily, but of course it may have been a migraine headache and I'm sure they can make you feel pretty sick."

"Hmm."

"And that Giles Johansson has been creeping around Lunna house too, I know I shouldn't say it but that lad was difficult enough in school and what with his father being the headmaster he thought he was the great untouchable. Lowry told me about your Pa catching him out during curfew with the stolen flashlight. He's a one to watch Tally and no mistake."

"Do you know what he was doing at Lunna house?"

"No, no one does."

CHAPTER SIXTEEN

Giles Johansson was sitting in his fathers cold wooden shed at the bottom of the garden. He was wiping his smelly, grimy hands on a piece of old cloth. It had taken him a while to cover the hole that he'd dug. This was his secret place that couldn't be seen from the house. It was hidden behind a pile of old fence posts and compost that was slowly rotting into the ground. He knew his father would have no reason to visit this particular corner much before the spring. It was damp and stunk of old vegetation and probably harboured the odd rat or two. The hole was about two feet square and a foot deep, he'd put some old planks over the top to disguise it. At the bottom of the hole was a wooden box wrapped in rags. In this box was a large knife, the type that gamekeepers used. It had lots of blades of different sizes, a hoof pick, a file and a sharp round spike. Not that Giles knew what to do with half of them but it was his prize possession and no one yet knew that he had it, or at least he hoped not. He'd stolen it from a shop in Lerwick. Picking it up when he thought no one was looking, and dropping it straight into his pocket without any intention of paying. Then walking out the door he got on to the bus as brazen as you like and went back to Hillswick. Grinning slyly to himself all the way home, he thought how stupid the owner Mrs Larsson was. All she did was talk all day to anyone who would listen and take no interest in customers like him. Although he did notice she gave him one of her dark looks at one point. He decided that she deserved to be robbed, and if he got the chance, he'd go back and do it again. Next time he'll take something better, it'll serve her right. He felt proud of himself but knew that if his father found out there would be hell to pay and he would probably get an ear bashing in more ways than one.

The day he met the foreigner on Lerwick harbour was a bit of luck for Giles. He could at last see himself being important though he doubted many others would see it that way. The foreigner had spotted Giles sitting on his own on a stonewall by the harbour offices and approached him asking where the nearest Police Station was.

Giles had looked up, squinting in the sunlight with his eyes beginning to water. He looked into the pale face of this stranger. Not saying a word he pointed toward the street running up to the town centre. Giles noticed the foreign accent but said nothing. Then the man sat down next to him appearing not to want the Police Station after all.

The grey green suit the man wore was old and worn and looked a bit like a uniform that had been altered.

"Nice day?"

Giles looked at him, "Aye, it is."

"Not working today then?" the foreigner asked taking a cigarette out of a packet and putting it between his thin lips.

"No, not today," lied Giles.

"So, not much to do then?" the cigarette flipping up and down in his mouth as he spoke.

"Not a lot, why?"

"Just wondering if a strong lad like you might want to earn some money, that's all."

Giles knew that the man was also lying because he knew he certainly didn't look like a 'strong lad'.

"Depends." Giles felt a flutter of excitement. Money was what he liked.

"Well, I need someone to help me build some hides. Not in Lerwick you understand but up the Island away." The man was standing now with his back to the sun and Giles found it hard to see his face properly so just kept on squinting at him.

"What's your name?" he asked casually.

"Jimmy," Giles lied again, "What's yours?"

"Where do you live?"

"Just outside of Hillswick," wonder why he's not telling me his name.

Giles thought he saw the man's dark eyes light up a little. There was a trace of a smile but not the sort of smile that made you feel very comfortable. Anyhow if he was going to get paid, who cares? He didn't know why he lied about his name but it seemed the wise thing to do, not that Giles knew what wise meant.

"Well Jimmy, do you want to earn yourself some easy money or not?"

Giles's thoughts were only on the money, "Yes, ok, when do you want to build your hides?"

"I will wait at the road ends at Hillswick next Sunday at nine o'clock in the morning and you'd better be there, oh and, don't tell anyone what you're doing, it has to be kept secret. I will explain it all later, do you understand?"

"Don't worry; just you bring the money mate," Giles never could sound threatening.

The man lit the strange smelling cigarette and walked away leaving Giles sitting on the wall feeling a little afraid. What a strange man and what kind of accent was that. He didn't spend too much time wondering, he was too keen to get his hands on some hard cash. Now he'll show Jac Smith who can afford to take Tally Gregor out on a date and show her a good time, he might even get her drunk. That would be fun.

Sunday morning arrived and Giles had left the house early saying he was meeting friends and they were all going crabbing. His father didn't believe him but asked all the same why he was going to the beach when he should be going to church. As always his stupid son just gave a mumbled reply and his father couldn't be bothered to argue. His poor mother too frightened to ask anything of him, said nothing.

Giles could see a car waiting at the road ends as planned and the foreigner sitting behind the wheel smoking the foul cigarettes again. He walked cautiously forward and climbed in the front and shut the door.

"Have you brought the money?" he asked straight away glancing sideways at the foreigner.

"Have you built the hides yet?" the reply was calm with an icy edge to the voice, his mouth showing a slit of a smile.

Giles sat quietly for the rest of the journey, which took them to Dale in the east. Then the car turned down a narrow lane. He was beginning to wonder just why someone would want to build hides when there were very few birds worth shooting especially at this time of year. As they reached the rise of a hill he could clearly see the RAF station below them at Sullom Voe. This large military base sat beside a wide sweep of water between the low-lying hills.

The car came to a halt and they both got out and looked down on the whole area which had been taken over by the British and Norwegian forces. They could quite plainly see three flying boats that were moored in the bay, two Catalina's and one Sunderland; the latter looked as if it was being prepared for its next mission. Four men were pushing a large trolley along the jetty. On it were two bombs to be fitted into the bay of the aircraft. Giles could just about hear their voices carried on the wind as they shouted to one another, carefully guiding their highly explosive cargo.

Catalinas and Sunderlands were being used to seek out and bomb German U boats that were prowling around the Shetlands, and they'd been proved successful. Giles turned to the man and was going to ask him about the hides and the money. Then he saw the dark look, he didn't know what it meant but it made him feel uneasy. He quickly changed his mind and just kept on looking at the base. The foreigner seemed to struggle to keep calm then a nasty smile crept slowly over his face as he looked at Giles. "Come on then, I'll take you to where I want you to start building." Giles followed quietly.

They drove to a field not far away and the foreigner got out, opened the boot of the car and pulled out a dirty rather heavy spade and handed it to Giles. He walked a few yards into the field and stopped beside some tape that had been laid on the ground. The yellow markers showed three small oblongs about ten feet apart. Each looked like the size of a hole being prepared for a coffin and pointed east to west toward the Base.

"Ok, I want you to dig three trenches where you see them marked out. They must be a foot deep but this ground is soft enough here so you won't have any trouble," he began to walk back to the car.

"Hang on a minute mister," Giles shouted, "where are you going?" his voice showing the first signs of panic, "I thought you said you needed a hand, not that I was doing all the work myself," he wiped spittle from his mouth.

"It has absolutely nothing to do with you where I am going, and may I suggest you start digging. I will be back for you later and you'd better be finished." Giles was trying to place the accent but couldn't. The man lit another smelly cigarette and flicked the match on to the peaty ground.

Giles has never felt so miserable. He had thought about asking for the money up front and then wait for the man to go away so he could just disappear but it slowly occurred to him that the foreigner knew where he lived. So here he was stuck out in the wind and incoming rain, digging trenches for someone he didn't know. Plus he was beginning to get hungry; with his mind on the money, he had forgotten to have his breakfast. He told himself to just think about the money, and stuck the spade into the ground and dug out his first sod.

CHAPTER SEVENTEEN

Peter Gregor was looking at the package still sitting on the large polished desk in front of him and wondered why Vasily hadn't even picked it up.

He had never been tempted to open it, nor to ask Captain Vickers what it contained; now he was beginning to think he should have done. He and many others had risked a lot getting it to where it now sat and he wondered if there was perhaps more to his journey that he first thought.

"So what happens now?" he asked quietly.

"Well, I think you probably want to return home as quickly as possible, do you not Peter?"

"Yes, of course but first I must visit my father and brother who are not many miles from here. If I could borrow some transport for a couple of days I would be very grateful."

"Of course, of course, we can sort you out something right away but first we must go and eat and celebrate the fact you have delivered Captain Vickers' papers safely."

"Do you want me to come with you Vasily or would you like Peter to yourself?" Zoya asked flashing a smile as she walked towards the door.

"You must come too my dear, I'm sure Peter will appreciate the conversation of a Russian woman after so long, eh?" he laughed and slapped Peter on the shoulder.

As they left, Peter noticed that the package was still on the desk but a door opened in the corner of the room and he saw a figure walk toward it.

The three of them went down to the yard and got into a big black saloon car that was sitting with a driver and the engine running ready to go.

"The Dacha if you please Uri," said Vasily, climbing into the front leaving Peter and Zoya to get into the spacious back seat.

They didn't have to travel far before they were on a dirt road driving through beautiful birch forests heading south into the midday sun. Soon they arrived at a clearing in a forest on which stood the most magnificent wooden dacha Peter had seen. It was a hexagonal shaped two storeys building, painted dark blue with white edged window frames and a rust red metal roof. Surrounding trees sheltered it from any winds. Views from the garden at the back were spectacular and looked south over the river Iset. Rolling hills stretched away into the distance. Peter stood for a while studying the house then looked over the lawn to the river, he turned and smiled at Zoya and Vasily

"Well, well this is really something."

"Ha, so you approve of my hideaway then Peter?"

"Approve, it really is beautiful Vasily, how long have you owned it?"

"It was handed down to me by my father; he 'acquired' it after the death of the Tsar many years ago. I use it as often as I can, it keeps me sane," he smiled.

The two men walked across the snowy lawn, Vasily brushed the snow from a large wooden seat underneath a birch tree and they sat down.

Peter, shielding his eyes from the sun, looked across the vast landscape, wishing somehow and strangely, that he was back on Shetland with his beloved daughter and his friends.

"You say you want to visit your father and brother, how long will you stay with them?" Peter got the distinct feeling that Vasily had some other plan.

"I'm not sure yet, my father is very old and in poor health, why do you ask?" he didn't think he was going to like the answer.

"Oh, it's just that before you leave for home I would like you to come with me to a factory on the outskirts of Sverdlovsk. I want you to have a look at some work that is being done there. I think you will find it very interesting."

"What sort of work, is it more guns?"

"No, not at all, better than that, but very specialised and has been moved here from Moscow. The Germans are creeping ever nearer to the capital and it was thought best that this particular type of production was removed quickly to a safer place. Our leader, Comrade Stalin is an ever-present threat to any new or radical development of any of our aircraft, ships and submarines. So much so that he has already executed many of the best brains in Russia. God alone knows why, because I'm sure as hell that he doesn't. The man's insane and I would also be shot if he or any of his secret army were to hear me," Vasily stood up sharply and kicked a stray stone into the bushes.

Peter considered what he had just said and was curious as to what was happening at this factory.

"Ok, I'll go to my father's in the morning. I will stay a couple of days, and then return to see the factory, is that ok with you?"

"Yes of course that's fine, now let us go and eat and enjoy some good food which I hope by now is ready for us," the two men turned and went back to the dacha.

CHAPTER EIGHTEEN

The war was taking its toll on Shetland and on much of the shipping around the islands. German U boats were homing in on defenceless fishing boats sending many of them to the bottom; the grief was tangible in the towns and villages.

Katy had visited Tally a few times but normal conversation was difficult. She knew that Tally was terrified her father may not return, and she also knew that there was a lot more to Peter's trip, because Lowry had hinted as much. He'd told Katy that Captain Vickers wanted to see Peter again to discuss his Russian connections. They all now had the feeling that Peter Gregor was probably somewhere back in his homeland.

Tally had visited Jac last week and saw that he was looking quite tired and his lovely smile did nothing to hide the paleness of his face and when he hugged her she could feel that his arms were not so strong.

"It's so lovely to see you Tally, what brings you here today?" his big blue eyes seemed to stare at her.

"Well, if you look outside you will see that I am now the proud owner of a bicycle. It's not a new one; I got it from Katy. It's been in her outhouse for years and she thought I would make good use of it, come and have a look." They walked slowly to the yard at the back of the house.

"Goodness Tally, it's great, and you rode all the way here, you must be careful there might be some nasty Germans about," he laughed.

"And I brought you these." She took a package from the wicker basket on the front of the bike and handed it to Jac.

"My favourite biscuits, thanks Tally, come on in and we'll have some tea, I'll get Ma."

Sitting in the big warm kitchen, Tally looked at Jac and knew there was something terribly wrong with him. He didn't seem to have any energy and even eating a biscuit took time.

"So! How have you been Jac?" she asked quite firmly, then, thinking she sounded like a matron softened a little, "I've been worried about you."

"I'm ok, but the doctor keeps asking me to go and see him and I haven't got the time what with work and all."

Tally glanced at Jac's mother who just sat folding a tea towel on her knee and looked at the floor.

"What does he think is wrong then?"

"I don't know. He wants to do some tests or other," Jac said rather dismissively.

"Is there anything I can do, I mean can I help on the farm, anything at all?"

Jac looked at this special girl and wanted to hug her again but there was nothing she could do, not now.

Tally knew she would have to go before it got dark but wanted to speak to Jac's Ma, Jac must have sensed it and got up and left the room,

"I'm going to have another look at your new mode of transport Tally," he smiled and walked quietly out of the kitchen.

"Mrs Smith, can you tell me what's wrong with Jac?" her voice quiet.

"My dear girl," she said with a tired smile, "if I told you, he would never speak to me again, so no, I can't tell you. All I will say is that any time you want to come and visit, you are more than welcome. I know that you are a very special friend to Jac and he talks well of you. Your father and my husband have been friends since you first arrived on Shetland and good friends are very precious. We should love them even when they are no longer with us. Precious Tally." Her voice was but a whisper. The ticking of the clock seemed to get suddenly louder and Tally could hear the rushing of blood in her ears. The crackling of the peat in the grate sounded like fireworks and it suddenly became blindingly clear that Mrs Smith was telling her Jac was soon going to die.

She left Jac and his Ma standing at the gate, and got back on her bicycle; hanging on to her emotions until she'd rounded the corner. Then the tears came easily, streaming down her cheeks. Her heart was breaking for dear Jac the boy she grew up with, who was so kind and gentle and had hoped one day their special relationship would become permanent. Tally peddled as hard as she could crying out Jacs name wanting to get home quickly and shut out the world. How could Jac be so ill, he was such a strong young man, outside in all weathers, working hard and never ailed a day in his life? All these questions she asked herself but knew it wasn't the hard work or the weather. It was an illness that no one had any control over that sucked out life, shattering the lives of families. She knew in her heart it was cancer, but that no one would say the word. The bicycle didn't seem so special now as it stood against the cottage wall. Oh how she wished her father was home.

CHAPTER NINETEEN

The road back to the Gregors old farm had changed little in the years Peter had been away. The beautiful birch forest was bare of leaves and looking monochrome and ghostly in the morning fog. Memories came crowding in; he could almost hear his brother's shouts from deep inside the woods as they played Cossacks as boys. Then their mother would call them home for supper and the two of them not wanting to leave the protection of their 'camp' just in case the 'enemy' were to catch them. Vivid memories of eating his mother's most delicious soup made with fresh caught rabbit followed by a mug of milk.

He pulled the wagon into the front yard and grabbed his bag. His brother had heard the engine and was already standing by the front door. There was no spoken greeting; just a hug to each other that said a thousand words and when they finally broke apart, both men were smiling with tears in their eyes. Peter quickly wiped his hand over his face and put an arm around his brother's shoulder as they walked into the house.

"He's not good Peter, as I told you in my letter. He cannot remember much and keeps asking for mother." Stefan said quietly as they went along a passage to a room at the rear of the house.

"Is he in pain?"

"No, the doctor has seen to that but his mind is leaving him, he may not know who you are so don't go getting upset."

"I'll try not too." They entered a dimly lit bedroom and Peter saw at once that his father was indeed very frail. The old man looked up as the two men came and stood by the bed. His face showed a glimmer of recognition when he looked at Peter but it seemed to be fleeting and he turned to Stefan.

"I see you've brought a friend to see me, that's very nice," his voice faint and rasping, with the merest of smiles, "ask mother to make some tea."

Peter had to swallow hard. His father had shrunk to the size of a boy and looked lost in the big wooden bed. His nightshirt crumpled around his thin shoulders, his hair long and grey. Peter sat down on an old familiar chair beside him.

"Hello Father," he said, gently taking hold of the bony hand that was slowly picking at the sheets.

His father looked closely at him with hollow rheumy eyes but Peter could see there was nothing there to give him any hope that his father may recognise him.

"Have you told Mother I'm going out tonight?" he said with a croaking voice and the hint of a smile.

"I will Father, I will," Peter laid his head on the bed beside his fathers hand and cried softly.

He stayed like that for a long time; just wanting to be near and feel the comfort of this mans presence. Quiet and safe, just like it was when he was a boy. He must have drifted off to sleep because Stefan came quietly back into the room to wake him asking him to come and eat. Peter was still holding his fathers hand although the old man was fast asleep his breathing quick and shallow. He slid his hand from his fathers and kissed his parchment coloured face.

Stephan had known of Peter's arrival through various means, which Peter took to be resistance workers, friends or agents. He didn't know which and didn't need to know, it was safer that way. The two of them talked, laughed and cried into the early hours of the following morning.

"Stefan, how do you manage to look after Father when you're working the farm?"

"Ah, well," Peter saw that his brother began to blush a little, "I have a woman dear brother. She is wonderful and kind, a good cook too. You will remember her as Anya Corin; she went to school with us? You'll meet her tomorrow."

"Good heavens, yes," said Peter.

"I couldn't have managed without her, she looks after father as if he was her own and he calls her Mother so all is well," Stefan smiled sadly.

"Will you marry her?"

"Of course," he laughed, "if she'll have me."

Peter stayed at the farm for another two days and met the lovely Anya. She was delightful and obviously cared a great deal for their father. She busied herself around the house always singing and when Stefan returned from working in the fields it was obvious by the hugs and the welcome that she had a great love for him.

Peter sat with his father the last afternoon before having to leave. He talked of old times, and the memories of summers when he and his brother helped at harvest time. And of the day he fell in the river and his father ran along the bank to rescue him. Watching his father's face closely, he could see nothing but a vacant stare and hear the soft voice asking for 'Mother' to make some more tea.

It came the time to leave. Peter said his goodbyes to his father, quietly and sadly, knowing there was little chance of ever seeing him alive again. Stefan and Anya waved him off as they stood smiling, hand in hand at the door of the farm. He wished them happiness, hoping his brother would find the same love that he had with Zhanna. He drove away from the safety of the old life into the uncertainty of the new, choking back his emotions.

As he drove back to Vasilys place, he was still thinking how strange it was that he'd travelled thousands of miles to deliver papers from the British Military in Shetland to a man in Russia he knew little about, and no one seemed to be in the least bit interested in the contents. There had to be more to this trip he thought.

He arrived at Vasilys dacha in the afternoon and parked up under some trees.

"Peter," Vasilys booming voice came from the porch way, as he stood smoking a fat cigar, "come my friend we have been waiting for you, tell me all about your trip." The two men walked to the house and into the welcoming warmth, not just of the house, but Zoyas smile.

The three of them sat in the comfortable dining room and ate the excellent meal that Zoya had prepared. It took Peter a while to tell them of his visit back to the farm. His emotions were riding on the surface and images of his father, frail and confused, lying in bed asking for 'Mother' were still vivid in his mind. Zoya watched him and saw the tenderness in the face of this big man as he spoke. She wanted to hold him, and needed to hold him.

She wanted to tell him she understood but instead just put her hand gently on top of his. He turned to her and smiled the action not unnoticed by Vasily who was topping up their wine glasses.

"Let us move to the other room and sit more comfortably, then you can tell us of your trip here Peter, and of the people you met." Vasily walked into the large cosy lounge where a log fire was burning and oil lamps filled the room with the softest of light. Vasily sat, quite deliberately Peter thought, in the middle of one of the two big dark red couches, Zoya looked at Vasily and smiled then sat next to Peter on the other.

"It was difficult Vasily, harder than I thought but it was wonderful to get the chance to return to my home. Everyone I met, everyone who helped me to get here, was amazingly courageous, with little thought of their own welfare. The war has not yet touched you here to the extent it has in the west so you have been lucky."

Vasily grunted and looked at Peter, "I'm not so sure of that. With Hitler's perseverance and Stalin's stupidity it will not be long in coming, though I pray it never will."

Peter told them of the resistance groups he had come into contact with and the hardships they'd suffered, losing friends and family to the Germans. Vasily listened intently.

They continued to talk amiably and drink the best pure Russian vodka until the warmth of the fire and the late hour began to tell and eyes began to close.

The morning sun shone into the house, filling the rooms with early gold. Zoya was already making breakfast when Peter walked in to the kitchen and stood behind her. Sensing his closeness she turned, smiling, and pecked him on the cheek, "Good morning Peter, are you feeling hungry?"

A good night's sleep in a big comfortable bed had worked wonders. He was feeling better than he had for a long time, plus the kiss from Zoya had been an unexpected bonus.

The previous evening Vasily had spoken of a factory in Sverdlovsk where some radical work was being undertaken. He did not go into a great detail but Peter got the feeling he could have done if he'd wanted.

"So, what are they making?" Peter had asked.

"It's experimental stuff as far as I know something to do with a new type of aircraft."

"But you said it was radical work, in what way?"

"I'm not too sure Peter but I do know it is important enough to have the scientists keeping their heads down."

Peter had heard that some designers and boffins, who came up with what were considered to be extreme solutions to help the war effort, did not always receive the backing of Stalin. He was becoming increasingly paranoid and to some close to him, unstable. It was a frightening time and some of these scientists were 'disappeared' never to be seen again.

"So if it's so secret, are we even going to get in?"

"Oh yes, we'll get in alright."

"Vasily, I must ask you a question, perhaps I should have asked it a long time before this."

"Then go ahead my friend."

"Well, I have travelled to Sverdlovsk with the help of some very special people. It was planned and thought out by someone who needed me to get papers from Captain Vickers to you. Now that I'm here I feel rather curious as to the total lack of interest being shown in them. They sat on the desk in your office while we chatted and past the time of day. We drank vodka as if it were Christmas. You didn't even pick them up or check to see if it was the correct package. You have made no mention of them. Now, tell me what is it all about?"

"What is what all about Peter? Firstly, we are very grateful that you made it here safely with the papers. We are very, very grateful that you did not come to any harm and on top of that we hope and pray that you return home just as safely," Vasily was beginning to look and sound rather serious. Peter felt there was going to be a sting at any minute.

"We will now go to the factory Peter, and there you will see, 'what it's all about."

They drove to a bleak part of the city, over to the east, where spoil heaps and scrub land were the landscape. Rows of factories stood empty behind crumbling brick walls. Windows were grimy and broken and weeds grew through cracks in the grey concrete of the yards. A length of guttering swung precariously from a corrugated roof. Nearly all the buildings looked abandoned. Where once busy gangs of workers suffered in the heat and dust of heavy machinery, but at least having the camaraderie of their friends, they were now suffering the heat of battle for their country with or without their friends.

Peter could see up ahead that there was smoke or steam floating gently from a rusting metal chimney into a clear blue sky. The huge building looked like an aeroplane hanger with big grey metal doors and a priest hole to one side. As they got out of the car, Peter could hear the clang of hammers and the screech of power tools. Wind whipped around them as they made for the priest hole and stepped in to the relative warmth of the building. Vasily shook the hand of a man who came forward to greet them, introducing Peter as his friend sent by Captain Vickers. It was at that point, Peter knew there was more to this visit than to look at something interesting, because of that simple reference to Vickers.

The vast dusty floor was covered in machinery, the air smelled of metal and oil. Huge round lights hung from the massive iron girders above. Heavy wooden tables set around the perimeter held all manner of tools. There was a cacophony of noise and sparks as a team of workers struggled with hammers and grinders and welding gear. Peter likened it to a scene from *'Dante's Inferno.'*

The focus of all this attention was a relatively small aircraft, which stood in the centre of things. It was a low-winged monoplane about six and a half metres long and roughly the same in width.

"Well, what have we here?" Peter asked of Vasily.

"This, is a rocket plane. A B2, which our friend Comrade Stalin hopes will bring forward the end of the war or at least cause a lot of damage to Germany. The engineers here are under the command of Comrade Dushkin. He has designed a fuel propulsion system which is now in the process of redevelopment, and I might add, giving us a lot of problems."

"I had no idea that Russian technology had moved so quickly," Peter said.

"At the moment work is going on day and night here to perfect this aircraft. It is very dangerous work as you can imagine, and these men are dealing with nitric acid and some have already suffered breathing problems and burns." He pointed to three metal containers standing on an iron-framed table, "We have tanks of sodium carbonate to neutralize any spills but work has to go on regardless." He stood next to Peter who was trying to take in the vastness and organisation of it all.

"We lost one of our best pilots a couple of months ago. He was flying over the test sight at Bilimbay Lake and had just about reached maximum power, then just plummeted into the ground. No warning, nothing, the instruments were so badly damaged we couldn't rescue any information." Vasily fell silent. "There are many problems to overcome with this rocket plane. We have to find the correct pumps and the metals to use, and work out the stress factors and aerodynamics of the plane to cope with the power. We know that the British are working on a very similar design and we need to share information. So getting our plans to them would be crucially important." He looked sideways at Peter. "Of course these plans are absolutely top secret and if they fell into the hands of the Germans, need I say that would be a disaster. Now do you see what it is all about Peter?"

CHAPTER TWENTY

The North Sea was at its worst. Huge rolling grey waves were thundering westward toward Shetland. The tiny islands of Yell, Fetlar and Unst were the first to feel their force. Winds howled over the savage sea and seagulls tumbled and screamed close to the tops of the waves. Their skilful wheeling dance was defiant in the face of the monstrous power beneath them.

Underneath this devils own cauldron was a lone Russian submarine, patrolling the icy waters on the hunt for German U-boats. A Northern Fleet boat, it had left the port of Archangel with a full compliment of men. Its young commander, Yuri Volkov, was already a veteran of war. He'd served four years on submarines with an exemplary record and had been feted by the hierarchy of the Soviet Navy. He had an excellent record of U-boat kills, although he himself felt that being rewarded for killing people, war or no war, seemed to have a hollow ring. For the last two years he'd been commander of this fifty-seven metre long Schuka class boat. He now considered it to be a dangerous rust bucket, badly made way back in nineteen thirty-four, and shoddily maintained. Emergency modifications had been made before they left on this last trip and the young commander made it known that he was not satisfied with the results. However, his complaints fell on deaf ears and he was told leave port as soon as possible and head for the North Sea and onward to the North Atlantic.

Problems had started within a few days of leaving. The submarine had a four hundred and fifty horsepower electric engine which enabled them to travel submerged at over six knots. It had another huge diesel engine for surface travel of up to twelve and half knots. Both engines, when running true were the most powerful in any submarine. It was on a Sunday; Commander Volkov was in his quarters studying the great pile of paperwork and charts that he'd been given by Naval Command. His telephone rang and the blue light showed him that it was the engine room; wearily he picked it up, "Captain Sir, one of the batteries is leaking. I strongly suggest that we steer a course to Murmansk for repair, otherwise this is going to be hell on earth down here, sir."

Volkov was already feeling the weight of his responsibilities and this just added to them.

"We can't Chief; you know we have to make good time to reach our rendezvous. See what you can do."

"Aye aye sir," the veteran engineer clicked off the radio and rubbed an oily hand over his head. This fucking boat should have been scrapped a long time ago he thought as he went to check on what may become a very serious problem. He'd survived this long and he prayed that his good fortune would last a bit longer. He made his way along the narrow metal passage, its walls running with condensation, and as he reached the engine room door, he gave an involuntary shiver.

The sea state was vicious even by a seaman's standards and the old submarine rolled and creaked as it forged ahead through the monstrous sea. Her metal hull made unnerving noises as she twisted and strained. Volkov didn't want to return to Murmansk for repairs, and he hoped that his grouchy but excellent engineer could work one of his many miracles. Time and again the wizard of the engine room would repair, coax and sometimes hammer the old machinery to keep it working. But he knew there was only so much the man could do.

Less than half an hour later the commander's phone rang again from the engine room and he suspected it was going to be bad news. He was right, no miracles today.

"Sir, it's impossible to seal the batteries, I've tried everything I know and it's not working. So can I respectfully suggest that you get us into Murmansk for repairs or you will have a very nasty and dangerous situation? Sir." There was heavy emphasis on the 'sir'. He'd already had a couple of run in's with the young Commander, not that he disliked the man but he knew what he was talking about when it came to his engines.

"Is that your final word Chief?"

"Yes it is Sir."

"Well then I suppose it's Murmansk, keep me informed of the situation down there."

"Sir," the chief by now was coughing and choking on the acrid fumes that were coming from the batteries and chlorine gas was soon to be an even bigger problem.

Murmansk in the middle of winter is not the ideal place to be but Volkov had no choice. He had radioed ahead and hopefully there would be all the equipment he'd asked for ready and waiting, with mechanics. Plus it was a chance to get some fresh food supplies, which would come as a bonus for the crew, God knows they deserved it, he thought.

Two days later they were back at sea and heading for the waters off the Norwegian coast where danger lurked in every kilometre and every fathom.

This was not one of Volkov's favourite places; many Russian submarines had met their fate here. Most of them colliding with one of the hundreds of German contact mines then going to the bottom. Unheard, unseen and in the darkest of horrors.

Progress was sickeningly slow. Volkov's only thought was to keep his submarine and his men safe, so, as on every trip, all noise on board was at a minimum and the listening equipment was working full-time. He had even watched as some crewmen took off their heavy shoes and continued to work in stocking feet on the freezing damp floor.

The engine was not running as smoothly as it should but the new batteries were doing their job. All crew were at battle stations, alert, quiet and careful. The captain had always maintained that carelessness cost lives, the slightest noise, a dropped spanner or a slammed door could be picked up by enemy ASDIC (Anti Submarine Detection Investigation Committee) above them. Then depth charges would be dropped and all they could do was say their prayers.

They crept westwards around the Finmark peninsula, turning south toward the Norwegian Sea.

The crew were jittery and worried about the problem with the engine and the tension swept through the boat like bad air. Now they were steering a course closer to the Norwegian coast than had first been planned, which meant there was more danger of mines.

Volkov was a good Commander and knew all of his crew. He liked every single one of them and the decision to take them into more dangerous waters was not an easy one but he had a feeling that the engine may give him more trouble. The Chief confirmed that when ten minutes later the phone rang. He sounded totally exasperated and emotional to the point where Volkov thought the man was going to cry.

"Sir, I have given all my love and attention to this confounded fucking engine. I have talked to it and in my worst hours I confess, have hit it. I'm not saying I don't love it but I am very tired of it, Sir. It is; and I hate to say this, Sir, rattling itself to pieces as I speak and if something is not done and done soon then we are all going to find ourselves floating in a boat going nowhere, and the Germans are going to come at us like bees around honey." His voice becoming a little steadier, "And that would not be good, Sir." Volkov allowed himself the shadow of a smile, he had had to deal with the excitable engineer on more than one occasion and there was always something in the way he tried to explain things that sounded rather humorous, even though there was certainly nothing to smile about today.

"Ok Chief, I'm on my way down," Volkov felt the first signs of anxiety. Something felt wrong though he didn't know what. He didn't believe in 'feelings of impending doom' but a shadow of uncertainty ran through his thoughts. He lifted his worn commander's hat and wiped a hand through his thick blond hair as he headed for the bowels of the boat. A couple of crewmen stood aside in the narrow corridor allowing him to pass. Both men looked at each other after Volkov had gone through the watertight doors. They'd seen the first signs of strain on the young commander's face.

"You see Sir, if repairs are done correctly then I would have very little to do but in this case the repairs have not been done properly. Here, for example," said the engineer who now had Volkov's full attention, and pointing to a pipe which contained diesel. Attached to it was a gauge, which showed the flow to the engine. He tapped it gently, and quite a bit of fuel dripped onto the floor. "There, how am I supposed to repair that joint, it has been soldered that many times it looks like pile of mashed potatoes."

Again Volkov smiled, but inwardly, and seeing the diesel running down the tank soon quelled any humour he may have felt.

"I will do my very best to seal that leak Sir, but I give you not one promise that it will last until breakfast," the chief stomped off leaving Volkov hating the damned submarine even more.

They made slow headway to the west and all systems appeared to be holding up. Volkov watching every light and dial on the command post desk, knowing the Chief would have stood with his finger in the leak if he had too.

He was half way back down to the engine room when suddenly the boat gave a mighty shudder. Volkov grabbed the nearest phone, which was hanging on the wall.

"What's happened number one?" he asked quickly.

"Mines sir, we're in a field of them," said his officer.

"I'm on my way, stop all engines," he slammed the phone back down and ran through the boat, his feet slipping where the leaking diesel had stuck to his shoes. He scrambled up the wet metal ladders, which took him to the control room. Everyone there stood silently. The sound of metal screeching and scraping on the massive hull could be heard quite clearly. It was as if a sea monster was trying to rip open the submarine with a giant tin opener. All eyes stared at the hull visualising what horror there was on the other side. A steel cable holding a mine that was hanging in the water like a box jellyfish, just waiting.

"It's moored mines sir, they must be at about fourteen fathoms and we've caught on a cable."

"Take her down slowly number one," Volkovs voice was steady and clear but he was now worrying even more about the engine and the leaking diesel.

"Aye sir," the huge submarine started its slow creaking descent to hopefully get clear of the cables.

"No soundings on these mines then?"

"No sir, nothing, they are too small, and we don't yet know if we're in the middle of the field or at the edge."

"Right, follow the bearing I gave you, and half speed number one," he hesitated, "and it looks like we may have another problem with the engine…again."

The scraping stopped and the relief was palpable. The air smelled of sweat and fear. No one spoke, the men just got on with their jobs but with ears now finely tuned to the slightest sound that may come again, from outside the hull…

The explosion when it came shook the boat from stem to stern. Men grabbed at the handholds in the walls or what ever was nearest, hanging on until the boat steadied itself again. Volkov watched the instruments as the huge groaning hulk hung in the water. Shouts from along the hollow sounding passageways informed him that the conning tower had been hit. He gave the order to 'take her up' and raise the periscope, he snapped down the handles and tried in vain to lift it, nothing happened. It was now firmly jammed in the down position. God in Heaven, thought Volkov, he now had to work blind. More shouts, this time voices raised in panic as water began spurting through splits in the metal hull above the men's heads. Claxton's sounded throughout the boat as men started running to their stations to close all watertight doors. Volkov looked grim as he told his number one to bring the boat up to the surface. The ballast tanks were emptied amid a frightening roar of noise. No one knew what other damage had been done. He knew now that the boat was effectively crippled and hope of rescue was minimal unless somewhere out there an allied ship was to pick up their distress calls. God forbid it should be a German vessel.

They were not many miles from the Shetland coast and he knew of the runs to Norway but didn't know how good or effective their equipment was when it came to listening to Russian submarines, suspecting they would travel without making any radio contact at all. He quickly relayed their position to the radio room and then made his way there. It was a stuffy cramped little cupboard of a room. In it sat an officer whose sweat was running down his nose onto the chart in front of him. He pounded out the boats Mayday message over and over again; Volkov then gave the order to use open radio messages. The officer looked at him and knew they were giving the Germans a gift if they heard it but he did as he was told. Volkov placed a supportive hand on the man's shoulder. The messages were urgent and unending. Volkov just prayed that friendly ears would hear them.

Somewhere in the bowels of the boat Volkov could hear the mournful sound of a crewman singing an old Russian folksong.

CHAPTER TWENTY-ONE

The tiny village of Mossbank is in the parish of Delting, which sits on the northeast coast of Shetland. It huddles along the shoreline and is blasted by easterly winds that show little mercy, relentless in winter and not much less in summer. Mossbank has a little stone pier, which is the only bit of shelter a boat could hope to find and even that is meagre. The driving wind is more likely to smash any vessel to pieces on the rocky beach than allow it sanctuary. Low grey stone cottages straddle away from the beach and are hunched down almost defying the winds to blow them away. Mossbank knew of hardship, knew of loss and knew of great sadness. On the twenty-first of October, in the year nineteen hundred, four fishing boats with twenty-two men and boys were lost to the sea. It was one of the worst storms ever to bring its fury to the Shetland Islands. Herring had been the prize but human life had been the cost, all men gone like snowflakes in the wind.

The memories were raw and vivid. Women thought they still heard the voices of their men folk, not wanting to believe they would never feel the strength and comfort their arms again. Women who had lost everything wondered where God was that day.

One such woman was Valerie Carlson. Her life changed suddenly as did many. Her man Eric set off in the morning to go and help crew one of the boats. He never came home; his body was found three days later. Her life became one of solitude and seclusion, living on her smallholding on the sand banks above the beach. Her father Edward had been a pillar of the local community, a ready smile and an ever-helping hand. He'd been a big man with an even bigger heart and had died not long before the tragedy, so did not see the desolation of his beloved daughter. Valerie Carlson tended her plot and looked after her few sheep keeping herself to herself. Becoming such a recluse, people didn't really know how to approach her, but felt there was a need. Folks knew that she had suffered along with others and therefore tried to talk but found the meeting difficult.

Years came and went; Valerie Carlson seemed not to want anyone to go near her. She even built a wooden fence around her little smallholding and put up a gate, which was not that common for Mossbank. People saw her tending her little vegetable garden and feeding the sheep and her few chickens so they knew she was still well, but invited no one in to sit with her and only occasionally said 'hello' over the fence.

One of the things that Valerie treasured among her little house full of belongings was an old radio her father had built. It had given him pleasure, listening intently to what was happening beyond Shetland. He told his daughter he'd heard things that he didn't think were true but he was going to keep a sharp ear out saying, "One of these days you or I might hear something 'really interesting'." He would say on many an occasion "Believe nowt of what yer hear and only half of what yer see." But his radio was slowly beginning to change his way of thinking, and he was going to have to believe something of what he heard. Mr Carlson was a hoarder too; his little shed was full of all sorts. There were rolls of wire, tins full of screws and nails, bits of string, valves, and parts from old crystal sets. Most of it in old boxes on dusty shelves, which sagged under the weight of them. He was not about to part with anything, except his life. When one day he knew he'd made a bit of a breakthrough with a newfound channel on his radio and couldn't wait to tell Valerie. He looked out to the blue sky through the dusty window of the shed and fell gently to the floor dreaming of greatness. The darkness, like a cloak folded around him and in that moment, Valerie lost the leading thread of her life.

It came when she was least expecting it, as things do. It was very faint at first. Valerie had chosen that morning to bring her fathers radio in to her little kitchen. There was neither rhyme nor reason for this decision; it was just done on the spur of the moment. It was something to do. She placed it on the oilcloth-covered table and dusted off the years of dirt and cobwebs. She fiddled with the big Bakelite knobs and various wires, waiting for it to 'warm up'. Then she wiggled the valves just as her father had told her. Not expecting anything to happen she was quite shocked when she heard a voice coming from the brown woven canvas speaker. It seemed a long way away and rather ghostly. She stood back from the table not quite believing what she'd heard.

Then it came again, a voice that sounded rather urgent but not an English voice. She listened intently trying to work out what was being said, but she couldn't. She bent down and put her ear to the speaker and turned the volume button slowly, trying desperately to hang on to the sound. Could it be one of the fishing boats that were plying between Shetland and Norway? Bravely running the gauntlet under the noses of the Germans? No, she thought, they wouldn't dare broadcast in the middle of the day; if ever. The accent was not Norwegian but Russian; she knew that from her trips into Lerwick where men from the Russian fishing boats often came to shop. She strained her ears and was holding her breath as if to hear better.

"May Day, May Day, this is…Soviet Su…Four zero… North Sea…Degrees east…Shetland…surface…conning tower damage…open line…May Day, May Day."

Valerie just stared at the radio her heart beginning to race, and for a minute she couldn't move.

"Oh my God, my God," she cried as she listened again. On the table were a pencil and a brown paper bag from the shop. She quickly wrote down everything she'd heard, and then shoved the bag in her pocket, pushing it right down to the bottom so it wouldn't fall out. Then, grabbing her coat she ran out of the cottage to the shed. There she pulled at her old bicycle until it untangled itself from the junk that was piled up in front of it. Eventually it landed on the grass with a clatter. The handlebars were covered in muck and needed a good hard tug to straighten them up. Then she found the front mudguard was rubbing on the old tyre so she kicked it and kicked it until it fell off and threw it in to the bushes. With a bit of an effort she climbed onto the saddle then started peddling off down the road toward Lunna House. Her heart was pounding and she was struggling to breathe as she attempted a little rise in the track. She had to make it; she had to keep going. Her lungs were fit to burst and her legs began to shake, she prayed that she wouldn't pass out with effort of it all. There were men out there, who desperately needed help, and she couldn't bear to think of what they were going through, she had nightmares still thinking of her Eric. Lunna House, Lunna House that was all she could think about, they would know what to do

The wind was blowing in from the east as Tally struggled to close the grain house door behind the cottage. Time was hanging heavy while her father was away. The days seemed endless and the work harder, and the only topic of any ones conversation was the war. Some boats that left quietly from Scalloway on their missions to Norway were never seen or heard of again. Torpedoed by German ships, or bombed by the regular sorties of German aircraft. She'd heard nothing from her father so made up her mind to go to Lunna House and see this Captain who sent him away, and just ask straight out where her father was.

CHAPTER TWENTY-TWO

Peter Gregor was sitting comfortably in the late afternoon sun on an old stone wall, looking out over the forests that surrounded the town of Sverdlovsk. He raised his hand to shade his eyes and pointed to a far off tower, "That is where I used to live." he said, looking again at Zoya who was sitting next to him.

"It's an old water tower not far from our farm, my brother and I tried to climb it many times but never made it to the top, I was too scared," he smiled as if it were something that he regretted.

"Were you happy there, on the farm?" asked Zoya.

"Oh yes, very happy. We had wonderful parents who gave us all they could. It was sometimes hard, you know, the weather could be cruel and keeping cattle, as my father did, was not easy but they managed," he sighed, "I don't know how, but they did."

She snuggled near to him trying to get some warmth, the same as she had done the night before. They had made love slowly and tenderly at first, but their hunger for each other took over and they rolled with a rhythm, which lasted all night. As the early morning light streamed through the windows they still clung to each other, Zoya kissing his chest and his fingers entwined in her long hair.

Now, the sun was going down and they'd been out for hours.

Peter pulled her closer and kissed the top of her head, she smelled of fresh air and flowers and he liked that.

Vasily was there at the door with the usual welcoming smile on his face and hugged Zoya as she entered the hallway and he then slapped Peter on the back, his familiar greeting.

Tonight was to be Peters last with his two friends; he was leaving early in the morning to make the long journey back to Shetland. He didn't want to leave Zoya, he was certain of that; she stirred in him old emotions that he thought had gone forever. No promises could be made, no wishes wished, nor feelings disclosed but they both knew of the love they felt for each other. No tears would be shed and no backward glances would be made in the morning, just two people meeting, loving and parting. He hoped though that she would find the note he'd left her under the pillow.

Peter understood the importance of his journey back to the Shetlands and it was only after he'd talked with Vasily last night that it had become clear.

The package he'd brought from Shetland was just plain white paper. Peter was at first, shocked and angry. He couldn't hide the fact from his friend, banging his big hands on the desk and staring down at Vasilys calm face his voice loud but controlled.

"You bastards, why the hell did I go through all that just to bring you paper, with no significance to you or anyone else for that matter. You'd better come up with a good story my friend, one that I can believe enough so I don't just kill you now?" Anger rising to the surface as he paced around the room looking first at Vasily then to Zoya who had no expression on her face but just looked him straight in the eyes.

"Please Peter, let me explain. The papers you brought were significant. It proved to us that the route you took, the route we have worked so hard to establish, was safe. We had planned it many months ago, and the people who helped you are the best. Good and trustworthy people who know the terrain and how to keep out of the Germans way. We are a long way off here Peter and we have to find ways of communicating away from the eyes of our enemies."

"Ok, how did you know about Captain Vickers and that I even existed?" He leaned forward onto the desk his face a few inches away from Vasilys.

"There are some things Peter that you are better off not knowing, God forbid that you may get caught and have to give up information," Vasily held the gaze.

Peter was silent for a minute, his emotions still raw. "So, tomorrow I go back, yes?" He knew now that he was finally returning home. He slumped into a chair suddenly feeling very tired.

The war still raged though Hitler was now finding out what it was like to feel cold steel. The Russians were advancing from the east and the allies were moving in from the west, it was only a matter of time before Germany fell.

CHAPTER TWENTY-THREE

Valerie Carlson was as red as a beetroot when she finally cycled the last hundred yards toward the front entrance of Lunna House. Her shaking legs almost collapsed underneath her as she climbed off her bicycle. Her heart was thumping and she gasped for air as she leaned the bike against the wall. It immediately fell over but she didn't stop to pick it up, and staggered to the door knocking frantically until her hands hurt and tears poured down her cheeks.

Captain Vickers had been watching all this from the upstairs window of his makeshift office and sent one of his young officers downstairs to see what all the fuss was about.

He moved to the top of the stairs. From there he could hear the urgency in Valerie's voice and he overheard the words 'Russian submarine' and the choking sobs as she tried to explain herself. The officer ushered her into a downstairs room and produced a chair for her to sit on and asked if she would like a drink of water. She nodded not yet able to speak coherently.

After she'd calmed down a little, Vickers appeared in the room and came to sit down beside her, smiling, he hoped after all this effort whatever she had to tell him, was important. He took her hand and asked what had brought her to Lunna House.

"I have an old radio; my father built it years ago. He used to listen to anything and everything," she had to stop to catch her breath. "Anyhow, it has been in the shed since he passed away," she sniffed, "and so I thought I'd get it out and well." She choked back the tears, "I just wanted to see if I could hear anything."

"Go on," said Vickers gently.

"Well, about an hour ago, I had just finished dusting it and had twiddled the knobs and valves, and there it was," she took a drink of water, her hands still shaking.

"There what was, Miss Carlson?"

"A voice, they're in trouble, all of them. They're out there in the sea, in a submarine and they are shouting for help," she could hardly keep the choking cry from her voice.

"Tell me exactly what you heard. Roberts," he snapped at the young officer, "take this down sharpish." The lad was soon stood at the side of Valerie, notebook and pen at the ready.

"Right Sir, sorry, Madam, fire away," the lad looked a little embarrassed and kept his head down.

"I can remember everything I heard and I've written it all down," Valerie said quickly producing the paper bag and giving it to Vickers. Telling them word for word as the young lad transferred it to his book. Finally Vickers stood up and thanked her. He shook her hand and said he would have to go immediately but that she could stay and have some tea if she wished. They would make sure to escort her and her bicycle safely back home whenever she was ready.

Valerie thanked him and sat back heavily in the chair, looking out from the big window towards the sea. She started to cry, great heart-breaking sobs. All the fears and tears brimming over, all the years she'd been on her own, missing her Eric, missing her father and now the thought of more men fighting for their very survival out there in the North Sea. It was almost too much for her; she wiped her sleeve across her eyes and just sat there, crying softly as the young officer tiptoed out of the room.

Tally was almost there, she could see Lunna House now so kept on peddling hard down the road. It wasn't a bad day the sun was even trying to peep through the clouds and she was glad of it. Any rain seemed to be over in the east but moving toward Shetland so she knew she might get a soaking on the way home. Arriving at the big house she leaned her bicycle against the wall and picked up the other one that was lying carelessly on the ground.

This meeting might not be easy she thought. In fact, the Captain may not even be here. What would she do then?

She banged on the door and waited. She banged again.

The young orderly, who had been with Captain Vickers earlier, opened the door and smiled when he saw Tally. Then his smile disappeared as caution entered his thoughts,

"Yes madam, can I help you?" he asked, feeling a little silly having called this lovely looking girl 'madam', why didn't he call her Miss?

"I'd like to speak with the Captain, if you'd please tell him I'm here. My name is Tally Gregor," she smiled back at him, but noticed how a shadow came over his face when she'd mentioned her name.

"Oh, I see, well, eh, yes, I mean no you can't speak to Captain Vickers, because he's not here," he stuttered.

"Are you supposed to let me know that Captain Vickers is not here? Surely you could have told me that he was just busy or something? I could be a German spy, and I didn't know his name was Vickers." she looked him straight in the eye. He wavered, trying frantically to think of something clever to say, but he couldn't. She had beautiful blue eyes.

"He is busy, he's just not here being busy." His stutter was getting worse, "what is it you want to see him about?"

"If you'll let me in, I'll tell you, but it's a bit too cold to be standing on the doorstep."

"Yes, sorry, come in and follow me, Miss," he led the way upstairs, pleased he had called her Miss, and then knocked on a large ornate brown door. They entered a room that looked as if it could once have been a drawing room. Long windows framed a view of the grey sea outside. There was a welcoming fire burning in the grate. A tall slim man in uniform was standing with his back to it and came forward to greet them as they walked in.

"My name is Sergeant Carter, how can I help?" he held out a slim white hand.

"I'm here to ask about my father. His name is Peter Gregor, you sent him somewhere, and I'm worried about him. He has been gone far longer than I thought and I would really like some answers. Where is Captain Vickers?" Tally walked around the room and sat herself on one of the large chairs by the window.

"I'm afraid I can give you no information about your father's whereabouts, nor can I tell you where Captain Vickers has gone." He watched her carefully; this young girl who he knew lived on her own while her father had been sent to Russia amidst a lot of secrecy. He also knew that Captain Vickers had gone to arrange the daring rescue of a Russian submarine, from right under the noses of the Germans.

"I'm not inclined to go until I get some information about my father. You know where he is and perhaps even how he is. So do not try to get rid of me by saying nothing." She met his smile with a stare and her mouth set.

"I am not obliged to tell you anything," his smile had disappeared.

"I know, but…" now it was Tally's turn to smile.

"All I can tell you is that your father is alive and well, other than that, I can tell you nothing." He sat at his desk and shuffled some papers, he glanced up at her, she hadn't moved. His look told her the conversation was over.

Tally said a silent prayer for her father and wondered if it were worth pushing for any more information, she thought not.

A knock on the door brought the young orderly in to the room. "Miss Carlson is ready to go home now, sir, shall I see to it Sir?"

"Valerie Carlson, what is she doing here?" Tally stood up surprise showing in her voice.

"She came to give us some information, that's all, I'll escort you downstairs," said the Sergeant taking Tally by the arm and leading her through the door.

"Valerie is that really you, how lovely to see you, how have you been?" Tally said, going up to Valerie and putting an arm gently around her shoulders. The two women stood in the yard, with the lad putting Valerie's bike into the back of a truck.

"I'm fine really, thanks for asking Tally, how are you?" she sniffed into an old handkerchief. Tally could see she was upset.

"What's the matter, can I help you, why are you here?"

"So many questions my dear, just let me get on my way. This kind chap is going to take me and my old bicycle home. It's been a awful day Tally, an awful day," she made to turn away but Tally kept her arm around her and looked down in to her face and could see the tears welling up again, so she steered her away from the house and they walked a little way toward the jetty.

"Tell me what's happened, please"

"I heard a message, Tally dear," and Valerie explained what had happened that morning and how she ended up at Lunna House and that she had spoken to Captain Vickers.

"And that's why he isn't here?"

"Yes, he's gone to start a search for the submarine, there's little we can do now my dear." Valerie sounded calmer and was quite relieved that she had managed to get to Captain Vickers and also that she had the chance to share her concerns and fears with Tally. Yes, she was pleased to see Tally Gregor.

Tally waved to the truck as it went slowly out of the yard, Valerie sitting up front with the young driver and her old bike rattling around in the back, and then she turned to go home. It was going to be a long time before she got there but at least she now knew her father was still alive. She stood for a while in the yard, watching the truck make its way slowly toward Mossbank, thinking about the rescue mission that was being organised. Tally decided that the first thing to do was go to Kate's and tell her what Valerie had heard on her radio. Then they should go to see Meg and Maisie Donaldson at the Post office, they had a radio and a telephone and may just have heard the some other news from the submarine.

CHAPTER TWENTY-FOUR

Giles Johansson sat watching. He had been sitting for a while on the wall above Mossbank and had seen the army truck trundling up the road into the village and Valerie Carlson getting out of it. Then he'd watched as an army lad lifted her bike out of the back. Now what was she doing and why had she got a lift in an army truck? He puzzled about this, but then Giles puzzled about lots of things and usually came to all the wrong conclusions. Well there was only one way to find out as he slid off the wall and started off down to Miss Carlson's place.

Valerie was not a stupid woman, nor was she the type to leave her doors open. It wasn't so much that she expected trouble; it was more to do with keeping the sheep and chickens out of her kitchen and keeping the precious heat in. But at this moment in time she suspected it might be trouble as she glimpsed Giles jumping over her new fence. She slid the bolt back on the front door and opened it quickly scaring a couple of hens that were scratching around.

"What do you want Giles?" she caught him off guard and he spun round hitting his head on the clothes prop.

"Oh, hello Miss Carlson, I was just wondering if you would like me to cut you some peat, you know, save your back. Heavy work cutting peat." He hopped from one leg to the other rubbing his head at the same time. He was trying not to look her straight in the eye because he knew how fierce she could be. Valerie thought how stupid this boy looked and was not in the mood to take any foolishness.

"And why would I want you to cut peat for me?" she stood with her hands firmly on her hips, "I've cut me own for years without any help from you or anyone else, so, no, I don't want ye to cut the peat. Now would you mind just leaving me be, I've work to do." she turned to go indoors.

"Aye, It's just I noticed you're getting out and about a bit more and maybe haven't got the time that's all." He still stood there, now with his hands in his pockets, watching her turn slowly at the door.

"And why would you be keeping an eye on my comings and goings young Giles Johansson? Because if ye are, I'll be across to see yer father and let him deal wi' ye."

"No, no I just saw you coming back in that army truck and wondered if you were all right, or if your bicycle needs fixing?" he was having to work hard at this.

"Oh, so now it's 'are you alright?' and 'is your bicycle alright?' get out of here before I put the broom over yer stupid head. I haven't got time to talk to ye, ye witless chump, go on!" She went back into the cottage, smiling to herself, well heck, she thought, that made her feel better. Tomorrow she would get that bike out and fix it properly and visit Tally Gregor, tell her about sneaky Giles and find out what was happening with the rescue.

CHAPTER TWENTY-FIVE

The massive submarine was rolling like a mortally wounded whale. Emergency alarms were still sounding in different parts of the boat. Volkov had stopped all engines to try and lessen the amount of water pouring down the damaged conning tower hatch. He knew time was running out. The top of the tower had been blown clean away. The forward hatch was badly twisted and by some Herculean effort from the crew, was still able to be opened. Water was beginning to seep into the lower levels. Officers and men were trying desperately to close off watertight doors but the explosion had caused much of the old hull to buckle. They were now like sitting ducks, riding on the surface.

"It was a bloody contact mine, sir," an engineer said angrily wiping his face.

"Yes, a damned rogue mine. It must have broken free of its chain. Bastard Germans," Volkov hurried toward the radio room to find out if anyone had answered any of their Mayday calls. No one had.

He realised that pretty soon there was only going to be one course of action and that was to abandon the boat and take to the life rafts. The sub was now leaking more water than any pumps could handle. He returned to his cabin and collected up all relevant papers and put them into a waterproof bag. He also grabbed a couple of small framed photographs. One of his smiling parents and one of his dear friend, Sergei Somova. Then he quickly grabbed his small flask of vodka looking at it for a couple of seconds then put it into his coat pocket, a sad smile on his face.

"Tell the men to release the life rafts, number one, and sound the 'abandon ship' as quick as you like."

"Yes sir," he replied.

The abandon ship alarm sounded loud and shrill. It was a wailing signal that triggered fear in the hearts of seamen all over the world. For those trapped in the bowels of a ship, it would be the last sound they heard. For others it was the start of a terrifying journey into the unknown, where training and trust in others may just save their lives.

All the crew who had been in the lower part of the submarine came charging up the steps. Others were already up top on the slippery hull. All were struggling into life jackets desperately trying to stay upright on the slowly turning metal surface.

Two men tried to get in to the life raft and misjudged the distance of their jump, they tumbled into the sea. One just lay on his back, looked up to his comrades, gave a weary salute, and floated away, his face white with shock and fear. The other man tried desperately to swim to the raft but was getting taken further and further away by the waves. Men on the hull were shouting and screaming at him to turn back but the wind was snatching at their words as they watched him. His energy gone he slowly turned face down and drifted toward the open sea, his big winter fur hat bobbing beside him like a faithful dog.

The first life raft was soon full of men, wet and miserable just hanging on. Terrified that at any minute they would be flipped over.

Volkov meantime was standing beside the radio officer who he'd just told to leave his station and get up on deck to save himself.

"Sir, I'll give it one more minute," he said, soon to be leaving this widow maker. He saluted Volkov who looked at the radio for a few seconds, then turned to go. He wondered if anyone would ever come to their rescue. "God help us all," he said to himself as he climbed up to the shattered conning tower and out onto the wind whipped hull, where he would wait for the rest of his men.

CHAPTER TWENTY-SIX

Peter climbed into the big black car which was waiting for him in the yard. He had said his goodbyes to Vasily and Zoya, and was about to say his goodbyes to Russia, again.

Vasily had given Peter a package, which was now firmly strapped against his waist in the same way that the envelope of plain paper had been when he arrived. Only this time Peter knew exactly what he was carrying and why. It was Top Secret plans for an experimental rocket plane, which a group of scientists in Sverdlovsk had been working on. There were facts and figures that Peter had studied over and over again, just in case anything should happen to the plans. All he wanted to do now was get home, so he settled himself and nodded to the driver who pulled quietly away and on to the road out of town. But first, there was visit he must make.

As she heard the car pull away, Zoya looked at the bed they had slept in. Her hand slid under the pillow, why? She didn't know. It was an instinctive move but there was the note. She ran to the window but Peter was gone. The little heart and the two crosses on that piece of paper told her everything she wanted to know.

CHAPTER TWENTY-SEVEN

It didn't take long for word of the stricken submarine to get about. Lowry Nicholson and his friend Duncan were already making their way to Lunna House where the focus of the rescue was to be.

Other local men downed tools to make themselves available. Captain Vickers was in the process of trying to get as much information as to the position of the sub. The big radio that sat in the operations room at Lunna House was being attended by a young officer whose ears were almost glued to the set listening to every squeak and blip. Next to him sat a radio telegraph officer who had managed to find the channel that the sub was using for its May Day. The problem was it was being sent on a ciphered system, which meant that the Germans were probably listening to every word. He decided to try a new emergency channel that was not widely known but 'nothing ventured, nothing gained' were his thoughts. He sent the message, and didn't have long to wait.

"Thank God." was the desparate reply. Then the message went on to give all the information that the rescue party needed to get the boats to them. Already a Catalina from Sullom Voe had been scrambled and was waiting for the coordinates so information could be sent back to Lunna House. The aircraft had been quickly packed with life rafts and flares to be dropped near the sub.

Storms that had raged over the North Sea were finally showing signs of easing. Two large fishing boats were being made ready to leave the anchorage at Lunna House. The men on board were sorting out the supplies that they would need, food, water, and medical equipment and bunks were being made ready.

"Grab all the blankets you can find lad and bring them to the boats." shouted Captain Vickers to a young officer, as he ran down the stairs. Out in the yard were the two skippers who had agreed to use their boats.

"Here are the last co-ordinates we have and here is the latest weather forecast, which as you can see gentlemen, could be better but at least the wind is easing slightly. They say that this will continue for the next couple days, so all I can say is good luck and may God go with you." He handed the men a copy each of the information and they shook hands.

Valerie and Tally had returned to Lunna House and were now preparing a large downstairs room ready for the submarines crew. They watched as the two boats left their moorings and set off into the North Sea. As soon as they were out of the shelter of land, the wind and swell took hold and lifted them up like toys. Only their dimmed little lights were visible as they quickly disappeared in to the gathering dusk.

There was nothing anyone could do now but wait...

CHAPTER TWENTY-EIGHT

Giles Johansson was even more curious when he'd seen Tally Gregor hurrying on her bicycle to Katy Graham's place. He watched from afar as she entered the little cottage, saw her being greeted by Katy and then heard the door shut behind them. Giles knew there was something up but couldn't work out what it was. So he decided to go to the Post Office and have a chat to the ugly sisters as he called them; not to their faces though, he knew better than that, but one day, he thought, one day they would all see. He smiled to himself as he raced down the road on his bike.

"Giles, how nice to see you." Maisie Donaldson lied through gritted teeth and a fixed smile. She had always tried to be civil to her customers but this lad she'd never liked. He had a nasty habit of making her feel very uncomfortable. He crept around the shop and picked things up, never wanting to buy and always ear wigging on other folk's conversation.

"What can we do for you today young man?"

"I want a stamp," he replied walking toward the counter.

"For a letter, and where is this letter going too?" Maisie asked.

"Who says it's a letter?" his voice defiant.

"I'm sorry, what is it you need a stamp for then?"

"Eh, it's for a parcel."

"Have you got the parcel with you Giles?"

"No, I just want a stamp." he sounded more agitated because he didn't know where this conversation was going and was beginning to wish he'd just asked for the time.

"Giles," Maisie said patiently, "bring me the parcel, I will weigh it, and then I will tell you how much the stamps will cost, ok?"

"Don't treat me like a child. I know what I'm doing and so will you all, and very soon, you'll see," his voice becoming louder and higher, spittle beginning to spray out of his mouth.

Maisie's sister Meg appeared from the back room wondering what all the noise was about. Giles walked away to the back of the shop and stood quietly, breathing deeply, trying to calm himself down. He wiped his sleeve across his wet mouth. Just then the milk delivery man, Jerry, walked into the Post Office. He was carrying a crate of milk, and not seeing Giles in the corner, shouted out, "The rescue boats left last night to go to the Russian sub. So hopefully we will hear something soon, you'll have to keep 'toot' on that radio of yours, ladies."

Maisie glared at Jerry then glanced sideways to where Giles was standing, Jerry, getting the message, saw the lad just as he made for the door pushing passed the milkman a triumphant look on his face.

"Well ladies, what was all that about?" Jerry asked, stacking the milk onto the shelves.

"I just don't trust that lad. He came in here ranting on about how we're all going to see what he's been doing. Oh I don't know I just know he's up to no good."

Jerry said his goodbyes to the sisters and climbed up into his delivery van. He thought about what they'd said, and remembered that his friend Peter Gregor had also told him of Giles hanging around Sullom Voe a while back and generally causing concern. Well, as he was going that way, he would stop off and talk to a few of his friends at the Base.

Giles was full of himself as he charged up north to a place near Sullom Voe. There were people up there who would be delighted to hear what he had to say. He was shaking with excitement. He'd be a hero telling them about the Russian sub and the rescue that was now under-way. He thought his new Belgian friends would be very pleased. It's just a pity he didn't know exactly where the sub was, he would make something up, make it sound genuine. He'd have them eating out of his hands. Then he would ask them for more money and everything...

CHAPTER TWENTY-NINE

Peter asked the driver to take him to an address in a quiet road which ran beside St Nicholas church at Slovak Park. It was to the east of the city near to his old home. As they drew up, Peter could clearly see Eva's cottage just as he remembered it all those years ago. There was still enough light as he focussed his attention on the small front door. His thinking was crystal clear. He knew exactly what he had to ask Eva. This visit had been on his mind since he first knew he would be back to his hometown. Thanks to Captain Vickers he was determined to solve, one way or another the mystery of his daughter's birth.

He had never been able to fight the feeling that Tally was not his daughter. Every night of his life he'd heard his wife's voice telling him to look after 'their son'…'call him Sergei'…that was the name of her father. He climbed out of the car telling the driver to wait for him, he wouldn't be long. Walking toward the cottage he saw a curtain move in the window. A face appeared. It was Eva. She saw him, staring, as if she'd seen a ghost. Her sunken eyes widening and her hand clamped over her mouth. She started to back away shaking her head from side to side. As he got closer Peter could hear her screaming, "No, no, no it wasn't me, it wasn't me, don't come in. He is the one…he forced me to…God will punish me...you must go and look after her...she will know one day. God is ready to punish me..."

Peter stopped before he got to the door and listened to the woman's ranting. He knew then. He knew he didn't have to go in and make her tell him. Tally was not his and he realised that Eva was living with the consequences of what she'd done. He didn't know whether his son had died or was still alive somewhere but his mind was in turmoil and he could see that Eva was in no fit state to talk to anyone. All he wanted to do was get out of there and return to Shetland. He left the wailing Eva to her torment.

He made good time and felt heartened by the news that the war may soon be over. His contacts in neutral Sweden were starting to round up and punish those who had joined forces with the Germans in the hope the Nazis would be triumphant. These traitors were sadly misled and were now paying the ultimate price. Those who were captured were taken to secret 'safe houses' where they would be kept in a darkened room for a few hours or days if they wouldn't talk. But usually after a little persuasion, gave the Resistance valuable information. One famous Swedish Resistance officer was more feared than most. He was a man in his thirty's, tall and blond. Small gold-rimmed glasses framed his steely pale blue eyes and a deep red scar on the right side of his face ran from his temple to his chin. He claimed he got it escaping the SS. He took a particular pride in the kind of torture he administered. He liked to call it 'counselling', saying that the term made him feel as if he was doing useful volunteer work for his country. Those he 'counselled', and gave all the information he felt they could, became useless to him, and were eventually taken into the garden at the back of the house. This fastidious officer loved his garden and he tended it whenever he could. There were beds full of seasonal flowers, and wholesome vegetables growing in neat rows. He liked to keep things neat. In one sunny corner was a beautiful greenhouse where he cultivated the most delicious grapes, for his own wine of course. He had a tendency to strut along the well-kept pathways picking up any stray leaves with the tip of his ever-present sword. His garden was his obsession as was his hatred of the Germans. He always felt a sickening sense of achievement when he brought traitors here. He would make them stand on the grass underneath a large pine tree. He did not want any blood spilled on the old beautifully worn stone path. There they would be ordered to tell him how nicely he kept the gardens. Then he told them how the soil needed plenty of shit to feed the plants. The last thing they saw was his gun raised to their heads. No one ever claimed to have seen him shoot anyone.

CHAPTER THIRTY

Peter was finally nearing the old wooden house of the twin brothers Lars and Jo who had helped him on his way to Russia. They would know he was not far away thanks to the 'underground' message carriers. As he neared the house he heard the sound of a generator as it chugged rhythmically away in the old shed and caught the faint smell of diesel. The 'guides' car had dropped him off at a road end half a kilometre away and he'd walked up the rough track carrying his few possessions and of course the precious package around his waist. Just then the door swung open and Lars appeared with a huge smile on his face, his arms outstretched toward Peter.

"My good friend, what a joy it is to see you again and looking very fit too," he laughed and took hold of Peter's bag and guided him toward the house. The two men sat in the kitchen and shared some food. Peter was very glad to be back in this man's company knowing it would not be long before he was home.

"I have good news for you," Lars said as he cleared away the few dishes, "we may get you home sooner than you think."

"Oh, how's that?" Peter asked drinking the welcome mug of hot coffee.

"Well, it just so happens that there's a drop tonight. We have a floatplane coming in with some ammunition and a few other supplies. They're going to land on the lake a mile from here at about ten o'clock. Friends will be helping with the unloading but there will be no time for me to give you any formal introductions you understand," he laughed. "They will appear and then disappear back to where they came from. The most important thing is that we arrive about an hour before, just to be on the safe side."

"That's good news Lars, and I can never thank you and your brother enough, and all the others who've put their lives on the line for me. It's been one hell of a journey, which I know is not over yet but I can at least feel is coming to an end, the same as the war, I hope," he raised his coffee and smiled warmly at his host.

"Right, I suggest you get an hour's shut eye then we'll get on our way. I'll wake you in good time." Lars showed Peter to a small back room which had an old bed with a pile of woollen blankets on it.

"Make yourself at home, it doesn't look much but it's comfortable," as he closed the door behind him.

Although Peter was pretty exhausted from his journey, he found it difficult to sleep or even close his eyes. His thoughts were with Tally who had no idea where he was or that he was on his way home. After an hour he got up and went through to the kitchen where Lars was stoking the fire and putting on another pot of coffee.

"That smells good," said Peter as he stood at the window looking out on to the darkening skies.

"We can wait a few more minutes then we must go," replied Lars.

"Where's the aircraft flying in from?" asked Peter as he hugged his cup of coffee, feelings it's warmth in his fingers.

"It's leaving from a small base on a reservoir about fifty miles north of Edinburgh." Lars put the blackened pot back onto the stove, "He should be going straight on to a site in Russia but we've diverted him and he's agreed to take you to the fjord near Bremanger Island. Someone will be there to meet you."

"I'm grateful to you my friend, and I tell you, I'm so happy to be going home. It has been very hard to leave my daughter and not to tell her anything."

"Is there no one she can speak to in Shetland?"

"No, we were both told that no one should know anything about my mission, nor was she to contact anyone," Peter gave a wry smile, "but she's quite headstrong so I would imagine by now she will have asked some questions. Whether she would have received any answers is another matter."

"One thing before we go Peter, I heard a few hours ago through various means, that there's a Russian sub in trouble in the North Sea just off the northeast coast of Shetland. It appears your friends and the R.A.F have put together a rescue, which is in progress as we speak. So I know you will have plenty to do when you get back." Lars put on his coat and grabbed a torch.

"Do you know what submarine it is or its number?"

"Not all of the numbers, that apparently has been blown off but it started with a four and I believe it is a Schuka class. Does that mean anything to you?"

"Yes, it means it's a floating death trap. Those things were made back in 1934 and were thrown together just so the powers that be could say they had the greatest navy in the world. God help all those men." Peter put on his coat and followed Lars out of the door.

The wind was slight and from the west. They walked down a narrow track keeping close to the hedges that towered either side. Lars signalled to Peter to stay quiet, but Peter knew better than to speak. His senses were alert and he kept his eyes ahead watching with the little fading light there was. There was a clear sky with a bright moon, which would help any pilot trying to find a small landing site. But of course it meant that any German patrols in the area would also know that a full moon meant possible aircraft movement. They arrived at the lake and from what Peter could make out it was about a mile long and half a mile wide with fields on all sides.

They stood in the shelter of some trees. He tapped Lars on the shoulder and whispered, "What type of aircraft can fly into here?"

"It's a Fairey Seafox, they're brilliant little planes and have been shuttling agents and ammo and all manner of things in and out of Norway for a long time." After they had sat quietly for nearly an hour he pointed to the West where the faint sound of an aeroplane engine could be heard. Then he put his hands together and blew, making the sound of an owl. At that moment two beams of light in an L shape lit up two sides of the lake so that the pilot could calculate where the landing area was. He came in quite fast and had to adjust his pitch before making the perfect landing. The little black Seafox with its double strutted wings left foaming white ripples as it turned toward the jetty. He was already to make a quick get away and head back west. Both landing torches were then extinguished and Peter sensed rather than saw that men were running to the aircraft to grab the supplies packed in the tiny fuselage. The only noise was that of the big single engine, which the pilot did not switch off. Lars then shouted to Peter, "Run, run, run, go and Gods speed." Peter hardly had time to shake his friends hand before he was sprinting down to the waters edge He clambered onto the wing then up into the single seat behind the pilot. He squeezed himself into the tiny space just big enough for his huge frame and gave the thumbs up. The pilot gunned the engine and the Seafox roared up the lake into the wind. Before he knew it, they were up in the air and flying over the moon lit fields and hills of Norway. The noise of the engine and the wind blasting into the open cockpit made conversation between him and the pilot impossible but he did feel strangely safe. An Old Russian folk song started playing in his head, and he smiled and thought of Zoya.

CHAPTER THIRTY-ONE

Winds from the west are usually strong and unforgiving as they whip across Shetland but now they had dropped to a steady force five or six allowing the two fishing boats to ride easier on their journey to the stricken submarine. With the wind behind them they made good time with all men keeping a sharp look out. It wasn't long before the huge hulk of the submarine could be seen wallowing in the waves. The bow pointed skyward and the stern underwater. A small bright orange life raft was being tossed around about twenty metres away from the hull; it was half full of water with the men inside hanging on for grim death. The captain of the first fishing boat to arrive could see that some of the protective cover had been ripped off either by the wind or had been damaged as it was thrown from the submarine. Either way the men who were huddled there were in danger of being swept overboard at any moment. He skilfully manoeuvred his vessel as near as he safely could and turned it so the raft had some protection from the wind. There were shouts and instructions in Russian and English as the second fishing boat came alongside. Rope ladders were flung over the rails and trailed in the water. More ropes snaked toward the raft in the hope that someone had the strength to pull them nearer.

"That looks like the sub captain standing on the hull," shouted one of the crew pointing over the bows of the second boat.

"Hang on lads this is going to be dangerous, keep yer wits about ye," shouted the captain as he powered the massive diesel toward what was left of the Russian submarine.

All he could see was part of the damaged conning tower and about ten metres of the bow that was rising up out of the sea. There were about thirty men, all trying desperately to stay upright. Every time a wave broke they were completely drenched and it was obvious that they were getting weaker by the minute. Commander Volkov was trying hard to keep their spirits up and when they'd seen the fishing boats arrive, a cheer went up. The subs chief engineer Ralf had fallen while down below and sustained a severe blow to his head. Volkov and the young radio officer were able to get him onto the deck and were now holding him tightly in a soaking wet blanket. Blood was oozing from his head wound as he drifted in and out of consciousness.

"Just let me go," said Ralf, his eye's closing and his breathing laboured.

"No, by God you're not going anywhere. We're going to get you to safety and then home to Russia, you'll see my friend, just hang on," Volkov cradled the man's head as more blood was washed over his uniform.

"Mother Russia," his voice was getting weaker as he looked at Volkov, his big oil stained hands grasping the sleeve of the commanders jacket. Volkov had known and worked with this fiery engineer for many years and knew him to be a good man in the truest sense of the word and it broke his heart to see him now.

"Please let me go, I'm done, you'll never get me off the deck. Save yourself man, you have the others to look after," he slipped into unconsciousness as a wave came over the hull and it took Volkov all his strength to hang on to him.

"Get this man off first," he shouted to his crew as the fishing boat came alongside.

It was as well that Ralf was unconscious because his journey from the deck of the rolling sub to the fishing boat was indeed perilous. His limp body was strapped into a makeshift stretcher and dragged through the waves toward the fishing boat. Many hands were ready to grab hold of him when he finally bumped over the rails, and was quickly taken below. Four other men who had been hanging onto the metal rails attached to the conning tower suddenly fell into the water. The rusted rivets had been damaged when the mine exploded and the rail could no longer hold their weight. Volkov looked in horror as his first officer and three crewmen were swept away. A wave brought them back to the sub but there was nothing for them to hold on too. The metal sides were smooth and slippery and the men who were on the hull couldn't reach down far enough to help them. Another wave came and swept them even further away. Two of them tried to swim to the fishing boats. One man managed to get to the rope ladders that were swinging over the side. He climbed up two rungs his body thudding against the side of the boat with each wave. His sodden clothes were adding to his weight. He finally fell back into the water and just sank out of sight. A second man also went under the boat, neither was ever seen again. The first officer and the other crewman almost made the life raft but the cold was too much and the waves too vicious. Volkov saw them look at each other; they opened their arms in a bear hug as the waves threw them together. It looked like a reunion of two long lost brothers. At that point, they both sank slowly beneath the waves.

It took the Shetland boats over two hours to get the last of the crew off the sinking submarine. Volkov was the last to leave. Totally exhausted he fell with great relief onto the heaving deck of the fishing boat. His first job was to see that all the men who had been rescued were accounted for and to gather the names of those who had been lost.

In all his years in the navy he had never felt so saddened and beaten. This was the first time he had lost any men under his command and it hit him very hard. Not only did he curse the Germans but he also cursed the fact that his submarine was not sea worthy, and by God he would let it be known when, or if he returned to Russia. He made his way to the captain's quarters, knocked on the door and waited.

"I cannot thank you enough Captain," he said holding out his hand to the giant of a man who was the owner and skipper.

"The names Mac, and we came as soon as we could Commander; it was all anyone would have done. You understand that we cannot start to look for the others, they're gone I'm afraid; there's no way they would have survived in the water for very long. May I suggest you go down below and change out of those wet cloths before you catch your death?" His handshake was tough and rough but his smile was warm and kindly. He returned to the wheel, "we'll be heading home now, go and see to your men, they're going to need you." His sad smile said it all.

"Yes, I know. Can I ask you to contact the other boat and get me the names of the rest of my crew?" said Volkov as he turned to go.

"Aye, of course, I'll do it right away."

Both boats were heading into the wind and a big swell but they road it out well. Men were sitting or lying where they could, some were smoking some drinking hot tea others sat staring into space. Volkov made sure he spoke to each and every one of them, giving them encouragement trying to bolster their spirits after what had been a nightmare. His biggest worry was Ralf the engineer. After being hauled on board, he'd been taken down below to the makeshift sick bay and treated for his head wound.

The medical officer, a doctor who had volunteered from the island, said there was not a lot he could do. Ralf had suffered a very severe head injury, with he believed, a massive amount of bleeding inside the brain itself. He was heavily bandaged and his face was porcelain white, his head supported on either side by rolled up towels lessening any movement that would aggravate his injuries.

"Truth Doctor, what are his chances?" asked a weary Volkov.

"Truth Commander, he has not regained consciousness since being brought aboard. I'm sorry to say he does not have very long. I have no facility to give him a blood transfusion or perform any operation to help stop any internal bleeding. I think you should just sit with him if you'd like, and perhaps pray." The doctor walked to the door, opened it and went quietly out into the corridor.

Volkov sat next to the bed of his friend, looking into the face of the man who had stood next to him for years. He'd given loyal and devoted service and had treated young Volkov almost like a son, and Volkov knew it. Ralf had come across as a man always in a bad temper, whether it was with the engines, the weather, the Navy, the war, the food, it was a constant moan, but never with the Commander. His respect for Volkov was gathered over the years. Seeing this young man work hard to bind a crew together, learn to trust them and in return gain their trust to lead them. Ralf knew the submarine should not have been at sea, particularly in such rough conditions, and he had repaired the engines so many times, they had almost been rebuilt.

Volkov picked up a damp cloth to wipe Ralf's clammy brow. As he did so the old man managed to open his eyes. Very slowly he looked at Volkov and Volkov took his hand.

"Hello my friend, you are safe now, try and rest. We'll soon be in Shetland and there you'll be taken to hospital, and soon be well again," he said gently.

"Sing for me please?" his eyes began filling with tears.

Volkov knew what he meant. He wanted him to sing the Old Russian folk song that Ralf sang all the time while on board with his beloved engines. So Volkov started to sing the sad song that spoke of the Ural Mountains its birds and its flowers. It was a song about the weary traveller longing to be back there again and walk once more in the sunshine and breathe the air that was as pure as Heaven itself. Volkov's voice was deep and rich as he sang; there was a glimmer of a smile on Ralf's face as he gently tightened his grip on the Commanders hand.

"I'm home," he said, as his last breath left his body.

Volkov stopped singing and still holding the older mans hand, leant forward to rest his head on the table, and wept softly.

CHAPTER THIRTY-TWO

After Peter Gregor and the baby had left Sverdlovsk, little did he know that the lives of his wife's maid Eva, and the local priest Father Dansik had turned into a nightmare. They had done what they thought they had to do for good reason. Now they were left to bring up a baby boy. The first few days saw Eva trying to pacify this crying child night and day. It was as if he knew what she had done after the death of his mother, and he was going to cry until he could be reunited with his father. Eva spent most of her time walking the child in the local park wondering how she'd ever got into this mess. She tried to stay away from other people and if anyone asked about the baby she had her story ready. He was the son of a niece who had been killed in the uprising and his father was away fighting with the revolutionary's. She had given him her family name Somova; it was easier that way. Better that than Gregor, which would take too much explaining. Father Dansik, who at first had helped with their plan, became less keen to be involved with the boy. Typical she thought, once she'd paid him a small amount of money to hide the boy in the church, he wanted no more to do with her. There was no more money, and now he knew what she'd done. He could hide behind the church and deny all knowledge of the event. But she was terrified.

When she had been maidservant to the most powerful family in Russia, she knew exactly what she had to do. It seemed simple at the time. Now she found herself alone with no one to turn too and a young boy to care for. What would become of her, but most importantly, what would become of the child that Peter Gregor had taken with him?

For years Eva struggled to bring the boy up and get him through school. He grew to be a big strong lad with a tendency to get himself into fights. Not that he ever came off worst; he was more than capable of looking after himself. He was nearly six foot by the time he was fifteen years old and admired by many of the girls at school and challenged by many of the boys. As soon as he was born and before she took him to the church, Eva called him Sergei as his mother had wished. She saw no reason not too. Only she and Father Dansik knew who his real parents were but she always pleaded ignorance when Sergei asked. He had questioned her long ago about them but Eva had been very convincing when she told him he had been left at the church. Father Dansik had taken him in and she had agreed to look after him and treat him like a son. Sergei seemed to accept this, although he still felt she'd not been totally honest. One day perhaps he would find out the truth.

His life with Eva was one of school and learning. She wished him to achieve the highest results and therefore be more able to acquire a good job when he finished college.

He found academic life very enjoyable and made many friends. These were friends who shared his wish for a better Russia and a better society. Especially for the farmers and peasants, the poorest of the country who had fought hard to make a life for themselves. The death of the Tsar and his family back in 1918 had been the start of the brave new Russia, but Sergei and his peers were yet to see positive change. Stalin had succeeded Lenin in 1924 and rumours of horrendous atrocities were rife. Members of the old Bolshevik regime were being rounded up and many were charged with collaborating with foreign powers to overturn Socialism. Subsequently found guilty they were executed. Thousands of others who supported the Bolsheviks either perished in camps, of which there were many, or were deported. The newly formed secret police bore the name 'Chief Administration of Corrective Labour Camps and Labour Settlements'. They were in charge of the notorious camps, and under Stalin, no one questioned them or their methods.

Young Sergei joined the local debating society and regularly met with a group of intellectuals who began to challenge decisions made by local government. His name was beginning to be heard in political circles and some didn't like what he was saying, calling him an anarchist. He and some of his friends were warned off by faceless political agents. Messages were left for him with no names or signatures. He was told not to ask so many leading questions in public, about Stalin and the ruling party. Nor to ask about decisions that were being made on behalf of the workers in the factories, and the peasants who were struggling on the land. Sergei took no heed of these petty warnings and pressed on with his questioning wherever he could be heard.

He eventually left the comfort of Eva's cottage and got himself rooms in the middle of town. This suited him well; there he could entertain his friends. They could eat, drink and argue politics through the night. One such friend was Yuri Volkov; a brilliant young mind who helped Sergei put speeches together for public debate. The two men shared the same visions and aspirations although young Yuri was set on going to sea. As soon as his education in Sverdlovsk ended, he would set off for Archangel to start his naval training.

It was a cold winter morning when Yuri was to catch the train to Archangel. His two large canvas bags were packed and ready beside his feet as he stood on the pavement outside the station. He was feeling cold and wanted to go into the little café and have a drink of coffee but he'd arranged to meet Sergei outside to say goodbye. The evening before, they had met up with friends and spent some time in a small bar off the main street. The night had been one of laughter and singing and telling of stories and jokes. Yuri's head felt a little delicate but he waited patiently for his friend, and then saw Sergei hurrying toward him with a big smile on his face. The two men embraced as Yuri guided them toward the coffee shop.

"My, my Yuri, you look a bit off colour this morning," Sergei laughed as he gently punched his friend's shoulder.

"It's nothing really, just had a bit too much vodka last night, anyhow how's your head?"

"The same as yours if I were to admit it, which I won't."

The café was not yet full and they found a table by the window. Sergei pulled back two chairs, which screeched on the floor, making Yuri wince

"Oh man, what a noise," he said holding his head.

"You're going to have to get used to drinking if you join the navy, it's expected of you." Sergei put the coffees on the table and as he took off his coat he glanced through the window.

"Who's that fellow there and what's he doing?"

Outside on the pavement, looking at them was a rough looking man. Tall and very thin with a pale face. His hair and beard were both long and black. He wore an old dark brown ragged overcoat that hung down around his ankles and a black felt hat that had no discernable shape. He had dark piercing eyes and was staring straight at Sergei. Both his hands were in his pockets but there was something about him that made Sergei shudder.

"I don't know my friend, sit down. Take no notice of him."

Time seemed to stand still, and then everything moved in slow motion. Sergei was still looking at the man when he saw the gun come slowly out of the pocket of the overcoat and point directly at him. Yuri had turned to look and saw the gun at the same time, shouting at Sergei to get down. The few people who were around just stared in disbelief as the gun went off and the huge glass window disintegrated in front of them. Sergei cried out as he hit the floor, blood oozing through his clothes. Yuri caught a glimpse of the man running down the street with three or four men in pursuit. He got down onto the floor and held Sergei's head and shouted to the manager of the coffee shop to get an ambulance straight away.

"Where have you been hit, just point and I'll have a look?"

"I know his face." Sergei whispered, as he felt his left side. He was shaking badly and going into shock.

"Don't try to speak my friend, we'll see you right, don't you worry and we'll catch the bastard who did this." It was the very first time Sergei had heard his friend use such language and he wanted to smile, but couldn't quite make it. He grimaced instead.

"It bloody hurts Yuri," Sergei was beginning to go very pale and sweat was forming on his forehead even though the temperature outside was freezing. With the big window gone, cold air came rushing into the café. People were gathering outside and Yuri could hear the odd scream and shout but wanted to hold onto his friend and keep him talking.

"I've seem him before Yuri, he was at the last meeting we had and I'm sure I saw him in the bar last night. He could have heard us making arrangements for today." his voice was weakening and his breathing becoming more laboured

The gathering crowd moved out of the way when the ambulance arrived. The two uniformed crew quickly put Sergei onto a stretcher and whisked him away to the local hospital. Yuri stood up looking at the blood that was now smudged into the tiles of the café floor.

"I'll follow you there Sergei, just hang on." He shouted as he picked up his bags and watched the ambulance leave to speed its way through the town. He then made his way to the bus stop. I guess the Navy will have to wait a few more hours, he said to himself.

It was clear by the look on the doctor's face when Yuri arrived that all was not good.

In his long white coat, he was quite an imposing man, who looked over the top of his spectacles at Yuri as if inspecting him.

"You're the friend who was with the young man who got himself shot?" he made it sound as if it was Sergei's fault.

"Yes sir, I am, how is he, can I see him please?"

"He is not well and no, I'm sorry, you can't," was the rather stern reply, though Yuri hoped the doctor wasn't as objectionable as he sounded.

"Then when would it be possible?"

"When we can retrieve the bullet. It is still embedded in him and is near his heart, he was obviously meant to die. Do you know who might have done this and why?"

"Your patient sir, is my friend Sergei Somova and is well known in this town for his rather outspoken views on Stalin's leadership. He has criticised the Party on many an occasion, so if Stalin's henchmen heard him and they'd been given orders to kill him, then it would be easy. Sergei told me he thought he knew who the man was that tried to shoot him and that he might have attended the meeting we were at last week." Yuri was beginning to wonder if his life may also be in danger and gave an involuntary glance over his shoulder toward the door.

"Ah, yes I have heard of this young speaker and I agree he may have made one or two enemies. Nevertheless, if he thinks he knows who did this then that is good. We may get some valuable information from him. Now, I must go and check the patient, please excuse me. I'll send word to you as soon as I can tell you anything. Leave your details at the desk on the way out eh?" with that he strode away down the corridor and out of sight, his heavy shoes echoing on the tiled floor.

Yuri sat down heavily on a metal chair next to the white tiled walls, putting his bags on the floor and wondering how his friend was going to come through this. A couple of nurses passed but paid no attention to him. It was an old hospital with huge long windows letting in the cold morning light. The corridors were white and endless and smelled of disinfectant. There were few people about. Yuri could hear some nurses not too far away, their laughter echoing and then being shushed by a man's voice. He sat there wondering how all this had happened. He'd helped with one or two of Sergei's speeches lately, and knew that they were anti Stalin questioning many decisions the leader was making. Never did he think it would ever come to this. Is it possible that Stalin had ordered Sergei to be killed; he found that hard to believe but did not dismiss it entirely?

He sat there for an hour just thinking of his friend and the times they had spent together and about the fragility of life itself. Then he tried to find someone to ask about Sergei. The nurses had left and the corridors were empty, so he started walking in the direction the doctor had gone. He past a couple of offices but there was no one there. He finally found him talking to a surgeon whose white operating gown was splashed with blood. They both turned as Yuri stood in the doorway. With his head bowed, the doctor told Yuri that they had done their best for his friend but the bullet had also punctured the edge of his lung. The damage was severe and it may be impossible to save him. Yuri felt hot tears come to his eyes as he sat on a chair offered to him by the surgeon.

"I can't believe it, I just don't understand, he's my best friend. Dear Mary, Mother of God," he wept.

"Can I see him, please?" he looked up at the doctor who nodded his head and asked him to follow him out.

Sergei lay in a small quiet side room; there was nothing to suggest the horrific violence he had just suffered. He looked peaceful in the white metal bed with its white starched sheets. To the side stood a white table, on it a white jug and a glass. His face was almost white; it was his shock of dark unruly hair that looked strangely out of place in this white world. Yuri felt faint. He held his friends barely warm hands and leaned toward him,

"I'm here old friend, don't you fret. Everything is going to be alright." He was choking back the tears as he looked at Sergei's face willing him to open his eyes or at least move his hand, but he did neither. It's not fair, it's not fair, he said to himself but realised he had said it out loud and the two doctors were looking at him as they stood by the door.

"Do you know of an address we can contact his parents?" one asked.

"Yes, yes, of course," Yuri still in a state of shock went back into the office. "He was brought up by a woman and a priest. They told him that when he was a baby he was left on the steps of St Nicholas's; you know the church by Slovak Park. He told me he never believed them, I don't know why. Sergei was never sure what to believe and he said it made things difficult for him at school, you know, 'you've got no mother or father' sort of thing. And he got into a lot of fights. I think he is desperate to find out but doesn't talk about it much, I mean where do you start? The name of the woman is Eva Somova and Sergei thinks she had been in the employ of the Romanovs. Sergei was the name she gave him." Yuri gave them his friend's address, "I'm sure she still lives there. We called him Sergei G, he doesn't know why but this woman Eva put the letter G after his first name." He sat silently staring at the floor.

"Do you want me to go and tell her?" he asked the doctors but dreading them saying yes.

"No, no my boy, leave that to the authorities. But thank you for the information; we would have struggled to work out who he was. He was carrying no identification which I thought was a little strange and as you can see he's not in the mood for talking, yet.

He shook his head slowly, "We will do our level best for him and get in touch when we have some news," he shook hands then left the office. Yuri left his address on the doctors' writing pad. Let me get out of this place, he thought as he walked back along the empty white corridor. Picking up his things he ran out in to the blinding light of the frosty winter sunshine tears stinging his eyes, and made his way slowly back to the railway station. "I'm so sorry Sergei but I have to go," he sobbed.

CHAPTER THIRTY-THREE

Tally had arranged to meet Valerie Carlson at Lunna House but on the way called to see Jac and his Ma. She wouldn't have a lot of time but Jac's health was worrying her and she knew her visits meant a lot to him. In her heart she knew he wasn't going to get better. He'd looked so frail when she last saw him, and the doctors treatments didn't seem to be making any difference. It was a cool day but the sun was trying to peep through the clouds as she peddled to the farm. Jac's Ma was in the yard hanging out the washing, her face strained and pale, "Hello Tally pet, how lovely to see you, come in, come in," she went into the kitchen carrying her flowered peg bag.

Tally could hardly keep from gasping with shock when she saw Jac. He was sitting in the big chair beside the fire, looking for the world like a little old man; his body seemed to have shrunk to half its size. Tally smiled at him and gave him a gentle hug.

"Jac it's good to see you, how have you been doing?" realising how stupid a question that was as she gave an apologetic smile.

"Well, Tally, I've been sitting here, while Ma has been looking after me. That's what I have been doing," his voice cut Tally like a knife.

"I'm sorry Jac, I shouldn't have been so insensitive is there anything I can do for you?"

"No Tally I'm sorry too. I just get so frustrated sitting here day after day watching Ma work herself into the ground." There was a deep silence between them.

"I'm going into hospital on Monday, it'll be better for Ma, I'll not be under her feet."

"Oh Jac, how long for?"

Jac just looked at Tally and with the tiniest shake of his head, said nothing. Just then his mother appeared at the door, "I'll put the kettle on." They sat in awkward silence and had their tea, small talk did not seem appropriate. Tally felt totally useless as she watched Jac hold his cup with both hands then struggle to place it back onto the saucer.

"I'm meeting Val Carlson at Lunna House, I think the boats are coming back today from the rescue," it broke the silence but her voice was shaking.

"I'd heard about that," said Jac, "how many men are coming in. We could take a couple here, couldn't we Ma, my room will be empty on Monday," again the silence hung in the air as Jac just smiled an 'its okay' to his Ma.

"Yes, I suppose we could, for a short while, until you're well enough to come home," she turned away to the sink saying no more.

"That's very kind of you Mrs Smith; I'll let them know at Lunna House. Now if you don't mind I must get going it's quite a way but I'll let you know as soon as I hear anything?" with that Tally made her way, with a feeling of great sadness, out into the sunshine, climbed on her bicycle and set off.

CHAPTER THIRTY-FOUR

Giles had spent most of the war years keeping out of his father's way. He would never have been able to explain why he'd been spending time with four Belgians up near Sullom Voe. They told him they were his new friends and he thought they had been very good to him. First, they bought him a great big torch saying that it was much darker in Shetland than where they lived in Belgium. He wasn't sure how dark it got in Belgium so didn't argue. Then they gave him some money to buy a new bicycle. Number one, the boss, said it was because the one he had rattled too much and could be heard miles away. He said he couldn't get a new bike because his father would ask too many questions, so they took the money back off him and told him to fix his old one. He didn't like that until they explained that they'd give him something bigger and better later.

He'd been going to the little shop nearby to get their groceries and because he didn't live in that part of Shetland the man in the shop didn't really take a lot of notice. Until one day Giles asked for four bottles of beer, "And what would you be wanting with all that drink young man?" he'd asked. "You don't look old enough to drink to me," his voice sounding suspicious, as he leaned closer to Giles to take a closer look.

"Well if you must know," lied Giles rather too defiantly, "It's for my Da and his friends."

He swallowed hard and looked the man straight in the eyes, the way his new friends had told him too.

"Well, I'll let you have it this time but I'll be checking up with your father," the shopkeeper put the four bottles in to a brown paper carrier bag and handed it to Giles, who was shaking that much he nearly dropped the lot. He paid and left the shop without another word and scurried back to the sheep shed; smiling to himself saying, "He'll have a job. He doesn't know who I am, and my new friends will be happy I've got their beer," yes, Giles was feeling good.

The shopkeeper was the kind of man who never forgot a face or a piece of gossip. His wife said he was worse than a woman when it came to tittle-tattle. She could talk with the best of them but he could remember things that even she hadn't heard of let alone talked about. He sat there in the shop racking his brain, searching his long memory for where he'd seen that young man before. It would come to him; he thought. It would come.

Giles arrived at the sheep shed and gave the men their beers.

"Did everything go ok?" asked one of them.

"Yer, fine, the man doesn't know me does he? I've told you, everything's fine," Giles was sounding more confident than he felt and wondered if they would give him a drink of beer. They didn't.

That afternoon, the boss man had given Giles a large canvas bag about the size of a rolled up blanket, but a lot heavier. He'd been told to leave straight away and put it into the farthest hide and to make sure no one saw him.

"Why, what is it?" he asked the man.

"It is part of our survey work. You see son, we have got to prove that the enemy could get to the base and blow it up. We are not the enemy you understand, but if we were, then we need to tell the military they are not safe. Get it?" Giles didn't really but nodded as the man put his arm on Giles's shoulder and gripped it with his bony fingers. There was another thing Giles didn't understand. These men didn't have names. It was always, number one or number four he never heard them call each other by their proper names. Maybe they are secret agents brought over by some powerful people in London Giles thought. And another thing, they had never once mentioned shooting birds.

He set off on his bike to the field where the 'hides' were. He kept looking around to see if anyone was following him but he was out in the middle of nowhere so felt safe enough. He leaned his bike up against the field gatepost and took the bag to where he had been instructed. Not knowing quite where to leave it, he stood for a while staring into the hole then just dropped it in the corner thinking it didn't matter so long as it was in the hide. He jumped back onto his bike and headed home. That's another shilling they owe me, he thought proudly.

"I've got it," shouted the shopkeeper to no one in particular, "I know who that lad is now." He rushed through the shop to his wife, who was in the kitchen, standing washing dishes at the pot sink. "I knew I'd get him eventually. He's that headmaster's son from Hillswick," he said triumphantly to his wife's back.

"Oh yes, and?" she replied not appearing terribly interested.

"He came in here and asked for four bottles of beer, said they were for his father. Well let me tell you, I know his father doesn't drink beer, only the finest whisky, Something to do with his crazy religious mother or some such, and she became an alcoholic," he was quite excited by the fact he'd remembered the lad and his fathers drinking habits.

"So he bought some beer, what does that prove? His father may have changed his mind. It's a long time since you've spoken to him," she looked at him sternly, drying her hands on her old worn pinny. Sometimes she got a little weary of his claims to have the best memory on Shetland.

"My dear, don't you see, he doesn't even live up here, he buys beer, tells lies so what's he up too?" the shopkeeper slowly pulled himself together, for his wife's sake.

"I don't know and frankly I don't care," she said as she walked through to the parlour and left her husband scratching his head.

"He's up to no good my dear and I'm going to find out what it is," He made a mental note of what the boy had been wearing, and the direction he went when he left the shop. Yes, tomorrow he will find out, first he will put the kettle on the stove and make his wife a nice cup of tea.

CHAPTER THIRTY-FIVE

Tally and Val stood on the jetty watching the two big fishing boats pull alongside and the mooring ropes quickly grabbed by many helping hands and made fast.

Within minutes the metal wheels of the gangways were resting on the jetty. It was a solid welcome to the men huddled in blankets and making their unsteady way onto terra firma. Many appeared able but others needed help to guide them on the short walk to Lunna House. Then came the stretchers with the injured, covered in blankets and being carried gently ashore. Val took the arm of one man who couldn't stop crying, whether it be for the comrades he'd lost or the fact he had been saved she didn't know but helped him slowly toward the house. Tally saw the last of the Russians to walk down the gangway. He was an imposing looking man, tall with a shock of blond hair. When he'd stepped onto the harbour, he turned to face the fishing boat. Tally could see the captain in the wheelhouse looking down at him. The Russian placed his battered cap on his head, stood to attention and gave a long salute to his rescuer, then turned to follow the others. Walking slowly, he looked up and saw Tally. His eyes were the most perfect blue and his face the most handsome that she'd ever seen. He gave her a small but tired smile and said, "Thank you," in perfect English then walked away.

Tally waited a few minutes before going into the house; she had to catch her breath. She pushed her hands through her tangled hair trying to tidy it then out of habit flattened the front of her skirt and walked into the big hallway of the house and along the stone passageway.

Inside, there was the murmur of voices and the chink of cups and plates. Most of the men were wrapped in big woollen blankets and being given hot food and dry clothes that had been hastily brought in by the villagers. Two of the local women were piling logs onto the already blazing fire making the room warm and cosy even though a little smoky. Many of the crew were talking quietly in groups some hugging each other just glad to be alive and safe. There were a few brief smiles but most faces showing strain and shock. One or two of them were sitting staring ahead not yet able to function. The local doctor, having been on board during the rescue, was quickly seeing to as many as possible and giving medical attention where needed. Tally soon realised that the officer she had watched earlier was the commander of the submarine. He was making it his job to talk to every one of his crew, comforting them and making sure they had all they needed. He looked exhausted as Tally walked toward him with a tray.

"Would you like some fresh tea?" she asked, "you look tired, perhaps you would like to sit for a while. You have seen to all of your men and they will be well looked after here. You know what they say, if you don't look after yourself, how can you look after others?" she quickly shut up thinking she's gone on too long, the poor man is dead on his feet, and what am I doing talking to him like that.

"Thank you," he smiled back at her, his voice was deep and rich, "and I would very much like some more of your Shetland tea. You are also right; I will try to look after myself because there will be lots to do." He took a cup of tea from the tray, held it in both hands and sat down heavily on a chair near the door. Tally put down the tray and was going to sit next to him, and then she saw a grim faced Captain Vickers walking briskly towards them.

"Commander Volkov," Vickers nodded to him. Volkov stood up. "Could I speak with you please, we will go up to my office, bring your tea." Captain Vickers whisked him away leaving Tally standing there feeling rather foolish. So his name is Volkov, she mused, that's Russian for wolf I think. She picked up the tray and went to give tea to the others.

CHAPTER THIRTY-SIX

Katy Graham was busy in her kitchen when Lowry Nicholson appeared at the back door of the cottage, "Good morning Katy, how are things with you this morning?" he gave a little smile and took off his hat which he twisted in his hands, a habit Katy had noticed before. He stood there like a pupil in front of the teacher.

"I'm very well Lowry, come in, I've just made some scones. Would you like one with a cup of tea?" she asked.

"Hm, sounds good, yes thanks that would be nice." He sat himself in one of the kitchen chairs. Katy could smell the cold morning air on his clothes. "Have you heard anything from Tally yet?" he asked.

"No, not yet, but I'm sure she'll be in touch when she can. Have you heard anything of Peter, it's been a long time now and that girl is so anxious. I know she hides it well and is running around looking after other folks, but, if he doesn't come home…"

"I've got some bad news for her Katy", Lorwy said grimly, "and I don't know how to tell her. I know you two are the best of friends and was wondering if you could, the next time you see her. I've just come away from Jac Smith's place," he hung his head and Katy knew what it was he was going to say.

"Oh no," Katy held her hands to her mouth and stared at Lowry, "don't tell me Jac has died, please God, no." Tears pricked her eyes and Lowry stood up to hold her and she cried quietly against his chest.

"An hour ago," he said softly, "he was in no pain at the end Katy, the doctor had seen to that. His ma has got her sister over to help out. I expect the funeral will be next week, I can let you know as soon as I hear." He held onto Katy as long as she wanted him too. The two of them locked in comfort in the little cottage kitchen, sun streaming through the window.

Finally Katy broke away and sat down still holding Lowry's big hands, he sat opposite her and looked into her lovely face, "Tally will be devastated, she just saw him yesterday, she called here on her way to Lunna House and said he was quite ill but able to talk. Mind you, he did tell her he would be going into hospital on Monday and indicated that he may not be coming out. Tally was upset by that and hoped he didn't mean it. Perhaps he knew better than all of us, just how ill he was." She kept hold of Lowry's hands.

Still looking at her, he said quite suddenly, "Katy, will you marry me?" he appeared to shock himself; he looked out of the window and smiled and squeezed her hands. "You and I have been friends for many a year and we know, I think, how we feel about each other. I have been in love with you since you took over the school and I've never been able to tell you. I'm such a lump when it comes to fancy speeches and fancy words." It was as if a great pressure had been released, he couldn't stop talking and Katy just sat there staring at him wondering if he was in his right mind. On the other hand her thoughts were racing, going over what he had just asked her. He was such a wonderful friend and had been over the years, always there if she needed him, always ready to do any job she asked. He was kind and gracious and gentle, never worrying her, never crowding her life, but she always knew he was there. Her heart was skipping a beat and she realised that she had loved him but was afraid to admit it to herself.

"I had to ask you Katy, I had to ask you today because if I didn't the World would pass us by and we'd have lost the time together that I know we should share. The war has made us all think differently, about our own mortality and that of others, our friends and our families." He now put his hand out and lifted her chin and saw that tears were running softly down her cheeks, he kissed them away and looked for his answer.

CHAPTER THIRTY-SEVEN

Hitler was trapped in Berlin. The Russians were bearing down on him from the east and the allies from the west. It was just a matter of time and Europe held its breath. Peter Gregor had finally reached the coast of Norway, having retraced his steps with the help of his good friends in the resistance and a daring pilot. He stood in the cave where he had met the first of his wonderful guides whose friendship and loyalty he would never ever forget. The boat to take him back to Shetland soon arrived at the jetty, showing no name or identifying marks. He made his way quickly down the path and walked onto the gangway. A huge man came out from the wheelhouse and grabbed Peter by the shoulders, "My God, it's good to see you again." It was one of the fishermen from Hillswick. Peter was never so happy to see a friend's face as he was this one.

The two big men hugged each other, "Heaven's above Tom, you're a sight for sore eyes," as the two men finally shook hands.

"Ok, let's go," the skipper started the old diesel and the boat slowly turned and headed out toward the North Sea and home. Peter had so many questions but just sat on the bench in the stern and looked to the west. They could wait he thought; they could wait, for now he was just glad to be alive and going back to Shetland and his daughter. A seed of panic about what he could possibly find on his return buried itself in a far corner of his mind. If we get home safely, he thought, everything is going to be alright from now on, and settled himself to try and sleep.

CHAPTER THIRTY-EIGHT

Duncan Cameron was slowly coming to terms with his sons' untimely death at the hands of the Germans. Now the days meant nothing to him, he spent most of them in the shack at Sullom Voe, just sitting watching life go by. His fishing boat sat unused in Hillswick. He was still full of anger, which he felt would never go away and though his friends and family had tried to help him move on, he found it too difficult. Time was filled with the mundane. Getting up, eating, walking to the shop and going to bed. He'd heard that Peter was away looking for a new boat, though he didn't believe it. He didn't know what to believe anymore. This lovely morning didn't make him feel any better; it fact it made him feel even more angry because his son was not here to see it. Just one bloody German he thought, just one will do. He pulled on his boots and set off for the shop.

The jolly welcome he received from the shopkeeper did nothing to lighten his mood and he just gave a grunt in reply. Picking up his bottle of milk and a loaf of bread he went to the little wooden counter to pay.

"I'll tell you, as I've told everyone else," said the shopkeeper regardless if anyone wanted to hear him and taking Duncan's money with a swift move of the hand, "that lad was up to no good, no good whatsoever, you mark my words. Thank you Mr Cameron, there's your change." Duncan forcing himself to be civil to the man said wearily, "What lad where?" putting his purchases into his shopping bag.

"That young Johansson lad can't quite remember his first name, posh funny name it is. He's been in here all times of the day, and on different days, buying this and that. He came in the other day and bought beer. Say's it were for his father, well, I'm telling you, his father don't drink beer and that lad is up to something," the shopkeeper put his hands on his hips and stuck out his chest as if defying anyone to question him.

"It's Giles, his name is Giles, and he's the son of the headmaster. What is he doing up here, do you know?"

"No, he's been coming in here for a while now, some-times on a Monday, sometimes on a Wednesday. No knowing when he'll come in again, real cocky he's getting. What's his father doing letting him wander around the place like that?" the shopkeeper loving the chance for a good old gossip just kept on going. He knew about Duncan Cameron's son and also that Duncan was trying to sniff out anyone with a hint of sympathy for the Germans. Was there to be something in this lads behav-iour, he didn't know but would like to think he was onto a juicy story. He told him what Giles had been wearing and which direction he'd gone after leaving the shop and of course the exact time the beer had been bought and how much was spent. Duncan had a feeling that Giles Johansson needed to be looked at more closely; his name was coming up just a little too often. This young man was moving freely about the island doing what he wanted without the knowledge of his father. That was obvious by the purchase of the beer, so what, Duncan thought, is the other mischief he may be getting in to. He went home with a growing sense of purpose.

CHAPTER THIRTY-NINE

Katy held onto Lowry's hand for a long time after he had proposed and kissed away her tears. Her feelings were rushing to the surface and she wanted to hold him so tightly so that he would never go away again. She wanted to but didn't, her heart was thumping. She looked at his rugged handsome face and wanted to kiss him but didn't.

"Yes, I will marry you Lowry, if that is what you want," she said in a very controlled voice.

"If it's what I want," he said sadly, "is it not what you want Katy? Because if it is not, then I'm truly sorry for causing you any embarrassment, please forgive me." He let go of her hand and sat back in his chair.

"No, Lowry please, don't get me wrong, I was just so surprised and a little shocked by your proposal. You had just told me of poor Jac and we know nothing of Peter yet and there are men at Lunna House in great need," she sat with her hands in her lap not knowing quite what to do.

"It is because of all the things that are happening around us, don't you understand? We have to grab our happiness now, we have no way of knowing what the future holds for us but at least we could share it. If that is what you would like."

Lowry stood up and Katy thought he was leaving, her heart flipped.

He took her hands and gently pulled her to her feet holding her tightly in his arms. It was the most wonderful feeling she'd ever had.

"I know you Katy Graham, your feelings are hidden like diamonds down a mine, but if one of us doesn't make the move, we will regret it. If you say no, then I'll still always be there for you and I'll never mention this day again," he held on to her for a few minutes then made to let go.

"I can't let you go Lowry, I love you too much and have done for a long while," she held him close with her head buried in his jacket. "I just love you, that's all," her heart was racing. "Yes, I'll marry you." She blinked back tears but this time they were tears of happiness as she looked up to his face. She stood on her tiptoes and kissed him on the lips. There was a silence filled only by the sound of the sea and the few gulls that were flying overhead.

This is what happiness feels like she thought.

"So, my beautiful woman, our wedding day will be very soon. I will have a word with old Samson the minister at Hillswick tomorrow. Get your posh frock out and pin up those lovely red curls." Lowry picked Katy up by the waist and swung her round the tiny kitchen sending the cups flying onto the floor and knocking over the chair. They both just laughed and clung onto each other.

"But Lowry I've so much to do, there are friends to ask and we must be mindful of poor Jacs funeral and Peter has not yet returned."

"I feel that Peter is on his way back. I have no knowledge of that but just an instinct, He has been away too long and an officer at Lunna House told Tally he was alive and well. So we will pray for his speedy return and our wonderful day will quickly follow. So be ready my love," he cupped her face in his hands and kissed her waiting lips.

CHAPTER FORTY

It was a pitch-dark night when Duncan Cameron set out to find Giles Johansson. The kindly shopkeeper had been very helpful with his information and it set Duncan's mind away. Why had the lad had been caught with the torch the night the German bomber had been able to hit the island. Who was he buying drink and food supplies for up this end of the island? Duncan went to visit the Johansson's and made some excuse as to why he wanted to speak with Giles.

"Oh aye," said an angry Mr Johansson, "what's he been up to now, I don't know where he is and I don't care. I've just about given up on him. Out all hours, sneaking around the garden in the night. He won't tell me what he's up too and his mother is useless, she can't get anything out of him. All he does here is sleep; and he must be getting fed somewhere else 'cos he's never hungry. Full of himself he is."

"What's he got in the garden then, why's he sneaking round there?" Duncan asked as casually as he could, hoping to hear something interesting.

"I haven't a clue and I'm not interested. You can go and look if you like; down by the old compost heap he has a camp or something. Don't suppose it's much. Help yourself, if you can see anything." Mr Johansson walked away seemingly uninterested and sat by the fire.

Duncan made his way out of the back door and into the cold air and the large old school garden. He got a tiny torch out of his pocket and made for the bottom corner where he soon spotted the rotting compost heap. Walking to the back of it he saw where the ground had been disturbed, and quite recently. He picked up a large stick and started poking away the stinking leaves and twigs. He saw a wooden box roughly hidden. He guessed Giles was getting a little careless. Duncan picked up the box. It was about two feet square and quite heavy and dirty. It had a cheap metal lock that fortunately was open. He flicked it up and lifted the lid. What he saw chilled him to the bone. He'd suspected that the lad was up to no good but nothing prepared him for this. He realised that he now had a problem. Should he tell the father straight away or should he go and look for Giles by himself. He knew if he did that he would kill him and he would have to live with that all his life. So, he would confront Mr Johansson and see what he was prepared to do. He picked up the box and walked slowly back up to the house where Mr Johansson was still sitting by the fire. He glanced slowly at Duncan as he entered the kitchen putting the dirty box on the table. Mrs Johansson had now joined the company her eyes fixed on the box. Her hands were fidgeting and her voice high and anxious. "What is it?" she cried.

"It's our Giles's stash of gold coins, what the hell do you think it is you stupid woman," Mr Johansson shouted dismissively at her as she turned and fled once more from her own kitchen.

"I think you should see this Johansson and I want to know what you're going to do about it." Duncan lifted the lid and more dirt fell onto the table. Mr Johansson stood up to get a better view, his curiosity roused just a little.

He soon sat down again with such a thump he nearly broke the chair.

"What in God's name is all this. This isn't Giles's he wouldn't get mixed up in this. He's just a young lad, he's stupid. No, no this isn't right," his voice was somewhere between anger and disbelief. His face began to go pale as he looked again into the box. Duncan started taking out the contents. First was the big torch that Giles was given by his 'friends,' after he'd told them of Peter Gregor taking the flashlight. Next a notebook with maps of Shetlands roads and lanes scribbled in it. A large vicious looking knife. Then came the metal water bottle covered in camouflage cloth. A shirt made of a grey woollen material with some red and black eagle insignia on the sleeve, a leather belt and a forage cap. Mr Johansson sat and stared not quite knowing what to do.

"So this is what he's been up too, siding with the bloody Germans, eh Duncan?" It appeared that Mr Johansson was slowly coming to his senses. "No wonder the little sod didn't want me or his mother to know what he was up too." his voice had become quiet as he continued to stare at the items from the box. It was as if he couldn't touch them. He put his hand near the shirt but quickly pulled it away in disgust. "What are you going to about it?" his eyes now focussed on Duncan.

"It's what you are going to do about it? You've now seen the evidence of your son's collusion. We can safely assume he is fraternising with a group who are presumably Germans, and who are on the island. We must first find Giles and then we can get to whoever it is he's with."

"How do we know where he is?" Johansson sat still on his chair with his head bowed.

"It's a pity you didn't take more notice of where he was going and who he was hanging around with but it's too late for that now. I'm heading home; I'll be in touch first thing in the morning and when that son of yours comes back, please, try not to kill him."

"I'm making no promises," said Johansson.

CHAPTER FORTY-ONE

Peter Gregor spotted land before the others. He'd been on lookout for the last two hours desperate to see his beloved Shetland. His friend and skipper steering the big heavy fishing vessel west and into Lerwick harbour gave him the thumbs up as he too saw the islands. Their arrival went unnoticed by many. But in an upstairs room of the Admiralty Offices a man was watching them through a large pair of binoculars.

"Send a message to Captain Vickers at Lunna House immediately. Our friend has returned from his mission and will be with him very soon," Captain Howard put down the binoculars and sat back in his chair smiling to himself. He lit his pipe and looked out of the window and started humming Jerusalem. The big man was back.

"Yes sir, right away sir," the young communications officer got to work straight away sensing the anticipation of the Russians return. He'd met his daughter once and she was very beautiful perhaps they would meet again.

CHAPTER FORTY-TWO

Tally and Val were quite exhausted by the time all the rescued men had been given food and dry clothes. All had been allocated beds and rooms for the coming days and weeks until they could all be debriefed and treated for any injuries. Val decided she had room for two men; she shocked herself to think of any man other than her Eric in her little house. But there was a war on she told herself so her help was needed as much as everybody else's. The army said they'd take the men to her place in the morning and she would get extra blankets and some food rations to help out. Val felt very much that her life suddenly had great purpose. She had been praised by the submarines Commander and presented with a beautiful silver badge with the boats class and number on it thanking her for acting so quickly when hearing their distress calls.

"It was all because of my father," she had said, "if it hadn't been for him making such a wonderful radio, no one would have heard you soon enough to do anything…" her voice trailed away, men dying at sea invaded her thoughts.

"Russia will grant you recognition when the authorities in Archangel hear of it," the young commander had told her.

"So your name is Tally, a pretty name for a pretty Shetlander," the deep dark voice in her ear was so close she could feel the warmth of his breath.

Tally spun round to see Volkov standing there with two cups of tea.

"Thought you might like one, now you are the one who looks exhausted," he handed her the cup.

"Thank you, that's very kind of you," she gave a half smile.

"Well, everyone is fed and watered and all have been given homes to go to so I am happy," Volkov looked around the room at his remaining crewmen with relief.

"Where will you be staying?" Tally asked, curious.

"I am staying here in Lunna House at the kind invitation of Captain Vickers We still have a lot to talk about and I must get letters written to the families of those who have lost loved ones. You know how it is?" he looked down with sadness at her.

"Where do you live on this lovely island?"

"Oh, I live in a place called Hillswick, just a way further north from here."

"Ah, and have you family there in Hillswick?"

"My father, he's a fisherman but away at sea at the moment, hopefully he'll be back soon," her heart lurched when she thought of her missing father.

"It must be very dangerous to be at sea in a small boat. There are still some rogue German planes out there trying to bomb anything out of the water, but I think with Hitler holed up in his bunker in the middle of Berlin, it is only a matter of time."

"Yes, I'm sure you're right and my father will be ok," Volkov heard the uncertainty in her voice.

CHAPTER FORTY-THREE

It was early morning and the pale sun was rising in the cold eastern sky. The winds had dropped and the seagulls were screaming their hunger over the wave tops and beaches. A couple of army trucks were being loaded with the men from the submarine and supplies from the storehouse ready to move out to their various digs. Volkov was overseeing his crewmen and some army lads were sorting boxes of food. Tally and Val were still there talking reassuringly to the men and helping with their bags.

Suddenly there was a commotion at the front gates as a staff car from Lerwick pulled into the yard. Everybody stopped and looked. The big cars engine was switched off. The passenger door opened and out stepped the tall figure of Peter Gregor. Tally clasped her hands over her mouth then cried out as she ran into his arms. Peter eyes were full of tears as he hugged his daughter. She laughed and cried as they made their way to see Captain Vickers who was watching from his window.

Val just stood with her hands on her hips and said, "well this is a happy day indeed. Come along men, off to the cottage, let me get you settled in."

The two Russians grinned and nodded at this lovely friendly woman. They weren't too sure what had just happened and why everyone was so happy, neither could they understand much English, but they climbed gratefully into the truck and left Lunna House for Mossbank.

Volkov, who had watched this from the corner of the yard, felt that there was bit more to the fishing story Tally had told him earlier. Why would a fisherman come to Lunna House and get such a welcome and why would Captain Vickers want to see him. Gregor, he thought, that is surely a Russian name

Peter was overwhelmed at seeing his daughter again. He wanted to tell her everything that had happened since he'd left but couldn't at this stage, if ever. So he entered Captain Vickers room on his own and started his debrief but first handed over the package he was so glad to relinquish.

"Peter, Peter my dear chap. How good it is to see you again," said Vickers, "come in, sit down and tell me all about it." He took the package and placed it in a drawer in his desk, locking it and putting the tiny key into his top pocket, which he patted then smiled at Peter. "Believe me, these papers are a lot more important than the ones you took to Russia."

"I'm pleased to hear it, I would not be happy to find out otherwise." Peter sat down gratefully into a large chair in front of the fire.

The two men talked well into the day with cups of tea and sandwiches going into the room at regular intervals. No one was allowed to interrupt the proceedings for any reason. Tally made herself busy downstairs in the room where all the rescued men had spent the evening. There were tables to be cleared and dishes to be washed and put away or given back to helpful neighbours. Blankets to be folded and then the floor swept. She was happy to stay because her father was upstairs. Outside the sun was bright and the sky looked clear. 'What a wonderful day it is,' she thought as she stood looking out to sea. The two boats that had braved the North Sea to save men's lives, sat quietly riding the gentle swell in the harbour.

It was over four hours before Peter finally emerged from Captain Vickers office and made his way downstairs to find Tally. She was sitting on the low stone wall in the yard of the house. He watched her for a couple of minutes then she slowly turned to see him. He walked towards her and put his arm around her. "How have you been girl, you don't know how I've missed you. I wish I could tell you everything but I can't just yet. Wait until we get home then at least I can give you some of my amazing journey." They walked away to a van that had stood there since Peter left, "We must call on Katy on our way home if that's ok?" Tally smiled.

"That's fine; we may be in time for some of her excellent baking," Peter started the van and they left Lunna House.

As usual, Katy's door was open so Peter and Tally went straight into the tidy little kitchen. Katy jumped up from Lowry's knee laughing when her visitors came in. "Oh, Peter," she ran toward him and gave him such a hug he laughed and pretended not to be able to breathe. "My, my girl, that's a real hug, it's good to see you too. What's going on here, you both look as if you've got some good news." Peter looked knowingly at Lowry who stood up and gave his friend an even bigger hug, both men blinked away tears.

"Firstly, let us have something to eat and drink," Katy said. "Lowry could you please put the kettle on?

Tally you come with me." Katy and her friend left the kitchen and stepped into the hallway closing the door softly behind them.

When she'd told her friend of Jac's death, she held her while the tears flowed. Tally went to sit on the step looking out into the garden. Katy joined her and held her hand in silence; a terrible sadness came over Tally. "He wanted to marry me you know Katy," she said through the tears.

"Yes I know, but it was not meant to be. Did you really love him enough, would you have married him Tally?" she asked gently.

"I don't know, I really don't know."

It was obvious by the looks on Lowry and Peters faces that Jac's death had been discussed in the last few minutes.

"Now we are all back together," said Katy, "let us say a prayer for our dear friend Jac." the four of them stood in the sunny room and said the Lords Prayer.

"But we have some good news too," said Lowry as he stood up with his cup of tea in his hand. "I would like the two of you to be the first to know, that this beautiful woman had just agreed to be my wife and we're going to be married as soon as it is possible. Peter my dear friend would you do me honour of being my best man?"

Katy then took hold of Tally's hand.

"Tally, I would love it if you would be my bridesmaid," she giggled.

"Oh Katy that's wonderful, I'm so happy for you both, yes I will be your bridesmaid, oh how exciting," her face suddenly solemn with thoughts of her poor Jac.

"When is Jac's funeral to be?" she asked .

"We don't know yet, but we will not be married until a respectful time has passed." said Katy looking at Lowry who gave a little nod.

"Well there is much to be done and we must get home Tally. Let us see what else has been happening in Hillswick," Peter said as they prepared to leave.

CHAPTER FORTY-FOUR

Duncan Cameron arrived at the Johansson house early in the morning hoping to catch Giles. He was out of luck. Mr Johansson was up and about and pacing the floor when he arrived, "He didn't come back home last night, the filthy spy." He spat the words out and appeared just as angry as ever. His face red and his breathing laboured. Duncan thought, any minute now this man is going to have a heart attack.

"No word at all from him?"

"No, damn him."

"Could he have come back and seen that the box had been moved?"

"What, I don't know, do I?" he wasn't calming down any.

"Mind if I go and have a look?"

"What difference will that make, he's not going to leave a visiting card is he?"

"I just asked if could go and look in the garden"

"Well, damn it if you want to, go and look all you need," spitting saliva as he shouted at Duncan.

Duncan walked down to the compost heap and started looking for the four small twigs he had set on the ground, knowing if someone had walked to the spot where the box was, they would have to disturb them. The twigs were not as he had left them, Giles had returned last night. So, the hunt was on he thought.

"It looks like your son came back last night," he said to Johansson who was hovering at the kitchen door. "I'd set a little trap and it's been sprung, so we need to find him with some urgency as he now knows you have knowledge of his secret box." Duncan made to leave the house.

"What are you going to do now, hunt down and kill my son?" the veins in his neck looked about to pop. Mrs Johansson appeared like a ghost at the kitchen door, not saying anything but rubbing her hands together. Then she tried to whisper something to her husband.

"What's that you said woman?" he shouted as if she were miles away.

Mrs Johansson walked into the room with her hands now in her pinafore pockets to stop them from shaking and said, "I heard Giles in the garden last night; well it was early this morning really. He went to his little camp by the compost heap and started rummaging around. Then I heard him cry out and run through the garden and away up the road." She just stood there as her husband looked at her with disbelief.

"Why on earth didn't you tell me? I'd have got up and strangled the blighter with my own hands. You know what I told you last night, the lads gone off in the head. He's siding with the bloody enemy, you stupid woman. Now he's gone to God knows where, and folks are out to kill him, if I don't get to him first."

"No," she cried, "he's just a boy; he's not helping the German's. I don't know where you get all this nonsense from. Just because he's got a box full of stuff doesn't mean he's the enemy. He's just pretending, he's playing, because lets face it he didn't get any attention out of you when he was little. Play was never in your vocabulary was it?" she stood quite still in the silence that followed. Mr Johansson looked as if his world was slowly falling apart. His son was fraternising with the Germans. His wife couldn't see what was happening in front of her, and he couldn't see a way out of this other than to find the boy himself.

CHAPTER FORTY-FIVE

During the day, Volkov had spent time in and around Lunna House, getting to know the place. He decided he would take a walk later; the chance to breathe in the beautiful sea air was not to be missed. Captain Vickers was upstairs in his office with the fisherman Peter Gregor, as yet a stranger to Volkov but not for long he hoped.

Walking along the beach north of the jetty he found peace and quiet. The sound of the waves over the shingle beach was calming, and Volkov knew he hadn't been so relaxed for years and was glad to just stand there with his bare feet in the sand. This island was showing him warmth, friendship and peace. What was there waiting for him back in Russia. Yes, he was on the 'winning' side, but some of the horror stories of Russian troops and their treatment of some prisoners, was to realise that being on the winning side meant very little. It did not sit well with him.

Tally was relaxing on the wall as he made his way back to Lunna House. The sun was shining on her and Volkov thought she looked serenely beautiful. At that moment Peter Gregor came out from the house and went towards her. Volkov saw them move away to the van and drive away. He waited, unseen, then started whistling and made his way back to the house.

CHAPTER FORTY-SIX

Jac's funeral was held at Hillswick church a day after his body had been released from Lerwick Hospital. The air was cold but the sky was as blue as a summer's day. Small white clouds raced west to east. His coffin was made of dark wood with traditional brass handles. Tally thought he wouldn't have liked that; it was too shiny and bright. Jac's Ma had chosen it and polished it the night before, when she and her husband had their son at home one last time. She said polishing his coffin had given her something to do, and anyhow what else was there, her world had crumbled. Almost everyone from Hillswick was there, apart from Giles Johansson. His absence caused humiliation to Mrs Johansson but not to her husband, who seemed not to notice. Later in the day darker clouds gathered and a light rain started to fall as the solemn procession made its way to the open hillside. Jac was to be buried in the shelter of the old stone wall that surrounded the graveyard. Freshly dug earth from the gravesite had been piled to one side onto an old grey canvas sheet. There it waited to cover young Jac. The wind blew softly as the coffin was lowered and Tally cried unashamedly, her father at her side united in grief. The mourning villagers stood quietly watching as Jac Smith was laid to rest. The minister proclaimed that he was now in a far better place than this war torn island. A thought that Mr and Mrs Smith had yet to come to terms with as they both stood holding each other as if one should fall. Tally stepped forward and placed a small bouquet of wild flowers on the dark coffin before the gravediggers continued with their solemn duty. "Goodbye dearest Jac," she said softly through her tears.

CHAPTER FORTY-SEVEN

It was pitch-black dark on the night Giles had agreed to meet his friends at the hides. He cycled quite happily to the field, humming a tune as he went.

"Shut up you stupid fool," came the voice from behind the big stone gatepost. He nearly fell off his bike with fright, "do you want the whole of Shetland to hear you? Get down here?" It was number one.

"You frightened the living daylights outta me," Giles said as he hid behind the hedge.

"We told you, didn't we, that we are pretending to be the enemy and its tonight we'll 'pretend' to attack the air force base down there," said number one as he pointed off into the distance toward Sullom Voe. There was not a lot to see because of blackout restrictions and the fact the darkness was almost total. The moon was hidden behind the fast moving clouds, and just the odd star shone through fleeting gaps. Giles was well aware of all the aircraft and ammunition down at the base because he'd been and had a good look around, as his friends had asked. Just wait until they find out that he was part of a secret mission to check their security; he was quite excited by the thought.

"Does it get as dark as this in Belgium where you lot come from?" Giles asked

"No Giles, not quite as dark as this but it makes good cover though doesn't it?" said another mocking voice though it wasn't number one. Number two perhaps thought Giles, who was now sitting on the damp ground waiting for his instructions.

"Here's what we want you to do Giles," just then a huge Catalina flying boat flew overhead shaking the ground beneath them. They looked up but saw only a black outline as the aircraft thundered closely over their heads and landed perfectly on the pitch-black water below.

CHAPTER FORTY-EIGHT

Duncan Cameron had visited Peter and Tally earlier, catching up on all that was happening in Europe. Duncan got little from his friend about his time away but knew that one day Peter would confide in him. Now was not the time.

He told them about his trip to the Johansson's house and what had been found in Giles's hiding place in the garden. Peter was horrified and keen to learn more. He didn't trust that lad and as Duncan had said, Mr Johansson seemed to have neither interest nor concern as to what his son was up too. The two men decided to go to the house later that evening and speak with old Johansson. They had to find out who Giles was seeing and obviously helping, albeit stupidly misguided.

Peter was driving the little van quite slowly to avoid the many pot holes as they approached the road ends near the Johansson house. It was getting quite dark and they nearly missed the illusive Giles as he came around the corner on his bicycle. He had his lights off and his head down. He'd heard the van but took no notice so didn't see that it was Peter and Duncan. He was on a mission and his thoughts were full of what the night was going to bring for him and his new friends. Shetland, he thought, was in for a shock. The two men gave him time to pull away up the road and then turned to follow at a respectable distance with the engine barely ticking over. It was quite difficult to follow him because he was going so slowly. There was a stiff head wind so hopefully it muffled the sound of the old engine. Giles didn't appear to hear them, and stopped beside a field. He jumped off his bike letting it fall to the ground as if he'd been given a shock, then he went through the gate. At that point Peter and Duncan pulled into the verge and switched off the engine. They crawled forward and sat quietly watching through their large field binoculars. It was a stroke of luck that a Catalina had decided to fly overhead toward Sullom Voe at that moment, covering up any noise they'd made. Luck indeed.

The two men moved cautiously to the field, where they heard the sound of voices, and one of them was Giles.

"So, you say we're going to attack the base tonight?" Giles asked excitedly.

"That was Giles," whispered Duncan as he touched Peters arm.

The two men were crouching down behind the hedge and could almost have touched Giles's back as he sat on the ground not five feet in front of them.

"Now Giles, what you have to remember is, we're only pretending. Whatever we ask you to do; it's just to check that we could have attacked, had we been the enemy. Remember what I told you a couple of weeks ago. We're not the enemy." The German accent made Peters blood run cold.

So, Giles had been with them for at least a couple of weeks. Damn the lad, he could've told them anything. He'd been sniffing around Sullom Voe so knew plenty about the base and he would no doubt have told them of the submarine rescue and the Russian crew who were now on the island. Peter was aware of Duncan reaching into the inside pocket of his jacket. He suspected that his friend had brought his gun, a pistol he'd got from a 'don't ask' source. Peter put his hand on Duncan's arm to stop him doing anything foolish. As they stared into the dark field a tiny light from a miniature torch came on and it picked out Giles who quickly stood up, almost clicking his heels to the man who stood in front of him.

The watchers could see there were five of them including Giles, just standing in a loose circle. Some men were stamping their feet and blowing onto their hands, trying to keep out the cold. Giles looked unsure of this man, the boss, Number One. Duncan wondered if Giles was going to tell them that his secret box had been taken and so their mission may have been compromised. He doubted he would.

Two of the men disappeared to the far corner of the field, stumbling and mumbling that they couldn't see where they were going. They returned a couple of minutes later with two long canvas bags and dragging a wooden box. The bags appeared to be quite heavy and contain some cylindrical objects. The box looked anonymous, and they dropped it onto the ground in front of Number One.

"Careful with those you idiots, do you want to damage them, because if you do, you will pay with your life?" he growled.

"Giles, come here," asked Number One, "this is what we want you to do." He again put his arm around Giles's shoulder; his bony fingers digging into his skin. Giles didn't like that but said nothing, and the man's breath stunk of those horrible cigarettes.

"Go and get the bag you put into the hide, and bring it to me?" his voice a vicious sharp command.

Giles stumbled off to the hole in the ground and stepped into it. He felt around in the peaty mud until he'd found what he was looking for, lifted it out and took it to the man.

"Good, good, now put it on the ground next to that box." Giles did so, quickly.

Number One then started giving orders to the others although Giles couldn't understand what was being said because they were talking in their own language, Belgian...he thought.

He stood a little away from the group and listened as number one became more and more agitated with his men. His voice was vicious and angry, spittle forming at the corners of his mouth. A film of sweat was glistening on his brow, even though it was very cold in the field. He kept pointing towards the air base below them where the flying boats were riding gently at their moorings. Giles began to feel a little nervous and swallowed hard clenching his teeth to stop them from chattering; his stomach started to churn, something didn't feel quite right.

CHAPTER FORTY-NINE

The doctor took a closer look at the drip bottle that hung above Sergei Somova's bed, tapping it to make sure the liquid was flowing freely. Satisfied, he picked up the chart that was hanging on a clipboard at the end of the bed. After reading it he turned to the nurse in attendance. "Looks like he's going to make it, God alone knows how but good news indeed, eh?" he grinned at her.

"Yes, Doctor, good news, I'll prepare his next feed right away," she turned to go.

"No, not yet, let's wait a while, say a couple of hours. I've got a feeling this young man is going to wake up sooner rather than later and he may manage a proper meal but thank you nurse." He stood beside the bed looking down on his patient for a few minutes, marvelling at the strength of the human body, then returned to his ward rounds.

It was indeed only one hour after the doctors' visit that young Sergei opened his eyes and looked at the white ceiling and then the lovely nurse standing at his bedside. "Well, I guess I'm alive." he said huskily, with a mouth as dry as sticks, trying to smile.

"Yes, I guess you are, welcome back. You are in Sverdlovsk main hospital and if you remember, you'd been shot," she said softly as she placed her hand on top of his.

"Ha, it's not the sort of thing you forget in a hurry," he replied as he tried to sit up.

"Argh!" he cried in pain and slowly lay back down again.

"My God that hurt," his voice became a whisper and sweat broke out on his brow.

Just then the doctor appeared at the door, "Yes, it hurts does it not young man, getting shot is not to be recommended, no certainly not?" The doctor took Sergei's temperature, wiping the thermometer on his white coat and putting it back into his top pocket. "All is well, you are an extremely lucky man but now you need to rest and eat if you want to get out of this place, which I'm sure you do. I'll talk to you later," he left the room.

"He doesn't hang around, does he?" Sergei said to the nurse.

"He's a very busy man," she said tucking in the bed sheets.

Sergei smiled back at her, Hm, nice eyes he thought, and put his head down to sleep.

It took nearly five weeks, before he was well enough to get out of bed. The wound had become infected and needed some vigorous treatment. Then he caught pneumonia and it was that that nearly killed him but he had youth and strength on his side.

He looked at the sun streaming in through the window and thought of his good friend Yuri Volkov, where was he now?

The doctors had told him of their search for his parents and with the information Yuri had given them, they visited the address where Eva Somova lived.

"We spoke to her at length about you and your circumstances, you know, the fact that she brought you up as it were," the doctor said hesitantly. Sergei wondered what was coming next. "She is not in the best of health as you probably know and she wanted to, shall we say, 'off load' some issues as they were clearly causing her some distress."

Sergei looked at the doctors with some concern, "What do you mean 'not in the best of health' it's not long ago that I visited her, and yes she's getting old but her health appeared well to me."

"Mr Somova, I am going to be totally honest with you and I would like you to be the same, is that understood?"

"Of course," Sergei waited.

"Do you know who your father and mother are?" he asked quietly looking Sergei straight in the eyes.

"No, no I don't. Eva told me that I was left at the church near to her cottage, and she and the local priest took me in. I believe my father may have been killed and I know nothing of my mother. If either had been still alive, you would think they'd come and look for me, wouldn't you. So I'm assuming they are both dead. Oh, I don't know. Eva has been very kind to me and I gave up asking questions about my parents. Although, as I got older and began to ask again. I always got the feeling she knew more than she was letting on and it seemed to make her very unhappy…and somewhat agitated but she still didn't say anything. Why do you ask?"

"I am asking because I have news of your parents," before he could say anymore Sergei stood up and walked to the window, his mind racing and his heart thumping.

"Then please tell me everything you know, please." He sat down again his legs shaking.

"It seems your father may still be alive." was as far as he got.

"What ... where, you must tell me?"

"It's a long story Sergei but I will do my best. Your mother had been quite ill before you were born and your father was in Archangel. He was a submarine commander and was due to return home. Then he received an urgent message telling him that she may not recover so he made haste back here to be with her. Eva was your mother's housemaid and was with her when your father arrived. What neither your mother nor your father knew was that Eva had swapped you as an hour old baby for a girl of a similar age."

"What? What are you saying? I don't understand. I was swapped. You're crazy; I've never heard such a thing. You mean Eva knew all along who my parents were and never told me, why?" the disbelief in Sergei's voice was like a desperate cry. He put his hands over his eyes in an attempt to hide his tears. He was heartbroken, what was so important that Eva should swap him for a girl. Who was the girl, where did she come from? He knew then that he had to find out.

"Please, go on, you must tell me everything you know, and then I must see if I can find my father."

For another hour the doctor went through all the information Eva had given him as Sergei sat and listened in silence. His head was spinning, trying to take it all in. Eventually he realised that what had been done was over. There was little he could do to change anything, except find his father and the grave of his mother.

He spent another two weeks in hospital until he was well enough to return home where he decided the only thing to do was to visit Eva and hear this amazing story from herself.

Soon he was standing on the steps of Eva's cottage, his former home. Feeling somewhat apprehensive at what he would ask her, and going over the information he already had from the doctor. He wondered what else she could tell him. It was more to hear a confirmation that it was all true, or not as the case may be.

He noticed that the little garden was unkempt and overgrown and the paint was beginning to peel off the familiar blue front door. His knock was unanswered so he looked through the small rather dirty window into the kitchen. There was no sign of life in fact it looked as if no one had lived there for a while. The table, which was normally covered in cups and dishes and always a breadbox, was bare. Cupboards, which held jars of food and all Eva's pots and pans were standing open and empty. The fireplace had been swept and no logs sat in the hearth. Sergei went round to the back of the cottage climbing over the long grass and broken chicken pen. He looked in the bedroom window. The same sight met him. Beds had been stripped and the cupboards empty, no carpet on the floor or fire in the grate. He felt a flutter of panic as he looked into the empty cottage. Where was Eva?

"She's gone, comrade, gone into the hospital. Five weeks ago now. Off her head they reckon, poor old soul." The man came and stood rather shakily at the fence, which bordered the garden. He was old and stooped, his clothes almost rags and his shoes held together with string. In his hand was a bottle of what Sergei suspected was locally brewed vodka. His face was weather-beaten and dirty.

"She looked out for me she did," he said wiping his watery eyes with a ragged sleeve. "Looked after me, gave me bread and a hot drink when I knocked at the door," he staggered slightly but held onto the fence.

"She was a good woman and so was the beautiful lady she looked after. She was an angel." he started snivelling again

Sergei walked towards him and put his hand on the man's arm, "Can you tell me what happened to Eva, I need to know?" he pleaded.

"She's gone to the hospital, I told you."

"What hospital?" Sergei felt sure he would have heard from the doctors at Sverdlovsk if Eva had been taken there.

"Well, it's not really a hospital is it? It's that big house where the mad people go." he took a drink from his bottle and looked at Sergei with his rheumy eyes.

"What big house, I don't know where you mean, where is it?

"No, because nobody wants to know, do they? No one wants to go to the mad house?" he said with a rasping voice as he looked up to the sky.

"Please, think; tell me where it is I must find Eva Somova."

"Ha! You might find her my friend but she will tell you nothing," he staggered forward and Sergei grabbed him before he fell headfirst over the fence.

Sergei climbed on to the other side and helped the man walk a short distance to a little wall where they sat down.

"Now, where is this house so that I can find Eva?" he was getting desperate.

"Over there," the man pointed vaguely up the road toward the outskirts of the city.

"Where for Gods sake, give me an address?"

"It's the big house, the one that used to belong to the artists. All those lovely people who painted those wonderful pictures," he was waving his arms around, vodka pouring from the bottle onto the ground and himself. He seemed not to notice, and Sergei again had to stop him from falling backwards over the wall but now knew exactly where he meant.

"Thank you my friend, thank you." Sergei stood up and shook the man's hand and gave him some money, although knew it would not go on a decent pair of shoes.

It was quite a walk to the artist's house which sat on a hill overlooking the town. By the time he arrived the sun had come out. The building was large and had obviously been a grand family home in its day but the conversion to an asylum had rid it of many of its old, elegant features. He walked determinedly up the path.

"Yes, Eva Somova lives here and can I ask who you are sir?" the nurse's voice was clipped and formal. She wore a drab blue uniform, which had a red star on the collar. She did not look in the mood for small talk so Sergei told her exactly who he was and why he was there.

"Well I'm afraid you may not get much conversation from her, Mr Somova but you can try. Please follow me," as she almost sprinted down the corridor to a room at the back of the house.

Eva lay in a large grey painted metal bed pushed up against the wall, a matching table sat to one side, on it a single glass of water. The long bay windows were hung with tired looking flowered curtains. The place was unlit and smelled of damp.

Odd gurgling noises were coming from an overworked and ancient heating system but no heat was apparent. Sergei walked towards Eva and called her name softly, there was no visible response. "Eva, it's me Sergei, Sergei Somova. I've come to talk with you," he took hold of her hand, it felt fragile and cold. She blinked once but did not turn her head or move her fingers. Sergei sat on a chair beside the bed and just looked at her. What could have happened? He realised it was just after the doctor had been to see her that she took ill. Was it because of that conversation? Just then a nurse came into the room.

"You are Mr Sergei Somova?" it was a firm statement rather than a question.

He stood up, "Yes, I am."

"Then this is for you," she handed him an envelope, sealed and with his name on the front. He did not recognise the writing. He opened it. Inside was one sheet of rather crumpled paper, the ink smudged and mistakes roughly crossed out, this writing he recognised.

He read it with tears stinging his eyes, it was clear that it had been written with a trembling hand and a frail mind.

'Sergei, my darling child, may you and God forgive me for what I did all those years ago? I hope one day you will understand. I did the right thing. I worshiped your mother, Zhanna, as I worshiped all the others, they didn't deserve to die like that. I escaped you see, with the girl. I ran away with her. They knew it was the only way. They were killed, shot, all of them. God will punish those with guns you'll see. Your mother, she knew she'd had a son but I told her she had a wonderful daughter. God forgive me. I will pay the cost, it is my entire fault... No...it's not, it is the priest's, he was the wicked one ... He is dead now...Paying his cost...He told me what to do...he knew how to get the girl out of the house and I helped him. God forgive us. My child, my wonderful

Sergei, your mother named you Sergei.' The writing became more and more erratic.

'I took the girl to save her life; I carried her out in a little basket while her mother screamed in pain and despair. She knew it was the end for all of them and I was the only one who could save the baby. You must look for her; you must find her and ask her to forgive me. God will forgive me I know, I am...' And that is where the letter finished, Sergei, still standing in the middle of the room stunned by what he'd read but not fully understanding all of it. Thoughts were forming in the back of his mind about who the girl was. He pushed them aside fearing what he may conclude from this rambling letter. He looked again at Eva, lying as still as death, staring upwards and living now in her own tormented mind. He knew he wasn't going to get anything from her, leaning forward he kissed her forehead and said his goodbyes. Eva continued to stare, motionless.

He met with the nurse again in the hallway, "Has Eva said anything to you since being here?"

"Not really, all she kept saying when she first came here, was she hoped that God would forgive her. That's about it, nothing else. She's had a complete mental breakdown and is very frail ... I'm so sorry," the nurse smiled gently as Sergei thanked her and left the house.

A single tear rolled down Eva's cheek as she slipped into darkness.

CHAPTER FIFTY

War had scarred the Shetland Islands and the islanders. Lerwick's buildings, especially the harbour and shipping, had been targeted regularly by German aircraft and submarines. Life became one of supporting friends and family but distrusting strangers, which is a lesson Giles Johansson never learned.

Here he was, and wishing he wasn't, in the field with his rather angry friends. Something didn't seem right but he couldn't work out what it was at the minute.

Peter and Duncan were listening and watching these suspected Germans as one of them took hold of a canvas bag. He shook it gently to tip out what was inside.

"Careful, I told you, you stupid oaf," Number One hissed.

Peter knew straight away what had fallen onto the ground from the bag. It was a 'Panzerfaust,' a hand held rocket launcher that could blow a hole in a tank or an aircraft. That particular weapon had a range of roughly thirty-three metres. The base was too far away but he was not about to find out what their plans were and touched Duncan's arm again signalling that he was going to move left around the hedge on the outside of the field. Just then, Number One gave Giles the launcher and attached a long rocket into the clip. Giles looked scared stiff and began to shake but part of him felt good holding such a powerful weapon in the belief that this was still an exercise.

"Are you sure about this, I don't think I want to do this anymore. Is that a real rocket?" Giles's voice was getting higher as he spoke.

"Look, yes, I mean no, it's not a real rocket don't be stupid," Number One showed him how to hold and fire the weapon then told him to go to the lower edge of the field and point it towards the base. When he shouted 'Fire' then Giles was to pull the trigger. Peter hearing all this whispered to Duncan that he was going to follow the farm track and catch Giles at the bottom of the field and stop him. Duncan nodded and kept watch on the others, his gun in his hand. Giles began to walk away from the group the rocket launcher resting on his right shoulder and pointing down toward the Catalinas. He couldn't really see where he was going but knowing he was heading in the right direction, tried not to trip over in the dark. Peter could just make him out so moved quickly and quietly to make sure he was in a position to halt the mayhem that Giles would surely cause. Duncan was horrified to see the others put together a machine gun that appeared in pieces from the three wooden boxes. It was very expertly clipped together and now sat mounted on a heavy metal stand in one of three holes cut into the ground and faced down the field to the base. Hundreds of rounds of ammunition were being lifted out of another box. When the staff and crews came out of their billets after hearing any enemy fire, they would be mown down by that machine gun. 'God almighty, lad, what have you done?' Duncan whispered to himself. There was no way for him to warn Peter.

The wind was slight and the moon came out from behind the clouds as Giles neared the edge of the field holding on tight to the rocket launcher. He could see men working on a motor torpedo boat below him and actually heard them laughing at some joke. He knew one of them. He worked at the local garage and fixed his father's car. Joe, that was it, Joe Tobin. Peter was already waiting at the bottom of the field having followed the tractor path, which was smoother than the furrows and tufts Giles was trying to negotiate. Duncan was weighing up his options, should he try and kill them all as quickly as he can, or will he shoot the man who looks to be the boss and hope the others will come to their senses. He knew that under cover of darkness they wouldn't see him and he might get away with killing all of them. But that was only if he was lucky and they didn't spin that gun around.

Giles's right foot went straight down a huge rabbit hole. Peter, who was close by, heard the bones in Giles's leg snap, then the lad scream out in agony. The rocket launcher rolled off Giles's shoulder as he fell but he didn't let go. His fingers tight with pain pulled the trigger and the rocket fired into the ground two feet away from him. At that moment the metal canister packed with high explosives, blew up in his face.

Peter was shocked for a couple of seconds when he saw him fall and automatically put his head down, which saved his life. All hell broke loose up the field where the others had heard Giles cry out and saw the explosion. Two of the men ran down the field to get a closer look, the other two stayed at the top and stood unmoving beside the machine gun. Just then Peter heard Duncan's pistol, two sharp cracks, and knew his friend had managed to kill or injure them. The other two Germans looked at what was left of Giles and didn't know which way to run. Not knowing who had fired the shots they foolishly ran back up the hill. Peter also ran but on the tractor path and arriving at the top could see the men looking around for signs of their comrades. Peter knew that Duncan was hiding behind the hedge and made his way to him. The two dead Germans were lying beside him and he had a great grin on his face and blew the end of his gun cowboy style. Peter pointed to the others and Duncan took careful aim through the hedge, fired twice in quick succession and the bodies fell silently to the ground.

Peter started waving his torch toward the base and sat and waited for the troops to arrive and it didn't take long. It seemed every vehicle they had was trying to get up the track to see what was happening. Giles's broken body was taken away in an unmarked vehicle. All the weaponry was packed carefully into a troop carrier and taken away for inspection. The base commander had requested that Peter and Duncan go straight away to brief him on the night's events and all the facts leading up to it. The pair could see the night stretching out before them but climbed gratefully back into their van out of the cold and followed an escort Landrover back to Sullom Voe.

Giles's parents were duly informed that evening. An officer from the base and two policeman from Lerwick called at the house just as Mr and Mrs Johansson were full flight into their third row of the evening. The knock on the door had stopped them in their tracks and when they saw the three men and the looks on their faces they stood frozen to the spot.

"May we come in Mr Johansson, we need to speak with you about your son?" said the policeman, taking off his helmet as the men entered the warm kitchen. Mrs Johansson, having just been screamed at by her husband regarding their errant son, was trying desperately to compose herself, and sat down by the fire.

"Make some tea woman, this looks as if it might be serious, am I right officer?" Johansson's anger was just under control.

"Yes, I'm afraid it's very serious and we don't have time for tea Mrs Johansson but thank you anyway. I'm sorry to have to tell you both," he coughed and tried again. "I'm sorry to be the bearer of bad news but your son Giles," he never got any further.

"For God's sake man, spit it out, what's he done now, is he still playing at spies?" Mr Johansson waved his hand towards his wife, his voice rising, "She won't believe he's caught up with some group of idiots who are sneaking around at night wearing some stupid uniform. I know he's up to something and if I catch him …" He walked around the kitchen with his fists clenched and his face getting redder.

"Mr Johansson, please. I think you'd better sit down and let me speak."

"Ok, ok just tell me where he is and I'll go and pick him up but by God he'll feel the back of my hand when I see him," he sat down at the big kitchen table.

"Your son has been killed in an accident," the policeman said quickly before being interrupted again. As the words came out of his mouth, Mrs Johansson let out a gasping scream and clamped a hand over her mouth. She made to stand up but her legs wouldn't carry her and she fell to the floor in front of the fire. One of the officers went to help her, but she rolled herself into a ball, holding her knees in front of her rocking back and forth sobbing uncontrollably.

Mr Johansson was stunned, and silent, just staring at the policeman.

"Dead, my son is dead and what do you mean an accident. Who did it, tell me and I'll get the law on them. I'll see my day in the courts whoever it is. Just you tell me now?" His anger was rising over any logical thoughts.

"He caused the accident, Mr Johansson. For a long while, we think, he has been working in cahoots with a group of Germans who infiltrated the island. He was their runner for the want of a better word. He did their dirty work and their shopping, helping to hide them in fact. We are in the process of finding out how they managed to land on the islands and stay hidden. Though I think Giles was helping them in that department too."

"You still haven't told me how he died; I'll get the bastards who caused the accident you mark my words."

"He caused the accident, Mr Johansson," repeated the policeman, "he fell onto a rocket launcher that he was going to fire at the base at Sullom Voe. It went off as he fell and it killed him."

There was total silence, even from Mrs Johansson. The policeman gave the couple time to let the horrific news sink in. Mrs Johansson was by now on her feet and feeling her way slowly and dreamlike around the table, finally stopping at the large wooden cupboard at the end of the kitchen. All eyes were on her silent mission as she opened the cupboard door. From there she took out Mr Johansson's two prized bottles of twenty-year-old single malt whisky and stood defiantly in front of her husband.

"What the hell are you doing with my whisky? Put it back and sit down you stupid woman," he yelled keeping his eyes on the shaking bottles.

Her voice was like the screech of the devil itself, "I'll bloody well show you what I'm doing with your whisky." Raising her arm high she smashed one onto the floor and unscrewed the top off the other, taking a long drink. She put her tear stained face just a few inches from his, "I'm doing what I should have done years ago. Standing up to you, you bastard. It's you who've killed our Giles. You said you were going too and now you've done it, you heap of shit. I hate you and have done for years." She took another drink and starting coughing it back up again. She tried again spilling more down the front of her pinafore. One of the young officers made to go to her but the older policeman put his arm out to stop him. It was only right the dear woman had her say, he thought to himself. After all she was upset and needed to get all this off her chest He had never liked the headmaster, but he had liked Mrs Johansson. Mr Johansson was rooted to his chair, his face was like red mottled parchment and his mouth fell open. He'd never heard his wife raise her voice to him let alone swear. He was in total shock and couldn't muster a reply. Mrs Johansson leaned on the table, bottle in hand and looked at the older officer, a satisfied drink filled grin on her face. He wanted to smile in support but didn't.

"I must ask one or both of you to accompany me to Sullom Voe Base to formally identify your son's body. If only one of you comes then I will leave an officer in the house. Mrs Johansson, are you ok?"

"No," she screamed, "I'm not bloody well ok. My only son has just been killed and you stand there asking if I'm ok, are you stupid too?" She swayed a little as she poured more whisky into a teacup and drank it straight down, crying and choking at the same time.

Mr Johansson sat with his head in his hands then looked up at the policeman.

"How badly injured is the body?" his voice now a croaking whisper

"Pretty bad I'm afraid, best for you to come and leave your wife here with sergeant Jobb."

"Ok, I'll get my coat. You will have to stay here," he said a little quieter to his wife who was sitting once more by the fire with another full cup of whisky. Her hands were shaking but the drink was beginning to dull the pain.

"I will not be here when you get back," she said it so quietly into her cup, only the young officer standing near her heard it.

The events of that night began an all out hunt to find out how the Germans had arrived unnoticed on Shetland. Questions were being asked of every man who owned a boat or knew someone who did. Had anyone seen any strange goings on in any of the many inlets around the coast or seen any craft that looked out of place?. For all the war was slowly coming to an end, vigilance was still the order of the day. Groups of locals set out and scoured the shoreline for clues, drag marks on the beaches where there shouldn't be any, ropes, anything that would show a boat had been landed. Crofters and locals looked in outhouses and sheds staying up at night watching, just in case there were more of them.

Finally, a crofter helping with the search became suspicious of footprints he'd spotted in an entrance to a field that he no longer used. He decided to go home first, get his shotgun and investigate. He met Lowry on his way back to the field, so the two men walked cautiously toward and old unused sheep pen. It was very quiet except for the flapping of an old piece of tarpaulin used to make a temporary roof.

"Bloody hell Lowry, what's been goin' on here?" as he took stock of what he was seeing. Lowry put his head down to a crack in the stonework and peered inside. No one was there. The two men went in and the crofter stood his gun against the wall and looked in amazement at what they saw.

"Talk about organised, look at this?" as he pointed to a small stack of stones that served as a fire and a cooker. One large flat stone on the ground, the others built up in a circle, with a piece of iron grating on the top to hold a cooking pot. There was metal ducting from the fire to the roof acting as a chimney. It went up in a spiral, that way the smoke would hopefully dissipate before it reached the outside and wouldn't be seen. There were old wooden fish boxes, stacked on one side of the room like shelves, which held their day-to-day stuff. There was cutlery, tins of food, bottles of vodka, bottles of beer, clothes, and fishing tackle. The whole place was set up almost like a permanent home. Four camp beds were laid around the walls all getting the benefit of the fire. The blankets were of heavy wool and there were plenty of them. On the floor beneath one of the beds were five wooden boxes. These were sturdy and well made and it was still possible to see where someone had tried unsuccessfully to rub out the markings from the lids.

"What does it say?" asked the crofter, as he blew some wood dust off the box.

"Gefahr Sprengstoff," (danger explosives) said Lowry. He tilted the box to one side and read the other letters, "Raketen Panzerfaust' 60, looks like it's the weapon of choice for these guys." He took his knife out of his belt and prized off the lid. Inside were four rockets lying in waxed paper and oiled steel wool? Each was about three foot long with a bulbous head and a narrow body. All were ready to be clipped into a shoulder launcher.

"Right, lets get these away from here and I'll go to the Post Office and call the Base," said Lowry. The crofter was only too happy to get out of that pen and into the daylight.

"Ok, I'll go and get the cart, it'll only take me a few minutes, and then I'll put them in the barn for safe keeping, 'til the authorities get here."

It was never discovered how the four men had managed to land on Shetland. They may have come in from Unst or one of the other smaller islands under cover of darkness but it made locals even more suspicious of strangers. The old sheep pen was destroyed after all the contents had been taken away. No paperwork of importance was found and the official conclusion was that they were rogue Germans who wanted a war of their own, well they got it.

CHAPTER FIFTY-ONE

Giles's funeral was a very simple and desolate affair with only his father and the minister in the church. No one else chose to attend the burial of a traitor. It was a wet and miserable morning as the gravediggers carried the coffin to its resting place. The two men stood by the graveside, the minister holding his black umbrella. He quietly read the burial ceremony as Mr Johansson looked on. His face was grey and drawn as he stood silently in the pouring rain. Mrs Johansson was a broken woman and had drunk herself into a stupor the night Giles had died. She left first thing in the morning. Her life, such as it was, she said, ended when her son was killed, and she'd no intention of staying on Shetland with 'that man' so moved down to Newcastle to live with her sister.

It was official. The war was over. Shetland was free from the threat of attack and the ships and fishing boats could sail safely once more. Celebrations were held in Lerwick for what seemed like days. People sang and danced in the streets and parties were held in almost every house all over the town. But there were those who had lost everything and had no heart to celebrate. Husbands, sons and brothers had set out to sea and had never returned. Shetland had become a very different place because of the war but different or not, life went on.

Valerie Carlson's life had certainly changed. One of the rescued submariners who were billeted to her little cottage, had taken a shine to her and was quite happy to stay on in Shetland, telling her he would be honoured to help her with the smallholding. He was hoping one day to marry this feisty woman who had shown him such gentleness and care when they first arrived. Valerie had never been happier than when he'd asked her, in broken English, to be his wife. Tears of joy ran down her face as he hugged her so tightly she could hardly breathe. Her life was good and she sent a prayer everyday, thanking her father for building the radio, which she knew was the beginning of her happiness.

Tally decided to visit Jac's grave. The day was bright and sunny and she'd picked a bunch of wild flowers that morning. The graveyard was not too far from her home so it would only take about an hour to get there and her father had once again gone out fishing with Lowry. She put the flowers on the headstone and stood for a couple of minutes remembering this wonderful friend who'd loved her so much. Her heart was full of all things he'd told her, the fantastic stories and dreams he had, and the fact she knew he'd wanted to marry her.

"Dear Jac, there was so much I wanted to share with you, things about me and who I am that no one knows but me."

Tears came easily as she realised she couldn't have married him, she didn't love him the way he'd loved her and knowing that would have broken his heart.

Tally didn't hear Volkov come up beside her, his footsteps silent on the soft grass.

"Am I disturbing you?" he asked looking into her face as she turned.

"Not really, I was just giving Jac some flowers and thinking about him," she replied.

"Thinking with tears in your eyes, he must have been very special."

"Oh, yes, he was, very special," she wiped her eyes with the corner of her shawl. Volkov thought how vulnerable she looked and wanted to put his arms about her.

"I can leave you if you wish, I didn't mean to intrude," he half turned away.

"No, it's alright, I'm going back home now, you needn't go."

"Can I at least see you home?"

"If you wish and it doesn't take you out of your way."

"No, don't worry it will not. I plan to get the bus back to Lunna Road ends later but for now I'm exploring the island while I can. Come, please take my arm?" With that they made their way to the village.

Tally and Volkov walked easily together down the lane as they approached her cottage. She asked him about his crew and what plans there were for returning home to Russia. Volkov said some men were desperate to get home, others, like one of his gunnery officers was quite happy to stay in Shetland and had proposed to Valerie Carlson. He had no intention of going back. They both laughed and she was delighted for Valerie. Tally was aware of the physical strength of this man as he guided her along the rough track and her heart quickened a little.

As they approached the cottage she could see Katy and Lowry pull up in their old van. She broke away from Volkov and with a backward smile ran down the lane. "Come on, I'll race you," as she lifted her skirt and set of at a great pace. Volkov laughed and took off after her arriving at the cottage a respectful second. Tally looked at him knowing he could have beaten her if he'd wanted; their glance to each other was long.

"Katy, Lowry, how great to see you both, come in and have some tea, Yuri please join us," she said going straight into the sink and filling the kettle.

"It's good to see you again Yuri," said Lowry shaking hands, "I take it you've been grilled by Captain Vickers and that plans are well under way for you and your crew to return to Russia?"

"Yes sir, they are and I may be returning within a couple of weeks but I still have some rather important business here in Shetland to clear up before I do," he looked at Tally, but she didn't notice. Katy did though.

The three of them chatted amiably for a couple of hours in the cosy room of the Gregor cottage. The war being the main topic of conversation, and Volkov quite happy to talk about his time in the Russian Navy and how the country was not fit to go to war when it did. Explaining that too many petty politicians making stupid decisions were costing lives, and of course Stalin who Volkov considered to be completely mad.

"My father was a submarine commander in the Russian navy just like yourself," it came from Tally who had been sitting quietly listening to the two men discuss the rights and wrongs of the war.

Volkov was shocked, he'd no idea that the fisherman Peter Gregor had any such background, but how would he; he hadn't spoken to the man.

"I didn't know, no one has told me, not even Captain Vickers. You must tell me more."

But as he said that, Peter walked in through the open door and was greeted by his friends.

"Ha-ha, what's this, a party to celebrate the end of the war or Lowry and Katy's wedding?" he walked to the table and heaved a big box of fish onto it.

"There's plenty there for everyone, and I see we have the good commander in our midst," he shook hands with Volkov and said something in Russian which made Volkov give a quick nod of the head, as if in salute. "We don't stand on ceremony here commander, get the vodka out Tally. I think this is a good time to drink a toast to the good friends we have around us this day." He got the glasses out and the five of them lifted their drinks,

"To Shetland."

"To Shetland."

Peter swallowed hard, looking at his beautiful daughter. The evening sun coming in through the window catching her rich dark hair and her lovely face and it filled his heart with love and pride.

Lowry had his arm around Katy and Volkov smiled at Tally. Peter's thoughts went to Zoya. Unbeknown to him she'd found his note, understood it and was now preparing to leave Russia and travel to Shetland.

"To Shetland," he said again, to himself.

CHAPTER FIFTY-TWO

Young Sergei Somova had travelled through Russia under the most difficult circumstances. He had been attacked at a railway station and robbed of some money. He had then hidden for two days in the ruins of a church realising it would be a miracle if he ever reached Archangel. But reach it he did, on the day he heard that Hitler had shot himself. He decided then that God was with him and everything was going to be alright. A letter he'd written to his best friend Yuri Volkov did not come back and he hoped that it was a good sign. It meant that Yuri was either at sea and hopefully would return or that he had received the letter and just hadn't had the opportunity to reply. Sergei was clinging on to the belief that he would have heard if his good friend had come to any harm.

Trying to find anyone in Archangel who could give him information about his friend was a nightmare. All he had was that Volkov had left on a course for the North Atlantic in the early part of January. It appeared that no one was willing to give this stranger any information, so he then asked about his own father, Commander Peter Gregor. That raised a few eyebrows and received some attention. He was ushered by a young representative to the offices of the Naval Yards Commander in Chief.

After showing his papers and going through his whole life story, once to the commander and then again to a secretary who wrote down every word he said, he was eventually told that his father had left Archangel in 1919 with his daughter Tally. Documents confirming this were shown to him and he could see that his father Commander Peter Gregor had indeed left for Shetland with a baby girl on the ship 'Saidy.' And by all accounts he had paid a very large amount of money to the captain for the trip.

"What do you know of the ship or the captain?" Sergei asked the commander.

"Not a lot really, except that the captain of the 'Saidy' was a particularly mean and very much disliked man who could never keep a decent crew for long. The ship, well, she sank on her return journey to Archangel with no survivors," he stayed silent for a while, "your father was a very good friend of mine and I was sad to see him leave but I could understand why. He had fought well and hard through the First World War and wanted to give his child a better life. After his wife died, well, something changed in him. He seemed to loose the will to fight, all he wanted was to keep his daughter safe." The commander poured them both a drink, and then went to the window, which looked out over the yard.

"All this, you see it?" he pointed from the window high up on the third floor, down onto the cranes, cabins and hardware below, "it's useless, old and rusting, it will all have to be broken up and new machinery and submarines built if Russia wants to keep ahead of the game." He looked very tired as he took a drink.

CHAPTER FIFTY-THREE

It was a lovely bright day when Katy, Jenny and Tally went to Lerwick to choose the wedding dress. They were all very excited even before they got onto the bus but even more so when they arrived in the town where Mrs Larsson met them. She told Katy she had, on loan from the mainland, six beautiful wedding dresses for her to choose from and would they all like to come and have tea and cakes in her private rooms. Mrs Larsson was never a woman to miss an opportunity and knew through the grapevine that Katy and her friends were coming to town today. She had managed to procure the dresses, which had arrived on that morning's ferry, just in time. The thought of having her friends in the shop after such a long time was wonderful and she was going to make a party of it. A sale of course would also be nice.

There were lots of 'oohs and ahs' during the fitting of the dresses but Katy soon made up her mind after only one try of a cream lace dress. It was ballerina length with a sweetheart neckline. The waist was tied with a cream satin bow and fitted her tiny figure perfectly.

"You don't think I look too much like Cinderella going to the ball, do you?" she asked of her friends, her face a little flushed as she stood looking in the long mirror.

"No, silly, you look exactly like Katy Graham who is going to get married, its perfect," replied Tally.

"Yes, yes, it is perfect my dear, Tally is right but you must try them all on just to make sure."

But Katy had made up her mind and the cream lace dress was the one.

It was duly wrapped in the finest tissue paper and placed into a large white box and presented to Katy with much ceremony and laughter, and of course the bill. After much jollity, tea and eating the finest of Mrs Larsson's cakes, they made their way back to the bus station and home.

The date had been set and all the hand-made wedding invitations sent out.

Tally and Jenny had picked armfuls of flowers to decorate the tiny church. On the end of every pew, they had fastened a tiny bouquet tied with a white ribbon, and the altar was bedecked with blue cornflowers.

"Do you know if Katy has invited Volkov to the wedding?" Jenny asked mischievously of Tally as they tidied up the mess from their flower arranging.

"Yes, Jenny she has," laughed Tally.

Are you pleased, he's rather handsome?"

"Of course I'm pleased, Katy and Lowry like him and they can ask who they want."

"You know what I mean Tally, he's lovely and you said he got on so well with your father. I bet they could talk for hours about Russia and the navy, how exciting. Oh how I wish I could meet a tall handsome stranger from Russia," she sighed.

"They've already met Jen, he came by again the other night to see Pa and the two of them were like old friends. They walked down to the harbour then visited Lowry and Katy."

"Hm, so he's making himself at home then?"

"I suppose he is, but you know he has to return to Russia, don't you?"

"What's the point, you said he has no family, and the war is over, for us anyhow. I don't see why he should. What would you do if he asked you to go with him?"

"Jenny," Tally gasped and went a little pale, "why would he do that, anyhow, I've no intention of going to Russia, my life is here in Shetland, you really are funny." No, she didn't want to go back to Russia, ever.

Jenny wondered why her friend was so jumpy about her mentioning Russia, but then thought 'that's just Tally'.

They finished up and left the church. Tomorrow was the wedding.

Mist hung over the fields the next morning, the sun was low but bright and it bode well for a warm day. Tally and her father were up early; she had brushed his best suit and hung it on the back of the door. Her lovely blue skirt and jacket were laid out on her bed. All she had to do now was tie up her hair and put on her shoes.

"Pa, it is such a special day, I'm going to wear my gold necklace," Tally shouted from her room. Her father had presented her with it on her eighteenth birthday and she had kept it safe in the little carved wooden box. On the end of a long heavy chain hung a beautiful golden egg. It appeared quite plain but for the four gold wires wrapped around it and a tiny catch. When her father gave it to her he said it must have been her mother's although cannot ever remember seeing it. She stood there in her room her hands were trembling a little, running the chain through her fingers. She was now having doubts as to whether to wear it or not. Its mystery locked inside.

Just then there was knock on the cottage door.

"I'll get it," said Peter trying to get his new boots on.

"Ah, good morning, I thought I'd come by and ask if I may walk with you both to the church?" Volkov looked every inch the commander with his uniform neatly pressed and his cap under his arm.

"Who is it Pa, we haven't got long?" Tally shouted from her room.

"Commander Volkov, he's coming with us to the wedding, do come in Yuri."

Tally was almost ready and walked into the room wearing her blue outfit and with the necklace in her hands. Volkov stood to attention and looked admiringly at this beautiful young woman.

"Good morning Yuri are you well?" her smile lit up her face.

"I am, yes and thank you for asking. I hope you won't mind me joining you today. I received a rather late invitation from Katy and Lowry."

"No, of course not, Pa can you fasten this chain for me please, the catch is so tight?" Tally held out the necklace and as her father went to take it from her the golden egg slipped off the end of the chain and fell to the floor where it burst open.

"Oh no," Tally gasped. "Goodness me, oh dear, sorry Pa … leave it, I'll get it," she began to panic and went to pick it up.

"Don't worry girl, it'll be fine, I'll get It," he went to bend down.

"Here, I can see it," said Volkov, "it's gone under the chair. Hm, looks like it's spilt into two." Volkov retrieved it slowly and held it in his hand.

"Oh no", she cried, "give it to me please; I'll fasten it" she held a shaking hand out to Volkov. "Please Yuri, give it to me," her voice becoming urgent.

Peter moved toward Yuri as Tally made her way slowly to her room.

He carefully took the necklace from Volkov who by now was looking very closely at the jewelled interior. Peters face began to go pale as he stepped back and sat down heavily on the big chair behind him. His mind was spinning and he could feel the blood rushing and pounding in his ears. His thoughts flew back to the cottage when his wife told him they had a son. He couldn't speak; he thought he was imagining all these crazy thoughts that were crowding his brain. It cannot be, it cannot be he kept repeating over and over in his mind. He was remembering Eva's words as she pushed the necklace in its bag into his hands as he took the baby away, 'protect it with your life; it is now the child's. She is the only one now'. He wondered at the time what it was she'd meant but now it was becoming clear. Now it all fitted into place. He could hear his wife's sad and frail voice telling him that she'd given birth to a boy and Eva was so determined for him to believe his wife was confused and that he was the father of a girl.

It took a while before Tally emerged from her room; her eyes were a little red. Yuri knew she'd been crying but said nothing.

"Pa, speak to me, please," she'd seen the shock on her fathers face and it frightened her. She went to hug him but Yuri took her arm, as her father stood up and walked slowly to the door.

"I'm ok girl, I just felt a bit faint," his voice hardly a whisper, "a couple of minutes outside is all I want, you put the kettle on, we've at least got time for a cup of tea before we go to the church." Peter still with the necklace in his hand went out of the cottage and walked to the garden fence. There he stood looking out to sea and the far horizon. From the kitchen they couldn't see he was weeping like a child.

"I know what it is Yuri. It's the necklace."

"I'm not sure Tally, only your father can tell you that and he will in his own time." Yuri had seen the double-headed eagle inside the golden egg when it burst open. Exquisitely decorated with emeralds, rubies and diamonds and knew immediately what it represented. Only Peter could decide whether to explain it all to his lovely Tally.

"This is the first time I've ever worn it," she sat at the table with her hands clasped in front of her avoiding Yuri's eyes.

"Where did it come from?" he asked.

My father gave it to me for my eighteenth birthday. He thought it had been my mothers, although he doesn't recollect ever seeing before. Do you know what is inside it?"

"No, I couldn't make it out?" he lied.

"I do," she said sadly and looked out of the window towards her father, shadows of concern on her face. He was now walking back and forward on the sandy grass that bordered the beach, "I hope he's alright."

Yuri puzzled over the connection between Peter and that amazing piece of jewellery. If it had belonged to his wife, how did she come to own it?

Perhaps, Yuri thought, Peter is now in the process of putting the pieces together, but Yuri had a feeling he already knew who Tally really was.

CHAPTER FIFTY-FOUR

Young Sergei Somova decided to change his name to Sergei Gregor. He now knew there was remote chance of his father still being alive. He didn't know how or where to do it legally, all administration offices were in disarray. Authority had all but broken down but he thought if people were looking for him or thought they could persuade him to toe the Party line then perhaps it would be better if he disappeared. So, he was now Sergei Gregor to anyone who asked. He had managed to find a room in Archangel. It was small and dingy with little heat but it would suffice until he could find a boat to take him to Britain. He spent the days walking the docks, looking for a likely ship. Fishing boats were going to be his best chance. They sailed and trawled in the North Sea and would stop and market their catches in Shetland. The little money he'd managed to hang on to was going to have to be enough to pay for his passage. After four days of searching, he found a friendly skipper who listened to his story and agreed to take him. Sergei couldn't thank him enough and explained that he didn't have much money but he was willing to give him what he had and work his passage too. The skipper laughed a told him he would have to work anyhow but he could hang on to his money, reminding him it would be no good in Shetland. The boat was to leave in three days giving the skipper time to see his wife and family and buy some supplies. Sergei returned to his room and wrote a letter to his good friend Yuri who he still hadn't heard from. He intended to leave it at the Navy Headquarters in Archangel and pray that someday it would find him. There was very little for him to pack, half a bottle of shampoo, a toothbrush, a change of clothes and his big coat, everything else had been stolen.

Three days on, found him putting his gear into a small wooden locker in a cabin below deck on the 'Olga'. The old boat had definitely seen better days; the smell of rotting fish invaded his nostrils. The decks were dirty and the hulls white, blue and red paintwork was all but nonexistent. His cabin was tiny and dark. The stink of stale tobacco hung in the air, and the windows yellow with nicotine but at this moment in time he didn't care. Supplies were on board and stowed away within an hour and the big, noisy diesel engines were running with a steady rhythm, vibrating the whole of the ship. A degree of heat was starting to surge through the boat via some extraordinary pipework that rattled and banged but was a luxury for the crew.

Sergei stood in the wheelhouse with the skipper as he navigated out of the harbour and into the gulf, then north to the White Sea. He felt excitement and trepidation, this was a journey he never thought he'd ever be making and could only pray that his father was still alive and in Shetland.

CHAPTER FIFTY-FIVE

Katy and Lowry's wedding went without a hitch. They said their vows in the little church in front of all their friends and relatives on one of the sunniest days for a long time. After the service everyone gathered on the grass outside. Captain Vickers produced a camera much to everybody's delight, so folks shuffled into groups amid lots of laughter and amusement and precious images of the day were captured. Volkov insisting that he and Tally have a picture taken of them together. Jenny fussed around Katy seeing that her hair and her dress were looking there best. Standing to one side, Volkov watched Peter and could see the man was greatly troubled but was doing well not to show it and kept smiling and nodding at the appropriate times. Yuri too was deeply concerned and felt something had gone terribly wrong.

Back in the village hall, the band began to play and the celebrations started. Valerie Carlson was there with her new man and she looked the picture of happiness. Now there's the next wedding thought Jenny. Peter took himself outside into the evening air, an earlier headache came pounding back again. His wife's voice still whispering that they had a son, a son, a son, a son, he couldn't get her words out of his head. Then Eva's wailing that he had a daughter, it was becoming a nightmare but a nightmare that was now a reality.

Tally was not his child but that of the Tsarina Alexandra of Russia. He suspected that Eva had taken his son and possibly given him to the church beside her cottage, then brought the Tsarina's daughter from the house in Impatiev where they were being held under house arrest. It was then that she told Zhanna she had given birth to a girl. He knew Eva had worked as a faithful servant for the Romanovs during their captivity in that 'House of Special Correction'. He remembered his wife Zhanna telling him Eva spoke of the family with a great passion. How she was desperate to help the mother who was trying to hide the fact she was heavily pregnant and the baby who would be in the gravest danger. He wished now that he could recall all that was said but it was a dull memory, which was disappearing fast.

It was almost more than he could take, if his wife gave birth to a boy then where was he now? A thousand questions were lining up to be answered but no answers came. All he knew was that he had to find out what happened to his son but first he had to explain all this to Tally. He was leaning against the cold stone wall when Yuri came out and stood beside him, he handed Peter a small glass of whisky and took a sip from his own.

"It's a beautiful evening," Volkov said in Russian.

"Is it?" Peter replied in the same.

"Yes, and it's a beautiful end to a beautiful day for your friends Lowry and Katy, and I think it would be prudent if you were to make an appearance. You are being missed and I suspect, forgive me if I'm wrong, you don't want people asking too many questions of you tonight, am I right?"

"You're right Yuri, and very astute of you. I'll tell you everything after I have spoken with Tally, but that may

not be tonight. Come on, let's go in and join the throng."
The two men went back into the hall where the dancing
was in full swing. Peter's smile gave nothing away.

At the end of the evening, which saw Tally and Yuri
dance nearly every dance together, he asked if he could
walk her home. She agreed and off they set. Peter
watched them go and thought how difficult it was going
to be, trying to explain what had happened all those
years ago.

He took his time, the night wasn't cold and he was
enjoying the walk. He wanted to get the past events clear
in his head so that he was able to explain every detail
without fear of doubt. He knew, and perhaps he'd
known all along that there was a difference between him
and his 'daughter' It was a difference he couldn't explain,
it was there but wasn't there. He sometimes felt it, and
then it was gone, unexplained. He loved her as his own,
he'd brought her up as his own but only a father or
mother knows when a tiny fleeting thought creates a
question that you cannot answer. He couldn't even tell
himself what that question was, but there was always
something that was missing from the picture. Sometimes
he tried to see his wife in Tally but each time it evaded
him. It was like looking through a window that had
become misted. Now it all made sense but caused him
great heartache. Should he even tell her? Would it cause
her to leave and go back to Russia to try and find her
past? The thought haunted him as he walked home but
he had made up his mind.

CHAPTER FIFTY-SIX

Young Sergei was standing in the wheelhouse when the skipper pointed out of the forward window, "There's Shetland for you, young man," he said expertly flicking his cigarette out of the small side door, sending it over the rails into the sea. They'd been fishing for the last week and Sergei really didn't have a clue where he was. Everyday he asked the skipper how long it would be before they reached Shetland and everyday he was laughingly told, they'd get there when they arrived. The hold was full of fish and the skipper was a happy man, he could probably sell half of the catch in Lerwick. Sergei had worked hard whilst on board, showing off his culinary skills and serving up good hearty meals for the crew. Then he would help up on deck hauling nets, stacking boxes, dodging swinging booms and trying to stay on his feet but now he could see his destination and was filled with excitement. It was a new challenge and a new adventure. Lots of questions filled his head but only by landing in Shetland would they ever be answered.

Finally the boat motored gently into the harbour and the skipper steered to a berth on the west wall near the fish sheds. Sergei was already packed and ready to go by the time the mooring ropes were secured. He shook hands with the skipper and thanked him for all his kindness and wished him a safe journey back to Russia.

The skipper in turn said he hoped that Sergei could find his father and things would work out for them.

The sun was shining and there was a light but cool breeze. People were out and about strolling along the harbour on this lovely morning. His first steps onto Shetlands soil made his pulse race he wanted to shout 'Peter Gregor where are you?' but he just stood and looked around him wondering where to start. Two people out for a walk smiled as they came toward him, he smiled back and put his bag on the ground. He must have looked a little lost because they stopped and asked him if he needed any help.

CHAPTER FIFTY-SEVEN

Even though it was Lowry's big day, he couldn't help but notice how withdrawn his friend Peter was, it worried him. They'd known each other for a long time and he sensed there was something very wrong and Peter's smiles and amiable conversations during the evening were barely masking his anguish.

Lowry had seen Peter, Tally and Yuri leaving the hall near the end of the festivities. Tally and Yuri walking happily arm in arm down the path toward home. Peter followed a little way behind.

Lowry shouted to Katy over the noise of the band that he was going to see Peter and wouldn't be too long, then hurried out.

Peter heard the footsteps and turned to Lowry, whose face was a little flushed.

"Well, what are you doing here; you have a new wife back there, what's up, has she kicked you out already?" he tried to sound cheerful.

"Look, Peter, tell me to mind my own business if you want but I know something's up, you haven't really been with us today, have you. I mean you look as if you're carrying the weight of the world on your shoulders. If there's anything I can do you know you just have to ask?" he could hardly see Peter's face in the gloom but could hear the big man starting to take great sobbing breaths and suddenly he found himself holding onto his friend before he collapsed on the ground.

"My God man, what is it?" He held on to Peter as they sat on a wall, "are you ill, do you want a doctor?"

"No, no, it's nothing like that," his sobbing had stopped but his whole body was shaking. Lowry stayed silent and waited.

"It's Tally, and there's no other way of saying it, but she's not my child, she's not my child Lowry."

Lowry was stunned, had he heard right. What on earth was Peter saying, what made him think such a thing, but there he was, breaking his heart, telling him Tally was not his daughter.

For nearly an hour the two men sat and Peter told Lowry everything. Right from the beginning, from when Tally was born to the discovery of the necklace and the fact that somewhere he had a son. Lowry was dumbfounded.

"How do you know that Tally is not your child just because of a necklace?"

"It was the necklace that confirmed to me something that has sat like a barb in my head since we came here from Sverdlovsk. My wife was dead, I was confused, and my world had turned upside down. Eva told me Zhanna had given birth to a girl, and there she was Lowry, lying there, like a little angel in her cot but Zhanna told me we'd a son. I should have believed her, God how I wish I had believed her and done something about it. She was so weak and there was nothing anyone could do for her, I just wanted to hold her," the tears came easily again as silence fell over the two friends sitting in the gathering darkness.

Tally and Yuri had arrived at the cottage and sat in front of the fire talking, easy in each others company.

"I have decided to stay on Shetland," Yuri said, "I see little point in returning to Russia, there is nothing for me there. I have given a full report to Captain Vickers and he is going to make sure it reaches the authorities in Archangel. I have no family and I don't know what has happened to my friends. I could easily get work here on the fishing boats; what do you think?" he looked eagerly into Tally's eyes.

"I think that may be a good idea, you could work with my father and Lowry," her look told him everything he wanted to know as he leaned across and kissed her on the lips. He took her hand and they both stood up and held each other for a long time, their kisses becoming more passionate as Tally, allowed herself to succumb to his warm and gentle touch.

CHAPTER FIFTY-EIGHT

It took young Sergei a little while before he found somewhere to stay for a few nights. The couple on the harbour had directed him toward the town centre but Lerwick was still suffering from the effects of the war and some folks were not too keen on taking in a foreigner. Nevertheless, he managed to find a nice little room above a bakery that overlooked the harbour. The landlady was a Mrs Strachan; who although fierce looking was kind and generous. She served Sergei a lovely hot meal as soon as he'd settled in and fussed around his room making sure he had plenty of blankets. Next morning, as he dressed, he watched the comings and goings of this busy little town. He could see lots of heavy equipment and army trucks being loaded onto the larger ships, going back where they came from. He could see a military man taking down the 'Admiralty Offices' sign from the harbour shed door. Perhaps he could look for work on one of the fishing boats. He needed money for his room and could do with some new clothes. It was a lovely day and his spirits were high, he liked what he saw of Shetland, but where was his father?

CHAPTER FIFTY-NINE

Peter walked in to the cottage and smiled when he saw the blushes on both Yuri and his daughters face; he went to the cupboard and took out a bottle of whisky.

"I think I should have been whistling as I came up the path," he kept smiling.

"We were just saying goodnight, weren't we Yuri?" she blushed even more.

"Join me in a nightcap please, the two of you," he sat in his big chair by the fire.

"Well, it's been a day to remember, Lowry and Katy seem very happy and everyone had a good time at the wedding, so here's to us." he lifted his glass to Tally and Yuri who touched their glasses together.

"Here's to us," she said looking at Yuri.

"Here's to us," he replied.

They sat for a while going over the wedding and the gathering afterwards, Peter noticing that Tally was not wearing the necklace.

"I see you have taken off your necklace," he felt unsettled, is this the time to tell her?

"Oh, it's too heavy and I couldn't open it again. I think it will stay in its box from now on; I could sell it I suppose. I might need some money for something important one day," she laughed and made a face at Yuri who made a face back at her.

Peter stared into the fire as Yuri stood up, "well, it is early morning and I must go, the sun will be coming up soon. Can I visit you again tomorrow or should I say today, Tally?"

"Of course you can," she walked with him to the door, kissed him on the lips and watched as he walked away.

Peter felt wretched, he had to get this right and it had to be done now, he had to tell her everything in a way she could understand. His head felt fit to burst as he took a drink and poured another into Tally's glass. His hands were beginning to sweat and his mouth felt dry. Tally came back into the room and sat down beside him.

"I don't know where to start girl, but I've got something to tell you that may change your life forever," he kept staring at the fire dreading the next few minutes or hours.

Tally put her hand gently on his arm feeling it shake, "I know what you're going to tell me Pa. I know about the necklace and what it means. I didn't want it to break open like that but I have already seen what is inside and I understand," her voice the gentlest Peter had ever heard. "I know you have never seen it before, so you wouldn't have been able to make sense of it. I have known for a long while and tried to keep it from you."

Peter just stared at her, his mouth ready to speak but he couldn't think of anything to say.

"When you gave me the necklace, you said it had belonged to my mother but you couldn't remember buying it or ever seeing it before. A long time ago when you were out fishing with Lowry, I prised it open and saw what was inside. It is such a beautiful piece of jewellery I wondered who would be able to afford such a gem. It made me think. I wanted to find out who my mother was. You had inadvertently pointed me in the right direction."

"What" Peter's voice incredulous, "Oh Tally no."

"Let me finish Pa," her voice steady, "so, I went to Lerwick without telling anyone and spent the morning in the library. I started looking for books about Russia. I knew there had to be a connection somewhere. There were a few and some articles about the Romanovs. I recognised the crest, the double-headed eagle. So I read everything and it didn't take long to find what I was looking for."

"Oh, Tally, and you didn't tell me."

"How could I, you didn't know yourself then, did you?"

"No, I didn't," he said not able to tell her of the doubts he'd had all his life.

"I found out that the crest is that of the Romanovs, and," she took a deep breath, "I have seen a picture of the Tsarina with her children not long before they were taken to 'the house' and she was wearing my Faberge necklace." It was as if a great weight had been lifted from her. She sat in the big chair and put her hands over her eyes. Peter didn't know what to say as he stood and put his arms around her and they held on to each other as if waiting for a hurricane to pass.

"I know who I am Pa; I knew there was something different about me. Things you used to say to me when I was little; things you probably don't even remember saying. I sometimes felt I didn't belong to you but I couldn't tell you why. Now I know who my mother is. Now I want to know everything you can tell me about how I came to be here with you. Please Pa?" her voice very calm.

The sun was up over the shimmering horizon by the time he'd finished his amazing story. Everything about his wife and Eva, and how he suspected she was lying to him. Tally asked about his son, wiping away his tears when he admitted he'd no idea where he was or even if he was still alive. They cried together and smiled together. He even sang her the Russian folk song that she'd heard him sing a long time ago explaining that his mother used to sing it to him when he was boy. He made no mention of Zoya singing the same song while he was in Sverdlovsk with her.

"Nothing changes Pa, nothing," she said firmly, "I don't want to know anything else; I want this to be the end of that part of my life. I know of the Romanovs but I don't know them as my family. I want to stay here in Shetland, I have no intention of going off to Russia, why should I, there's nothing there for me. You are my family, I love you and I love Yuri Volkov." She smiled her biggest smile at him, "Now we have to find your son, my new brother." She leant forward and kissed her father on his cheek.

Peter couldn't believe the strength of this girl. She had just found out that she was born into the house of the Romanovs, knowing that her father, mother, brother and sisters had all been brutally murdered just days after she was born. Now here she was telling him that they were going to find his son. Tally went to her room exhausted and sat on the edge of her bed looking out over the sea; she could hear the calming sound of the waves breaking on the beach below. There was one thing she was determined to do very soon but she would wait for Yuri to call. She lay back fully clothed onto her bed and fell fast asleep.

Peter was tired, but sleep eluded him as he sat in his chair going over the night's events, praying that they could find his son, Sergei.

Yuri called a little after ten o'clock and stepped inside the kitchen to see Peter still in his chair, "come in young man, I'm not asleep. Put the kettle on will you?"

"Yes, of course, are you ok?" he asked.

"I'm fine thank you Yuri. I don't know what to say to you so I'll leave that up to Tally; she may tell you things, she may not. He got up slowly and went to his room.

Just then Tally came into the kitchen; Yuri thought she looked remarkably bright, considering they had stayed up until the early hours.

"Yuri," she ran to him and hugged him fiercely, kissing his neck, "I must talk to you, and it may change things between us, but you've got to know, let's go outside." She tugged at his hand and they went into the sunshine. Peter watched them through the window.

She led him to the spot her father had stood earlier, looking out to sea. She took hold of Yuri's hands and watched his face, "I'm not who you think I am, I am not Peters daughter. He brought me from Russia to take care of me but his son got left behind. It sounds impossible I know but that is what happened. I can't tell you everything now it would take forever but one day I will, I promise, do you believe me?" she looked pleadingly into his face, the sun catching her dark blue eyes.

"Yes, I believe you and I'm glad to hear that there is going to be 'one day' in our future," Yuri took hold of her in his powerful arms, telling her everything will be alright. She felt so safe and wanted this moment to last forever.

"Of course you will have to marry me first," he lifted her chin and kissed her gently.

CHAPTER SIXTY

Mrs Strachan was busy in the shop when young Sergei came downstairs. The smell of freshly baked bread filled the room and customers were collecting their daily loaves. Mrs Strachan looked up and gave him one of her toothless smiles.

"Have you had your breakfast, it's going to be a raw cold day today lad?."

"Yes thank you Mrs Strachan, it was delicious," he couldn't help smiling at her.

"Oh get away with you, it was only a bowl of porridge," she blushed.

"Yes, but you'd put a drop of whisky in, it was very good." he winked at her and she blushed even more, much to the great amusement of the customers in the shop.

He headed out and made his way through the narrow lanes in the oldest part of the town before he passed the solid stone cross in the middle of the market square. The narrow streets were glistening with early morning rain but now the sun was beginning to make its way over the rooftops. He followed Mrs Strachan's instructions and walked up Market Street. Soon he could see the large stone Police Station with its blue and white sign. Going straight in off the street he came into a reception area and behind the green painted counter sat a rather large policeman. He stood up when he saw Sergei come in and put his sandwich back in its paper bag. He wiped his mouth with his sleeve, "Ahem, and what can I do for you young man?" he finished chewing.

"I'm looking for my father, Peter Gregor. He came to Shetland in 1919 with his daughter and I believe he may still be here, have you heard of him?"

"And who told you he may still be living here?" trying out his authoritative voice but all he did was spit the odd piece of bread onto the counter.

"Naval headquarters in Archangel. They said he left there on the fishing boat 'Saidy' and arrived in Lerwick. Do you know anywhere I could check to see if he's still on the island?"

"You don't mean Archangel in Russia do you?" the policeman sounded amazed.

"Yes sir, I do"

"Good grief, now then, let me get a bit of paper and we'll go through it all again. What is your name son?" The policeman obviously having a slow morning was going to make a meal of this enquiry. His boss had told him to pull his socks up, well, up they were being pulled, he thought. He licked the end of his pencil and started writing.

By the time Sergei had left the Police Station his head was spinning with all the questions. Half way through the session the officer had to go to the toilet then he took a phone call from his wife, and of course he was eating his sandwich. Sergei headed back to the harbour hoping there would be someone he could ask who might be a touch more efficient.

CHAPTER SIXTY-ONE

Yuri and Tally had spoken for a long while in the garden. He assured her that he loved her for being Tally and not where she came from. He wanted to marry her as soon as possible. They finally came back into the cottage to have some lunch. Tally was so excited she said she was going to see Katy. "You must wait for me here Yuri, I will not be long," and off she ran down the track to Hillswick.

"My word Yuri," said Peter, "things must happen for a reason but don't ask me what that reason is because I couldn't tell you. Did Tally tell you anything of importance out there in the garden?"

"Not much about herself, no, but she said that you have a son you want to find. I hope you will allow me to help in any way I can. She said you've looked after her and loved her all her life but that you're not her father. I love her too and if one day she wants to tell me more then 'so be it.' Until that day comes, I want us to be married and begin our lives together here on Shetland. In fact I've an idea to put to you. Is there any possibility of me coming into partnership with you, or you and Lowry and buying a new fishing boat between us?"

"Well, that's an interesting proposition Yuri. What do you know of fishing or boats that aren't submarines?" Peter laughed for the first time in a while.

The two men chatted about the possibility of a new fishing venture. It sounded good to Peter, "But first, I must find my son."

"Of course," said Yuri, "where do you want to start, what is his name?"

"I've no idea where to start Yuri. I suppose going back to Sverdlovsk would be sensible. As for his name, his mother wanted me to call him Sergei, but if he was brought up by the church, St Nicholas's I believe, then they could've changed it."

"Mary Mother of God," said Yuri, his face was ashen, "I don't think I can believe what I am hearing." He pulled his chair nearer to Peters and reached into his inside pocket. The two photographs, which he had rescued from his cabin on the submarine had been with him ever since, and now he brought them out and showed one of them to Peter.

"I think this could be your son Sergei," his hand was shaking slightly.

Peter took it and looked at the smiling face of a tall handsome dark haired young man. He was standing on the steps of a beautiful theatre in the middle of Sverdlovsk. He could clearly see a resemblance to his wife, the thick dark hair and the warm brown eyes and the smile. It was the smile of Zhanna. Peter gave a huge gasping sob as he looked at Yuri

"Tell me how you know him, where is he, how can I find him?" Peter was still trying to come to terms with the happenings of the last few days and this was almost too much.

"It was when you said he was called Sergei and had been brought up by the church, St. Nicholas's in Sverdlovsk, who else could it be? Was the maid called Eva Somova?"

"Yes Yuri, yes, she was," Peter's voice was almost breaking.

Yuri went through everything, their days at school and college, how Sergei lived with his 'mother' Eva Somova in the cottage beside the church. How he later became involved in politics and how Yuri had to leave his friend in hospital after the shooting. Memories of Sergei lying in the hospital bed came flooding back to him and he found it hard to go on but he told Peter which hospital he was in and it would be wise to start his search there. Yuri prayed that Sergei had survived.

Tally hurried back to the cottage and was met by Yuri and a very emotional Peter, who quickly explained everything saying that he wanted to get to the Post Office and try to make contact with the main hospital in Sverdlovsk.

"I can't believe this is happening," Tally said, "I don't know whether to laugh or cry but both with happiness. You mean you have known Sergei all this time and we hadn't even asked you about your friends. Pa, this is the most wonderful news, oh Yuri I love you," she said.

Peter had already decided not to give too much away to the sisters at the post office. He'll tell them he's about to enquire about a relative and hope the news is good. They were of course delighted to see their friends, the Gregors but especially the young commander. They had heard about him but had never met him and wasn't he handsome.

When Peter explained why he was there, they treated the request as if it was the most important of their lives. Meg immediately went through to the back of the shop and came bustling back with a few phonebooks and sheets of paper with various exchange numbers.

This was important business. Maisie shooed away a woman who was just about to make a call and pulled Peter up to the big black telephone and made him stand in front of it. He grinned at Tally and Yuri.

After a long time they came up with a couple of numbers, the first was no good as it was the annexe of another hospital. The second though got him through to the Sverdlovsk main hospital reception. Yuri had his fingers crossed behind his back and held on tightly to Tally's hand. Peter spoke in Russian and was obviously trying to explain who he was to a total stranger. He wiped his hand over his face in frustration and raised his voice. Tally went to his side and put her arm through his.

"It must be a very close relative to go to all this bother," Meg whispered to Maisie who was doing a bit of casual dusting around the phone, but her knowledge of Russian was minimal.

Finally, the smile on Peters face said it all, he turned to Tally and kissed the top of her head in sheer joy. Yuri swallowed hard knowing that his friend was still alive. He had been listening to Peter's side of the conversation and trying to interpret what the other person was saying. What he did find out was that Sergei had survived and had left the hospital heading for Archangel. This was brilliant news indeed although why Sergei had gone to Archangel was a mystery.

"What wonderful news, he's alive. I spoke to one of the doctors who were treating him and they don't know how he survived the shooting, but he did. He's also changed his name to Gregor." Peter hugged Tally and Yuri leaving Meg and Maisie Donaldson a little bemused and wondering who Sergei was. Peter paid for the phone call and they left without saying much more.

"I suspect he's followed your trail to try and find you."

"That means he knows about me," Tally said quietly.

"I think he may have gone to see Eva," Yuri said, "and she's told him something about you. If he went to Archangel he could be anywhere by now."

"Unless he went to the naval headquarters and managed to speak to somebody who remembers me," Peter said thoughtfully.

"I can help you there; I still have a couple of phone numbers for Archangel. It's worth a try." Yuri was gripping Tally's hand not knowing how all this was going to affect her.

"Ok, Yuri but I think I'll do it from Lerwick. I have a sneaking suspicion that my phone call from the post office will already be hot news." He couldn't help smiling.

They set off for the town and went to the main telephone exchange and Yuri offered to do the talking this time as he would probably know a few of the people who still worked there. It would also give him a chance to speak with his commanding officer.

This was agreed so after speaking to a few operators he finally got through to his old offices.

Yes, Sergei Gregor had called and was given basic information about his father leaving with a baby girl. He had hung around the yards for a few days finally getting a working passage on a local fishing boat going to Shetland. They didn't know if he made it or not as the boat was still out working.

As soon as Peter and Tally heard the word Shetland they looked at each other not quite knowing what to say.

Yuri spoke briefly with his superior officer but Peter and Tally were now oblivious to the call.

"Well it is even better than we thought," said Yuri, "Sergei left over two weeks ago on a fishing boat called the 'Olga', going to Lerwick. It should have arrived to sell some of its catch, pick up fresh supplies and is now back out at sea. So my friend, it sounds as if your son could already be here." Peter could hardly believe his ears, his brain was in a whirl, so near yet so far, his own son, possibly, just possibly on the island.

"What now Pa, where do we go now?"

"I suggest the nearest police station, he would have had to start somewhere," said Yuri.

They parked the van on the harbour front and began to walk. Yuri was looking everywhere and at everybody but keeping tight hold of Tally. She had kept the photograph of Sergei and was making sure she got a good look at all the passing young men; some gave her a quizzical smile. She was actually getting used to the idea of having a brother figure in her life, and it felt good.

The big policeman was just about to bite into a hot meat pie, when three people walked into the station. Sensing something important, he stood up and stuck out his rather rotund stomach and put his hands behind his back.

"Now then gentlemen and lady of course, how may I help you?" he looked longingly at his quickly cooling pie.

As soon as Peter mentioned his name, the police officer became all hot and bothered. His search began, looking for the papers that he'd filled in when the young chap with the same name called earlier. Managing to find them in his rather untidy filing system he placed them on the counter for Peter to look at. There was the lads name, he pointed with his stubby finger, and there was the address he was staying. It was only a short walk back down the hill into the town.

They wrote down the address, thanked him and left the building. The police officer picked up his pie and sat down placing his big feet on the counter. He leaned back in his chair and dreamed of promotion, then fell over backwards.

Mrs Strachan was very happy to see Peter Gregor. His son had told her about him but she hadn't known where on the island to look. She told them that Sergei had left to go to what had been the Admiralty Office to see if he could pick up a lead there, then he was going to ask at any boats that were moored up.

The three of them walked quickly to the building and made there way up the stairs, Peter leading the way. He went straight to the office at the end of the corridor where he'd had his meetings with Bill Howard. Knocking on the door he heard an immediate "Come in" from the familiar voice, "How lovely to see you again and I see you have Tally and Commander Volkov with you. Welcome all of you, would you like some tea, Jackson tea if you please, and sort some of these chairs out will you?" his voice booming into the next office.

"Captain Howard, I just don't know where to begin," Peter looking to sit down but all the furniture had been pushed to one corner, and the floor was covered in boxes of equipment obviously ready to be shipped out.

Young Sergeant Jackson came in and started putting chairs in a circle around the fire knowing what was going to happen. He winked at Tally as he left the room.

"Why don't you begin by saying hello to your son, Sergei?" said Bill Howard looking beyond Peter and the others to the door behind them. They all turned around and there in the doorway stood this tall imposing young man with tears in his eyes and his arms outstretched to his father. Tally went too, to hug this man who had had such a journey, in every sense of the word to get here. Yuri stood choking back the tears and then slowly moved toward his friend to join in the celebrations. Bill Howard busied himself with some papers on his desk and waited for the tea.

The tears and the laughter went on for over an hour; Peter couldn't keep his eyes off his son. There were a million questions, which would no doubt be answered over the coming weeks and months, even years. Yuri explained that he was now going to stay in Shetland and marry Tally. And now he had his good friend with him, he was the happiest man in the world. Yuri pulled the tiny flask of vodka from his pocket, "Remember this?" he asked Sergei.

"Goodness, is that our celebratory flask of vodka?"

"Yes, and it was to be drunk when we met again. Well I think that is definitely now."

"Absolutely." the two men hugged each other, took a quick drink then handed it round, everyone had a drink including Captain Howard.

Any feelings of uncertainty that Tally had were washed away by this wonderful brother who had just entered her life. Sergei sat beside her and held her hand, "I'm so happy to meet you, can I call you sister?" he smiled a wonderful smile and she knew he had accepted all that had happened and that neither of them had any control over their lives all those years ago.

"Yes Sergei that would be wonderful," she kissed his cheek.

"Well, Peter, it has certainly been an interesting year for you, has it not?" Bill Howard emerged from behind his desk, holding his cup of tea.

Peter stood up and rubbed his hands through his hair, "You can say that again, and it's going to be an interesting time ahead when folks try to work out what's happened. But, we will deal with all that. Firstly I want to get my family home and I must thank you for allowing us this time, I know you're a very busy man but I couldn't think of a better place to have been reunited with my son."

"It was Sergei who came here. He had seen the Admiralty sign being taken down and thought there may be someone here with a little more information than our loveable policeman up at the station," he laughed. "Sergei was being shown around what is left of our operation here, and in you walked. Things happen for a reason Peter, things happen," the two shook hands and Peter turned to his family.

"Come on you lot, time to go home and celebrate."

They laughed, they cried, they ate and they drank and the day turned into evening and still they talked. Plans were made, memories were cherished, they were all safe and what ever the future held they would embrace it.

As the sun was setting Tally stood up and went over to Yuri, "You remember I asked you to wait for me because I wanted to do something important, well, will you come with me now?" she took hold of his hand.

"Of course," Yuri stood up and went with her out of the cottage, leaving Peter and Sergei rather puzzled.

"I will explain everything when we get back," she shouted as they walked down the path.

It didn't take long for Tally and Yuri to get to the cliffs at Eshaness, the wind was light and the sun was shimmering on the horizon. The waves still crashed and thundered onto the rocks below and the puffins dived and chattered to each other over the cliff tops.

Together they stood, their new life was just beginning, but first she had to get rid of the old. Pulling the little cotton bag out of her pocket she took out the necklace and held it tightly in her hand, then with one swift movement threw it over the cliff and watched as it went spinning and flashing like a golden planet hundreds of feet into the cauldron below.

"We can go home now Yuri, we can go home."

Yuri and Tally Volkov live quietly on Shetland.

THE END

Lightning Source UK Ltd.
Milton Keynes UK
UKOW04f13071 11217

3 14238UK00001B/2/P